The Fury

The Fury

ALEX MICHAELIDES

MICHAEL JOSEPH

MICHAEL JOSEPH

UK | USA | Canada | Ireland | Australia
India | New Zealand | South Africa

Penguin Michael Joseph is part of the Penguin Random House group of companies
whose addresses can be found at global.penguinrandomhouse.com

First published 2024
001

Copyright © Alex Michaelides, 2024

The moral right of the author has been asserted

Set in 14.5/17pt Garamond MT Std
Typeset by Jouve (UK), Milton Keynes
Printed and bound in Great Britain by Clays Ltd, Elcograf S.p.A.

The authorized representative in the EEA is Penguin Random House Ireland,
Morrison Chambers, 32 Nassau Street, Dublin D02 YH68

A CIP catalogue record for this book is available from the British Library

HARDBACK ISBN: 978–0–241–57553–6
OM PAPERBACK ISBN: 978–0–241–57554–3

www.greenpenguin.co.uk

for Uma

ἦθος ἀνθρώπῳ δαίμων
Character is destiny

—Heraclitus

Prologue

Never open a book with the weather.

Who was it who said that? I can't remember – some famous writer, I expect.

Whoever it was, they were right. Weather is boring. Nobody wants to read about weather, particularly in England, where we have so much of it. People want to read about *people* – and they generally skip descriptive paragraphs, in my experience.

Avoiding the weather is good advice – which I now disregard at my peril. An exception to prove the rule, I hope. Don't worry, my story isn't set in England, so I'm not talking about rain, here. I draw the line at rain – no book should start with rain, ever. No exceptions.

I'm talking about wind. The wind that whirls around the Greek islands. Wild, unpredictable Greek wind. Wind that drives you mad.

The wind was fierce that night – the night of the murder. It was ferocious, furious – crashing through trees, tearing along pathways, whistling, wailing, snatching all other sound and racing off with it.

Leo was outside when he heard the gunshots. He was on his hands and knees, at the back of the house, being sick in the vegetable garden. He wasn't drunk, just stoned. (*Mea culpa*, I'm afraid. He'd never smoked weed before; I probably shouldn't have given him any.) After an initial semi-ecstatic experience – apparently involving a supernatural vision – he felt nauseous, and started throwing up.

Just then, the wind sped towards him – hurling the sound straight at him: *bang, bang, bang.* Three gunshots, in quick succession.

Leo pulled himself up. As steadily as he could, he battled his way against the gale, in the direction of the gunfire – away from the house, along the path, through the olive grove, towards the ruin.

And there, in the clearing, sprawled on the ground . . . was a body.

The body lay in a widening pool of blood, surrounded by the semi circle of ruined marble columns, casting it partially in shadow. Leo cautiously approached it, peering at the face. Then he staggered backwards, his expression contorted in horror – opening his mouth to scream.

I arrived at that moment, along with the others – in time to hear the beginnings of Leo's howl, before the wind grabbed the sound from his lips and ran off with it, disappearing into the dark.

We all stood still for a second, silent. It was a horrifying moment, terrifying – like the climactic scene in a Greek tragedy.

But the tragedy didn't end there.

It was just beginning.

Act One

This is the saddest story I have ever heard.

—Ford Madox Ford, *The Good Soldier*

I

This is a tale of murder.

Or maybe that's not quite true. At its heart, it's a love story, isn't it? The saddest kind of love story – about the end of love; the death of love.

So I guess I was right the first time.

You may think you know this story. You probably read about it at the time – the tabloids loved it, if you recall: 'MURDER ISLAND' was a popular headline. Unsurprising, really, as it had all the perfect ingredients for a press sensation: a reclusive ex-movie star, a private Greek island cut off by the wind . . . and, of course, a murder.

There was a lot of rubbish written about that night. All kinds of wild, inaccurate theories about what may or may not have taken place. I avoided all of it. I had no interest in reading misinformed speculation about what might have happened on the island.

I knew what happened. I was there.

Who am I? Well, I am the narrator of this tale – and also a character in it.

There were seven of us, in all, trapped on the island.

One of us was a murderer.

But before you start laying bets on which of us did it, I feel duty-bound to inform you that this is not a *whodunnit*. Thanks to Agatha Christie, we all know how this kind of story is meant to play out: a baffling crime, followed by dogged investigation, an ingenious solution – then, if you're lucky, a twist in the tail. But this is a true story, not a work of fiction. It's about real people, in a real place. If anything, it's a *whydunnit* – a character study, an examination of who we are, and why we do the things we do.

What follows is my sincere and heartfelt attempt to reconstruct the events of that terrible night – the murder itself, and everything that led up to it. I pledge to present you with the plain unvarnished truth – or as near to it as I can get. Everything we did, said and thought.

But how? I hear you ask. *How is it possible?* How can I possibly know it *all*? Not just every action taken, everything said and done – but everything *undone, unsaid,* all the private thoughts in each other's minds?

For the most part, I am relying on the conversations we had, before the murder, and afterwards – those of us who survived, that is. As for the dead, I trust you'll grant me artistic licence regarding their interior life. Given I am a playwright by trade, I am perhaps better qualified than most for this particular task.

My account is also based on my notes – taken both before and after the murder. A word of explanation regarding this. I have been in the habit of keeping notebooks for some years now. I wouldn't call them diaries, they're not as structured as that. Just a record of my thoughts, ideas, dreams, snatches of conversations I overhear, my observations of the world. The notebooks themselves are nothing fancy, just plain black Moleskines. I have the relevant notebook from that year open now, by my side – and will no doubt consult it as we proceed.

I stress all this so that, if at any point during this narrative I mislead you, you will understand that it is by accident, not design – because I am clumsily skewing the events too much from my own point of view. An occupational hazard, perhaps, when one narrates a story in which one happens to play a minor role.

Nonetheless, I'll do my best not to hijack the narrative too often. Even so, I hope you'll indulge me the odd digression, here and there. And before you accuse me of telling my story in a labyrinthine manner, let me remind you this is a true story – and in real life, that's how we communicate, isn't it? We're all over the place: we jump back and forth in time; slow down and expand on some moments; fast-forward through others, editing as we go, minimizing flaws and maximizing assets. We are all the unreliable narrators of our own lives.

It's funny, I feel that you and I should be sitting together on a couple of bar stools, right now, as I tell you this tale – like two old friends, drinking at the bar.

This is a story for anyone who has ever loved, I say, sliding a drink in your direction – a large one, you'll need it – as you settle down, and I begin.

I ask you not to interrupt too much, at least not at first. There will be plenty of opportunity for debate afterwards. For now, I request you politely hear me out – as you might indulge a good friend's rather lengthy anecdote.

It's time to meet our cast of suspects – in order of importance. And therefore, for the moment, I must reluctantly remain offstage. I'll hover in the wings, waiting for my cue.

Let us begin – as we should – with the star.

Let's begin with Lana.

2

Lana Farrar was a movie star.

Lana was a big star. She became a star when she was very young, back in the days when stardom still meant something – before anyone with an internet connection could become a celebrity.

No doubt many of you will know her name, or have seen her movies. She made too many to mention. If you're anything like me, one or two of them are very dear to your heart.

Despite retiring a decade before our story begins, Lana's fame endured – and no doubt long after I am dead and forgotten, as though I never existed, Lana Farrar will be remembered, and rightly so. As Shakespeare wrote about Cleopatra, she has earned her 'place i' the story'.

Lana was discovered at the age of nineteen, by the fabled, Oscar-winning Hollywood producer, Otto Krantz – whom she later married. And until his untimely death, Otto dedicated his considerable energy and clout to furthering Lana's career, designing entire movies as showcases for her talents. But Lana was destined to be a star, with or without Otto.

It wasn't just her flawless face, the sheer, luminous beauty of a Botticelli angel – those eyes of endless blue – or the way she held herself, or spoke, or her famous smile. No, there was some *other* quality about Lana – something intangible, the trace of a demi-goddess; something mythical, magical – it made her endlessly, compulsively watchable. In the presence of such beauty, all you wanted to do was gaze.

Lana made a lot of movies when she was very young – and there was, to be honest, a slight sense of mud being slung at a wall, to see what would stick. And while her romantic comedies were hit or miss, in my opinion, and her thrillers came and went, gold was finally struck when Lana played her first tragedy. She was Ophelia in a modern-day adaptation of *Hamlet*, and received her first Oscar nomination. From then on, suffering nobly became Lana's speciality. Call them tear-jerkers or weepies, Lana excelled as every doomed romantic heroine from Anna Karenina to Joan of Arc. She never got the guy; she rarely made it out alive – and we loved her for it.

As you can imagine, Lana made an enormous amount of money for a lot of people. When she was thirty-five, during an otherwise financially catastrophic couple of years for Paramount, the profits from one of her biggest successes kept the studio afloat. Which is why there was a sizeable ripple of shock within the industry when Lana suddenly announced her retirement – at the height of her fame and beauty, at the tender age of forty.

It was a mystery why she had decided to quit – and destined to remain one, for Lana offered no explanation. Not then, nor in the years to come. She never spoke about it publicly.

She told me, though, one wintry night in London, as we drank whisky by the fire, watching snowflakes drift past the window. She told me the whole story, and I told her about the –

Damn. There I go again – already worming my way back into the narrative. It seems that, despite my best intentions, I'm failing to keep myself out of Lana's story. Perhaps I should admit defeat – accept we are inseparably intertwined, she and I, knotted up like a ball of matted string, impossible to tell apart or disentangle.

Even if that's true, however, our friendship came later. At this point in the story, we hadn't met. In those days, I was living with Barbara West in London. And Lana, of course, was in Los Angeles.

Lana was a Californian, born and bred. She lived there, worked there, made the majority of her movies there. However, once Otto died, and she had retired, Lana decided to leave Los Angeles, for a fresh start.

But where to go?

Tennessee Williams famously said there is nowhere to go, when you retire from the movies – unless you go to the moon.

But Lana didn't go to the moon. She went to England instead.

She moved to London with her young son, Leo. She bought them a massive house in Mayfair, six storeys high. She didn't intend to stay for long – certainly not forever: it was a temporary experiment in a new style of living, while Lana worked out what to do with the rest of her life.

The problem was, without her all-consuming career

to define her, Lana had the uncomfortable realization that she didn't know who she was or what she wanted to do with herself. She felt lost, she told me.

It's hard for those of us who remember Lana Farrar's movies to picture her as being 'lost'. On screen, she suffered a great deal but did so with stoicism, inner fortitude and tremendous guts. She would face her destiny without flinching and go down fighting. She was everything you want in a hero.

In real life, Lana couldn't be more different from her screen persona. Once you got to know her intimately, you began to glimpse another person hidden behind the façade: a more fragile and complicated self. Someone who was much less sure of herself. Most people never encountered this other person. But as this story unfolds, we must keep a lookout for her, you and I. For she holds all its secrets.

This discrepancy, for want of a better word, between Lana's public and private selves, was something I struggled with over the years. I know Lana struggled with it too. Particularly when she first left Hollywood and moved to London.

Thankfully she didn't have to struggle too long, before fate intervened, and Lana fell in love – with an Englishman; a slightly younger, handsome business-man named Jason Miller.

Whether this falling in love was, in fact, fate, or just a convenient distraction – a way for Lana to postpone, perhaps indefinitely, all those tricky existential dilem-mas about herself and her future – is open to question. In my mind, at least.

Anyway, Lana and Jason were married. London became Lana's permanent home.

Lana liked London. She liked it largely, I suspect, because of the English reserve – people tended to leave her alone there. It's not in the English national character to accost ex-movie stars on the street, demanding selfies and autographs, no matter how famous they might be. So, for the most part, Lana could walk around the city undisturbed.

She walked a lot. Lana enjoyed walking – when the weather allowed it.

Ah, the weather. Like anyone else who spends any length of time in Britain, Lana developed an unhealthy preoccupation with the climate. As the years passed, it became a constant source of frustration for her. She liked London but, after nearly ten years of living there, the city and its weather had become synonymous in her mind. They were inextricably linked: London equalled *wet*, equalled *rain*, equalled *grey*.

This year had been particularly gloomy. It was nearly Easter and, so far, not a hint of spring had material-ized. Currently, it was threatening rain.

Lana glanced up at the blackening skies as she wandered through Soho. Sure enough, she then felt a spot of rain on her face – and another on her hand. *Damn.* She had better turn back now, before it got worse.

Lana started retracing her steps – and her thoughts. She returned to the thorny problem she had been mulling over earlier. Something was bothering her, but she didn't know what it was. She had been feeling anxious for several days. She felt restless, uneasy, as if pursued by something and trying to give it the slip – keeping her head down in the narrow streets, evading what was tailing her. But what was it?

Think, she told herself. *Work it out.*

As she walked, Lana made an inventory of her life, searching for any glaring dissatisfactions or worries. Was it her marriage? Unlikely. Jason was stressed about work, but that was nothing new – their relationship was in a good place at the moment. The problem wasn't there. Then where? Her son, Leo? Was it their conversation the other day? It was just an amicable chat about his future, wasn't it?

Or was it, in fact, far more complicated?

Another spot of rain distracted her. Lana glared resentfully at the clouds. No wonder she couldn't think straight. If only she could see the sky . . . see the *sun*.

As she walked, her mind played on this idea of escaping the weather. Here, at least, there was something that could be done.

How about a change of scene? It was Easter next weekend. What if they took a last-minute trip, in search of sunshine?

Why not go to Greece for a few days? To the island?

Why not, indeed? It would do them good – Jason, Leo, and Lana in particular. She could invite Kate and Elliot, too, she thought.

Yes, that would be fun. Lana smiled. The promise of sunlight and blue skies instantly brightened her mood.

She pulled her phone out of her pocket.

She'd call Kate straight away.

3

Kate was in the middle of a rehearsal.

She was due to open in just over a week, at the Old Vic – in a new, highly anticipated production of *Agamemnon*, the tragedy by Aeschylus. Kate was playing Clytemnestra.

This was the first run-through of the play in the actual theatre, and it was not going well. Kate was still struggling with her performance – more specifically, with her lines, which, at this late stage of the game, was not a good sign.

'For Christ's sake, Kate,' yelled the director, Gordon, from the stalls, in his booming Glaswegian accent. 'We open in ten days! Can you not, for the love of God, sit down with the fucking book and learn the lines?'

Kate was equally exasperated. 'I know the lines, Gordon. That's not the problem.'

'Then what is? Pray enlighten me, love.' But Gordon was being heavily sarcastic and not waiting for an answer. 'Keep going,' he shouted.

Between you and me – *entre nous*, as Barbara West used to say – I don't blame Gordon for losing his temper.

You see, despite Kate's immense talent – and she was hugely talented, let's make no mistake about that – she was also chaotic; messy; temperamental; usually tardy; often belligerent; not always sober; as well as, of course, brilliant, charismatic, funny – and possessed of an unerring instinct for truth, both on and off stage. All of which combined meant – as poor Gordon had discovered – she was a bloody nightmare to work with.

Ah . . . but that's not fair, is it? Slipping in my judgement of Kate like that – under the radar, so to speak – as if you wouldn't notice. I'm a sly one, aren't I?

I've sworn to be objective, in as much as it's possible, and let you make up your own mind. So, I must honour that vow. Henceforth, I will endeavour to keep my opinions to myself.

I will stick to the facts:

Kate Crosby was a British theatre actor. She grew up in London, in a working-class family, south of the river, though any trace of an accent had long since been obliterated by years of drama school and voice training. Kate spoke with what used to be known as a BBC accent – rather refined and hard to place – though, it must be said, her vocabulary remained as earthy as ever. She was deliberately provocative, with a touch of 'the end of the pier', as Barbara West put it. *Bawdy* is the word I'd use.

There was a famous story, about how Kate once met King Charles, when he was still Prince of Wales, at a charity luncheon he was hosting. Kate asked Charles how far away the toilets were – adding that she was so desperate, sir, if she had to, she'd piss in the sink. Charles roared with laughter, apparently, entirely charmed. Kate's eventual damehood was no doubt secured, there and then.

Kate was in her late forties when our story begins. Or possibly older – it's hard to know exactly. Like many actors, the precise date of her birth was a moveable feast. She didn't look her age, anyway. She was lovely to look at, as dark as Lana was fair – dark eyes, dark hair. In her own way, Kate was every inch as attractive as her American friend. But unlike Lana, she used a great deal of make-up, heavy use of eye-liner and several layers of thick black mascara accentuating her big eyes. The mascara never came off, to my knowledge; I think she just added a layer or two daily.

Kate's whole look was more 'actressy' than Lana's – lots of jewellery, chains, bracelets, scarves, boots, big coats – as if she was doing everything she could to be noticed. Whereas Lana, who in many ways was truly extraordinary, always dressed in as simple a manner as possible – as if drawing undue attention to herself would be in bad taste, somehow.

Kate was a dramatic person, larger than life, with a restless energy. She drank and smoked constantly. In this, and every other regard, I suppose, Lana and Kate must be regarded as each other's opposite. Their friendship was always a bit of a mystery to me, I'll admit. They seemed to have so little in common, yet were the very best of friends – and had been for a long time.

In fact, of all the several intertwining love stories in this tale, Lana and Kate's relationship was the earliest, endured the longest – and was perhaps the saddest of all.

How did two such different people ever become friends?

I suspect *youth* has a lot to do with it. The friends we make when young are rarely the kind of people we seek out later in life. The length of time we have known them accords them a kind of nostalgia in our eyes, if you will; an indulgence; a 'free pass' in our lives.

Kate and Lana met thirty years ago – on a film set. An independent movie being shot in London: an adaptation of *The Awkward Age*, by Henry James. Vanessa Redgrave was playing the lead, Mrs Brook, and Lana was her daughter, the ingénue, Nanda Brookenham. Kate had the comic supporting role of the Italian cousin, Aggie. Kate made Lana laugh off-camera as well as on, and over the summer shoot, the two young women became friends. Kate introduced Lana to London nightlife and they were soon out every night, having a raucous time – turning up on set hung-over; sometimes, no doubt, knowing Kate, still drunk.

It's like falling in love, isn't it, when you make a new friend? And Kate was Lana's first close female friend. Her first ally in life.

Where was I? Forgive me, it's proving rather a tricky thing to keep hold of, a linear narrative. I must endeavour to master it, or we'll never make it to the island – let alone the murder.

Kate's rehearsal, that's it.

Well, it struggled on limply, and she kept stumbling through her speeches. But the reason wasn't that she didn't know the lines. She knew the lines. She just didn't feel comfortable in the part – she felt lost.

Clytemnestra is an iconic character. The original femme fatale. She killed her husband and his mistress. A monster – or a victim, depending on how you look at it. What a gift to an actor. Something to really sink your teeth into. You'd think so, anyway. But Kate's performance was remaining bloodless. She seemed unable to summon up the requisite Greek fire in her belly. Somehow, she needed to burrow her way inside the skin, into the heart and mind of the character; discover a small chink of connection that would allow her to inhabit her. Acting, for Kate, was a muddy, magical process. But right now, there was no magic – just mud.

They staggered on to the end. Kate put a brave face on it, but she felt wretched. Thank God she had a few days off now, for Easter, before the tech and dress rehearsals. A few days to regroup, rethink – and pray.

Gordon announced at the end of rehearsal that he wanted everyone word-perfect after Easter. 'Or I will not be responsible for my actions. Is that clear?' He addressed this to the whole cast, but everyone knew he meant Kate.

Kate gave him a big smile and a pretend kiss on the cheek. 'Gordon, love. Don't worry, it's all under control. *Promise.*'

Gordon rolled his eyes, unconvinced.

Kate went backstage to get her stuff. She was still in the process of moving into the star's dressing room and it was a mess: half-unpacked bags, make-up and clothes everywhere.

The first thing Kate did in any dressing room was light the jasmine candle she always bought, for good luck, and to banish that stuffy backstage smell of stale air, old wood, carpet, damp exposed brick – not to mention the sneaky cigarettes she would puff on out of the window.

Having relit the candle, Kate rummaged inside her bag, pulling out a bottle of pills. She shook a Xanax into her hand. She didn't want the whole pill, just a little bit, a *nibble* – to take the edge off her anxiety. She broke it in half, then bit off a quarter. She let the fragment of bitter pill dissolve on her tongue. She rather enjoyed the harsh chemical taste of it; she imagined the nasty taste meant it was working.

Kate glanced out of the window. It was raining. It didn't look heavy – it might brighten up soon. She'd go for a walk along the river. A walk would be good. She needed to clear her head. She had so much on her mind, she felt quite dizzy with it all ... So much ahead – so much to think about, to worry about – but she couldn't bear to face it just now.

Perhaps a drink would help. She opened the little fridge under the dressing table and took out a bottle of white wine.

She poured herself a glass and perched on the dressing table. And she lit a cigarette, strictly against theatre rules, punishable by death, but fuck it – the way things were looking, this was the last time she'd act in this theatre; or any other, come to that.

She threw a look of hatred at the script. It glared back at her from the dressing table. She reached over and turned it face-down. *What a disaster.* Whatever made her think *Agamemnon* was a good idea? She must have been high when she agreed to it. She cringed, visualizing the vicious reviews. *The Times'* theatre critic already hated her; she'd have a field day, tearing her apart. So would that bastard at the *Evening Standard*.

Her phone rang – a welcome distraction from her thoughts. She reached for it and checked the screen. It was Lana.

Kate answered. 'Hey. You okay?'

'I will be,' Lana said. 'I've worked out what we all need is some sunshine. Will you come?'

'What?'

'To the island – for Easter?'

Lana went on before Kate could respond: 'Don't say no. It'll be just us. You, me, Jason and Leo. And Agathi, of course . . . I'm not sure if I'll ask Elliot – he's been annoying me lately. Well, what do you say?'

Kate pretended to deliberate. She tossed her cigarette butt out of the window, into the falling rain.

'I'm booking my flight right now.'

4

Lana's island was a gift. A gift of love.

It was given to her by Otto, as a wedding present. A ridiculously extravagant present, admittedly – but that was typical of Otto, apparently. By all accounts he was quite a character.

The island was in Greece, in the southern part of the Aegean Sea, in a loose group of islands known as the Cyclades. The famous ones you've heard of – Mykonos and Santorini – but the majority of the islands are uninhabited, and uninhabitable. A few are privately owned, like the one Otto bought for Lana.

The island didn't actually cost as much as you might think. Beyond the wildest dreams of most ordinary people, of course, but, taken in its own context – as islands go – it wasn't that expensive to buy, or maintain.

It was tiny, for one thing – a couple of hundred acres in size – barely a rock. And considering the fact its new owners were a Hollywood movie producer and his muse, Otto and Lana ran a fairly humble household. They only hired one full-time member of staff – a caretaker – which was a story in itself, an anecdote Otto loved to tell – delighting, as he did, in the idiosyncrasies of the Greeks. He was entirely captivated by them. And here, far from mainland Greece, it must be said, the islanders could be quite eccentric.

The nearest inhabited island was Mykonos – twenty minutes away by boat. So, naturally, this was where Otto went in search of a caretaker for Lana's island. But finding one proved harder than expected. No one, it seemed, was prepared to live on the island, not even for the generous wage being offered.

It wasn't just that the caretaker would have to endure an isolated and lonely life. There was also a myth – a local ghost story – that the island had been haunted since Roman times. It was considered bad luck to set foot on the island, let alone live there. A superstitious lot, these Mykonians.

In the end, there was only one volunteer for the job: Nikos, a young fisherman.

Nikos was about twenty-five, and recently widowed. He was a silent, sombre person. Lana told me she thought he was seriously depressed. All he wanted, he told Otto, was to be alone.

Nikos was barely literate and he spoke only broken English – but he and Otto managed to make themselves understood, often employing elaborate hand gestures. No contract was drawn up, just a handshake.

And from then on, all year round, Nikos lived alone on the island. Caretaker of the property, and unofficial gardener. There wasn't much of a garden, initially. He had been living there for a couple of years before he started growing vegetables – but when he did, it was with immediate success.

The following year, Otto, inspired by Nikos's efforts, arranged for a small orchard to be imported from Athens – hanging on ropes, suspended from helicopters – apple, pear, peach and cherry trees, all planted in a walled garden. They too thrived. Everything seemed to bloom, on this island of love.

Sounds blissful, doesn't it? Idyllic, I know. Even now, it's so tempting to romanticize it. No one wants reality; we all want a fairytale – and that's how Lana's story seemed to the outside world. A charmed, magical life. But if there's one thing I've learned, it's that things are seldom as they seem.

One night, years later, Lana told me the truth about her and Otto; how their fairytale marriage wasn't all it was cracked up to be. Perhaps it was inevitable; along with Otto's larger-than-life personality, his generosity, relentless drive and ambition came other, less attractive qualities. He was much older than Lana, for one thing, and had a paternal, even patriarchal attitude towards her. He was controlling of her actions, dictating what she ate and what she wore, relentlessly critical of any choice she might make, undermining her, bullying her – and, when drunk, emotionally and even physically abusive.

I can't help but suspect, if they had stayed together for longer, that Lana would have eventually rebelled, as she grew older and more independent. Surely, one day, she would have left him?

We'll never know. Only a few years into their marriage, Otto had a fatal heart attack – in LAX airport, of all places. He was on his way to meet Lana on the island, to rest, on doctor's orders. Sadly he never made it to his destination.

Following Otto's death, Lana kept away from the island for several years. The memories and associations were too upsetting for her. But, as time passed, she became able to remember the island, and all the good times they had shared, without too much pain. So she decided to return.

From then on, Lana visited at least twice a year, sometimes more often. Particularly once she moved to England and needed a refuge from its climate.

Before we move on, I must tell you about the ruin. It plays an important part in our story, as you will see.

The ruin was my favourite spot on the island. A semi circle of six broken, weathered marble columns in a clearing, surrounded by olive trees. An atmospheric spot, easy to imbue with magic. A perfect spot for contemplation. I would often sit on one of the stones, just breathe, and listen to the silence.

The ruin was the remains of an ancient villa complex that once stood on the island, over a thousand years ago. It had belonged to a wealthy Roman family. All that remained were these broken columns – which, Lana and Otto were told, had once housed an intimate theatre, a small auditorium, used for private performances.

A nice story – if a little contrived, in my opinion. I couldn't help but suspect it was invented by an over-zealous real estate agent, hoping to pique Lana's imagination. If so, it worked. Lana was instantly captivated: she always called the ruin 'the theatre' from then on.

And, for a while, she and Otto revived this ancient tradition: performing sketches and playlets at the ruin in the summer evenings, written and acted by the family and their guests. A practice that was mercifully abandoned long before I ever went to the island. The prospect of having to indulge visiting movie stars in their amateur dramatics is, frankly, more than I could bear.

Apart from the ruin, there were only a couple of structures on the island, both fairly recent: a caretaker's cottage, where Nikos resided; and the main house itself.

The house was in the middle of the island – a sandstone monster, over a hundred years old. It had pale yellow walls, a red terracotta roof and green wooden shutters. Otto and Lana added to it, extending it, renovating the more dilapidated areas. They built a swimming pool and a guest house in the garden, and a stone jetty on the most accessible beach, where they kept their speedboat.

It's hard to describe how lovely the island is – *was?* I'm struggling a little with my tenses here. I'm not sure where I am – the present, or the past? I know where I would be, given half a chance. I'd give anything to be back there right now.

I can picture it all so clearly. If I shut my eyes, I can be there: on the terrace at the house, a cool drink in my hand, looking out at that view. It's pretty flat for the most part, so you can see a long way: past the olive trees, all the way down to the beaches and coves, and the clear turquoise water. The water, when calm, is blue and glass-like, almost translucent. But, like most things in life, it has more than one nature. When the wind comes, which it does, frequently, the churning waves and currents stir up all the sand in the seabed, turning the water murky, dark and dangerous.

The wind plagues that part of the world. It hits it all the year round; not continuously though, or with the same intensity – but every so often, it works itself into a rage and tears across the water, battering the islands. Agathi's grandmother used to call the Aegean wind *to menos*: which means 'the fury' in English.

The island also has a name, by the way.

The island was named Aura, after the Greek goddess of the 'morning air' or the 'breeze'. A pretty name, which belied the ferocity of the wind, and of the goddess herself.

Aura was a minor deity, a nymph, a huntress, a companion of Artemis. She didn't like men very much and would slaughter them for sport. When she gave birth to two boys, she proceeded to eat one of them, before Artemis quickly spirited away the other.

That's how the locals spoke about the wind, incidentally – as monstrous and devouring. No wonder it made it into their myths, their stories, as personified by Aura.

I was lucky enough never to have personally experienced it – the wind, I mean. I visited the island over several years and was always blessed with unusually docile weather – often missing a gale by a day or two.

But not this year. This year, the fury caught up with me.

5

Lana did invite me to the island, in the end – despite saying to Kate that I was annoying her.

I'm Elliot, by the way, in case you hadn't guessed.

And Lana was only joking when she said that. That's the kind of relationship she and I had. We played around a lot. We kept it light, like the bubbles in a glass of Bollinger.

Not that I was offered champagne, or even cava, on my flight to Greece. Unlike Lana and her family, presumably – who travelled to the island the same way Lana went everywhere, on a private jet. Mere mortals like myself flew commercial; or more often than not, these days, sadly, budget airlines.

And so it is here, at a distinctly down-to-earth check-in desk at Gatwick airport, that I enter this story. As you know, I've been waiting impatiently to introduce myself. Now at last, we can get properly acquainted.

I hope I won't prove disappointing as a narrator. I like to think I'm considered decent company – fairly entertaining; pretty straightforward, good-natured; even occasionally profound – once I've bought you a few drinks, that is.

I'm about forty years old, give or take a year or two. I'm told I look younger. That's down to my refusal to grow up, no doubt – never mind grow old. I still feel like a kid inside. Doesn't everyone?

I'm about average height, perhaps a bit taller. I have a slim build, but am not as razor-thin as I used to be. I used to vanish if I turned sideways. That had a lot to do with cigarettes, of course. I've got it under control now, just the odd joint and the very occasional cigarette, but during my twenties and early thirties, my God, I had a fierce tobacco habit. I used to exist solely on smoke and coffee. I was skinny, wired, edgy and anxious. What a joy I must have been to be around. I've calmed down now, thankfully.

That's the only good thing I'll say about getting older. I'm finally calming down.

I have dark eyes and dark hair, like my old man. Average looks, I'd say. Some have described me as handsome; but I don't think of myself that way at all – unless I'm in good lighting.

Barbara West always said the two most important things in life were lighting and timing. She was right. If the light's too glaring, I see only my flaws. I hate my profile, for instance, and the way my hair sticks up in a weird angle at the back, and my small chin. It's always an unpleasant shock when I catch sight of myself in a side mirror in a department-store changing room, with my bad hair, big nose and no jaw. I don't have movie-star looks, put it like that. Unlike the others in this story.

I grew up outside London. The less said about my childhood, the better. Let's dispense with it in as few words as possible, shall we? How about three?

It was darkness. That about sums it up.

My father was a brute; my mother drank. Together they lived surrounded by filth, squalor and ugliness – like two drunken children squabbling in a gutter.

Don't feel bad for me; this isn't a misery memoir. Just a simple statement of fact. It's a familiar enough tale, I suspect. Like all too many children, I endured an upbringing characterized by long periods of abandonment and neglect, both physical and emotional. I was rarely touched, or played with, barely held by my mother – and the only time my father laid a hand on me was in anger.

This I find harder to forgive. Not the physical violence, you understand, which I soon learned to accept as a part of life, but the lack of *touch* – and its repercussions for me, later, as an adult. How can I put it? It left me unused to – even afraid of? – the touch of another. And it has made intimate relationships, emotional or physical, extremely difficult.

I couldn't wait to leave home. My parents were strangers to me; it felt inconceivable that I was even related to them. I felt like an alien, an extraterrestrial, adopted by an inferior life form – with no choice but to flee and find others of my own species.

If that sounds arrogant, forgive me. It's just when you spend years marooned on the desert island of childhood, trapped with parents who are angry, alcoholic, endlessly sarcastic, full of contempt; who never encourage you, who bully and belittle you, mock you for loving learning or art; who ridicule anything remotely sensitive, emotional or intellectual . . . then you grow up a little angry, a little prickly and defensive.

You grow up determined to defend your right to be – what, exactly? *Different?* An *individual?* A *freak?*

In case I am speaking to a young person now, let me give you something to hold on to: do not despair at being different. For that very difference, initially such a source of shame, so humiliating, and painful, will one day become a badge of honour and pride.

The reality is, these days, I am proud to be different – I thank God I am. And even when I was a child, and full of self-loathing, I sensed there was another world out there. A better world, where I might belong. A brighter world – beyond the darkness, lit by spotlights.

What am I talking about? *The theatre,* of course. Think of that moment the auditorium darkens, the curtain glows, the audience clears its collective throat, settling down, tingling with anticipation. It's magic, pure and simple; more addictive than any drug I ever tried. I knew from a young age, glimpsing it on school trips to plays by the Royal Shakespeare Company, the National Theatre, or West End matinees, that I had to belong to this world.

Also I understood, just as clearly, that if I wanted to be accepted by this world, if I wanted to fit in, I had to change.

Who I was simply wasn't good enough. I had to become someone else.

It seems absurd, writing that now – even painful – but I believed it then, with all my heart. I believed I had to change everything about me: my name, my appearance, how I carried myself, how I spoke, what I talked about, thought about. In order to be part of this brave new world, I needed to become a different person – a better one.

And eventually, one day, I succeeded.

Well, almost – a few tinges of the old me remained, like a bloodstain on a wooden floorboard, leaving a pale red mark, no matter how much you scrub at it.

My full name, by the way, is Elliot Chase.

I flatter myself that my name might not be unknown to you – if you're a theatre-goer? If you don't know the name, you may have heard of my play – or seen it? *The Miserabilists* was a big hit, on both sides of the Atlantic. It ran for a year and a half on Broadway, winning several awards. I was even nominated for a Tony, he says modestly.

Not bad for a first-time dramatist, eh?

Of course, there were the inevitable snide, bitchy comments and malicious stories, spread around by a surprising number of bitter, older, more established writers, envious of this young man's immediate critical and commercial success; accusing me of all kinds of nasty things, ranging from plagiarism to downright theft. I suppose it's understandable. I'm an easy target. You see, for many years, until her death, I lived with Barbara West, the novelist.

Unlike me, Barbara needs no introduction. They probably taught her to you at school. The short stories are always on the curriculum; even though, in my unpopular opinion, she's vastly overrated.

Barbara was many years older than me when we met, and her health was failing. I stayed with her until the end.

I didn't love her – in case you're wondering. Our

relationship was more transactional than romantic. I was her escort; servant; chauffeur; enabler; punching-bag. I once asked her to marry me – but she declined. Nor would she consent to a civil partnership. So we weren't lovers or partners: we weren't even friends – not towards the end, anyway.

Barbara did leave me her house in her will, though. That rotting old mansion in Holland Park. It was enormous and hideous, and I couldn't afford to run it – so I sold it and lived very happily on the proceeds for several years.

What she failed to leave me was the royalties to any of her bestselling books, which would have given me financial security for life. Instead, she dispersed them among various charities and second-hand cousins in Nova Scotia she barely knew.

This disinheritance by Barbara was her last act of spite towards me, in a relationship dominated by petty cruelties. I couldn't forgive her for this. That's why I wrote the play, based on our life together. An act of vengeance, you might say.

I'm not hot-headed. When I become angry, I don't rage – I sit down, very quietly, very still, armed with pen and paper – and plot my revenge with ice-cold precision. I skewered her with that play, exposing our relationship as a sham, and Barbara as the vain, ridiculous old fool that she was.

Between you and me, I'll admit, I was even more delighted with the outraged fury it caused among Barbara's devoted fans worldwide, than I was with its commercial success.

Well, perhaps that's not quite true.

I'll never forget that night my play first premiered in the West End. Lana was on my arm, as my date. And, for a moment, I experienced what it must be like to be famous. Cameras flashing, thunderous applause – and a standing ovation. It was the proudest night of my life. I often remember it, these days, and smile.

Which seems a good place to end this digression. Let us return to our central narrative – back to me and Kate, and our journey from rainy London to sunny Greece.

6

I spotted Kate at Gatwick airport before she saw me. Even at this time in the morning, she looked gorgeous, if somewhat dishevelled.

Her face fell slightly when she noticed me at the check-in desk. She pretended not to see me, heading straight for the back of the queue. But I waved and loudly called her name – enough times for other people to turn around. She had no choice but to look up and acknowledge me. She feigned surprise, and fixed a smile on her face.

Kate came and found me at the front. Her smile didn't waver.

'Elliot, hi. I didn't see you.'

'Didn't you? Funny, I saw you straight away.' I grinned. 'Good morning. Fancy bumping into you here.'

'Are we on the same flight?'

'Looks like it. We can sit together and have a good old gossip.'

'I can't.' Kate held up her script to her chest like a shield. 'I need to work on my lines. I promised Gordon.'

'Don't worry – I'll test you on them. We can work all the way there. Now, give us your passport.'

Kate had no choice, we both knew that – if she

refused to sit with me, it would start the weekend off on a bad note. So her smile remained firm, and she handed me her passport. We checked in together.

No sooner had we taken off, however, and the plane emerged above the clouds, than it became obvious Kate had no intention of practising her lines. She stuffed the script into her bag.

'Do you mind if we don't? I have a terrible headache.'

'Hangover?'

'Always.'

I laughed. 'I know a cure for that. A little vodka.'

Kate shook her head. 'I can't possibly face vodka at this time in the morning.'

'Nonsense, it'll wake you up. Like a punch in the face.'

Ignoring Kate's protestations, I flagged down a passing flight attendant and asked him for a couple of glasses of ice – ice being the only thing on this flight that was offered for free – and though he gave me a funny look, he didn't refuse. Then I produced a handful of miniature vodka bottles I had smuggled on to the plane in my bag. Given the lack of choice of alcohol on airplanes these days, not to mention the exorbitant cost, I find it more convenient – and economical – to travel with my own.

If that sounds irredeemably debauched, I assure you the bottles were tiny. And besides, if Kate and I were forced to spend the rest of this long journey together, we could both probably use an anaesthetic.

I poured some vodka into the two plastic cups. I raised my glass.

'Here's to an entertaining weekend. Cheers.'

'Bottoms up.' Kate drank the vodka in one go, and winced. 'Ugh.'

'That'll cure your headache. Now, tell me about *Agamemnon*. How's it going?'

Kate forced a smile. 'Oh. Really good. *Great.*'

'Is it? *Good.*'

'Why?' Kate dropped the smile and peered at me, suspiciously. 'What have you heard?'

'Nothing. Nothing at all.'

'Elliot, spit it out.'

I hesitated. 'It's just a rumour, that's all . . . that you and Gordon haven't exactly been hitting it off.'

'What? That's absolute bollocks.'

'I thought it must be.'

'Total crap.' Kate opened another mini-bottle of vodka. She refreshed her glass. 'Gordon and I get on like a house on fire.' She knocked back her drink.

'I'm relieved to hear it,' I said. 'I can't wait for the first night. Lana and I will be there, in the front row, cheering you on.'

I smiled at her.

Kate didn't smile back. She looked at me for a moment – an unfriendly look, and silent. I can't bear an awkward pause, so I filled it with an anecdote about a mutual friend going through an absurdly vengeful divorce, involving death threats and email-hacking and all kinds of insanity. A long, complicated story, which I exaggerated for comic effect.

The whole time I spoke, Kate watched me stonily. I could see she didn't find me or the story funny.

As I looked into her eyes, I saw into her mind . . . and read her thoughts:

God, I wish he'd shut up. Elliot thinks he's so bloody funny, so witty – he thinks he's Noël Coward. But he's not. He's just a fucking cun—

Kate didn't like me much – as you may have guessed.

Let's just say she was immune to my particular brand of charm. She thought she hid her dislike well, but like most actresses – particularly ones who like to think of themselves as enigmatic – she was incredibly easy to read.

I met Kate long before I met Lana. Kate was a great favourite of Barbara West's, both on and off stage, and frequently invited to the house in Holland Park, to the famous soirées, euphemistically known as 'dinner parties' but actually debauched free-for-alls for hundreds of people.

Kate intimidated me even then. I'd feel nervous when she'd seek me out at a party – spraying cigarette ash and booze in her wake – taking my arm, leading me aside, leading me astray, making me laugh by mercilessly mocking the other guests. I sensed that Kate was aligning herself with me as another outsider. *I'm not like the others, love,* she seemed to be saying. *Don't be fooled by the cut-glass vowels, I ain't no lady.*

She was keen for me to know she was as much an imposter as I was – the only difference being I was ashamed of my past, not my present. Unlike Kate, I desperately wanted to shed my former skin, to inhabit my current role and fit in with the other guests. By including me in all her jokes, all the nudges, winks and asides, Kate was firmly letting me know that I wasn't succeeding.

To be honest, although I'm wary of criticizing Lana, as she never gave me cause – so this isn't really a criticism – I laughed more often with Kate. Kate was always trying for a laugh – always looking for the joke in everything; always arch and sarcastic. Whereas Lana – well, Lana was a serious person in many ways – extremely direct, always sincere. They were like oil and water, those two, they really were.

Or perhaps it's just a cultural difference? All the Americans I have known have tended to be straight-forward, almost blunt. I respect that – there's a kind of purity to that honesty. ('Scratch a Yank and you'll find a Puritan,' Barbara West used to say. 'Don't forget they all went over on the bloody *Mayflower*.') Unlike we Brits, that is – pathologically polite, almost servile, always agreeing with you to your face, only to bitch about you viciously the moment you turn your back.

Kate and I were much more similar creatures; if it hadn't been for Lana, we might have ended up as friends. That is my only reproach to Lana and all her kindness to me; that she accidentally came between us. As soon as Lana and I started becoming close, you see, Kate began to view me as a threat. I could see it in her eyes – a new hostility, a competitiveness for Lana's attention.

Regardless of how she felt about me, I found Kate to be fascinating and obviously talented – but also complicated and volatile. She made me feel uneasy, or perhaps *cautious* is a better word – the way you feel around an unpredictable, bad-tempered cat, liable to lash out at you with no warning. I don't believe you can ever truly be friends with someone if they frighten you. How can you be yourself? If you're afraid, you can't be authentic.

And, *yes* – I was afraid of Kate. I had good reason to be, as it transpired.

Ah. Have I revealed that too soon? Possibly.

But there it is, I have said it. I must let it stand.

We landed at Mykonos airport – a glorified landing strip, which made it feel even more exotic. Then we took a cab to Mykonos old port, to pick up the water-taxi to the island.

It was late afternoon when we arrived at the port. It was the stuff of picture postcards: blue-and-white fishing boats; tangled nets like balls of wool; the sound of wood creaking on water; the thin smell of gasoline on the sea breeze. The bustling waterfront cafes were packed; there were the sounds of chatter and laughter, and the strong aromas of sludgy Greek coffee and deep-fried squid. I loved it all – it felt so alive; part of me wanted to linger on there forever.

But my destination – or should I say my destiny? – lay elsewhere. So I clambered into the water-taxi after Kate.

We began our trip across the water. The sky was turning violet as we crossed. It was getting blacker by the second.

Soon, the island appeared ahead, a darkening mass of land in the distance. It was almost ominous in the dusk light. Its austere beauty never failed to fill me with something akin to awe.

There she is, I thought. *Aura.*

7

As Kate and I neared the island, another speedboat was leaving it.

It was being driven by Babis – a short, tanned, bald man in his sixties, very smartly dressed. He ran Yialos restaurant in Mykonos – and, subject to a decades-long agreement initiated by Otto, Agathi would phone ahead with a grocery list, which Babis would then deliver, as well as arrange for the house to be aired and cleaned. I was glad to have missed him – he was a bore and a snob, in my opinion.

As he passed us, Babis slowed down his boat. He made a performative show of bowing deeply and cere-moniously to Kate. Three elderly cleaning women were sitting in the back of his boat, next to a pile of empty grocery baskets. As he bowed, the old women exchanged stony looks behind his back.

I bet they hate him, I thought. I was about to comment on this to Kate – but one glance at her told me to keep quiet. She hadn't even noticed Babis. She was staring ahead at the island, a deep frown on her face. She had become increasingly morose as the journey went on. There was clearly something on her mind. I wondered what it was.

We arrived on Aura, and carried our bags in weary silence up the long driveway.

And there, at the end of the path, was the house. It was all lit up, a beacon of light, surrounded by darkness.

Lana and Leo welcomed us warmly. Champagne was opened; and, apart from Leo, we all drank a glass. Lana asked if we might like to unpack and freshen up before dinner?

I asked for the same room I always had – in the main house, the room next to Lana's. Kate requested the summerhouse, where she had slept so well last summer.

Lana nodded at Leo. 'Darling, will you help Kate with her bags?'

Leo, ever gallant, was already on his feet. But Kate declined.

'It's fine, love. I don't need any help. I'm a tough old bird. I can manage. I'll just finish my drink.'

At that moment, Jason wandered in, staring at his phone. He had a deep scowl on his face. He was about to say something to Lana, when he saw Kate and stopped. He didn't see me.

'Oh, it's you.' Jason gave Kate a smile that seemed a little forced. 'Didn't know you were coming.'

'Ta-dah.'

'Darling, I told you I invited Kate,' said Lana. 'You've forgotten, that's all.'

'Who else is here?' Jason sighed. 'Jesus, Lana, I told you – I need to work.'

'No one's going to disturb you, I promise.'

'As long as you didn't invite that prick Elliot.'

'Hello, Jason,' I said, behind him. 'Lovely to see you, too.'

Jason was startled, and had the grace to look

embarrassed. Kate roared with laughter. Lana laughed too. So did Agathi.

We all did – apart from Jason.

And so I come to Jason.

I may as well admit it's impossible for me to write about him with anything approaching objectivity. I'll do my best, of course. But it's difficult. Suffice to say, Jason wasn't my cup of tea. Which is a very English way of saying I couldn't stand the man.

Jason was a funny chap. And I don't mean amusing. He was handsome – well-built, with a strong jaw, clear blue eyes, dark hair. But his personal manner was a constant puzzle to me. I couldn't tell if he was being deliberately brusque – that's a polite word – and didn't give a damn that he was being rude. Or if he just wasn't conscious of how he made other people feel. Sadly, I suspect the former.

Agathi in particular resented the way Jason spoke to her. He used such a condescending tone with her, as if addressing a servant, when it was clear she was so much more than that. She would glare at him: *I was here before you,* her eyes screamed, *and I'll be here after you.*

But Agathi never spoke out of turn. She never criticised Jason to Lana – who remained blind to all of his faults. Lana had a stubborn habit of always seeing the best in everyone – even the worst of people.

'Okay,' Kate said. 'I'm going to unpack. See you lot at dinner.'

She downed the rest of her champagne. Then she slung her bag over her shoulder. She left the kitchen.

*

Weighed down by her bags, Kate descended the narrow flight of stone steps to the lower level.

The summerhouse was at the end of the swimming pool. The pool was made of green marble, surrounded by cypress trees. Otto had it designed to blend in with the original architecture of the main house.

Kate liked staying down here – it was away from the main house and offered her privacy, somewhere removed, where she could retreat.

She let herself into the summerhouse and dropped her bags on the floor. She considered unpacking but it was too much effort. She caught her breath.

Kate felt like crying, suddenly. She'd been feeling emotional all day, and just now, the sight of Lana and Leo together – so happy in each other's company, such easy, intimate affection – made her feel a pang of sorrow, mingled with envy, and strangely tearful.

Why was that? Why, when Leo took his mother's hand, or touched her shoulder, or sweetly kissed her cheek, did Kate want to cry? Because she felt so desperately lonely herself?

No, that was bullshit. It was more than that, and she knew it.

It was being here, on the island – that's what bothered her. Being here, knowing what she had come to do. Was it a mistake? A wrong idea? Possibly . . . Probably.

Too late now, she thought. *Come on, Katie, get it together.*

Something was needed to steady her nerves. What did she bring with her? Klonopin? Xanax? Suddenly, she remembered the little present she'd left herself, last time she was on the island. Could it still be here?

Kate hurried over to the bookcase, running her fingers along the spines. She found the battered yellow book she was looking for:

The Doors of Perception by Aldous Huxley.

She took it from the shelf. It fell open at the right page – revealing a little flattened bag of cocaine. Her eyes lit up. *Bingo.*

Smiling to herself, Kate emptied the cocaine on to the bedside table. Then she used her credit card, and started chopping it up.

8

In the kitchen, Agathi was using a small, sharp knife to deftly gut a sea bream. She pulled out the murky grey entrails in the sink. Dark red blood mingled with running water as she washed out the inside cavity.

She could practically feel her grandmother's hands working through hers; her spirit guiding her fingers as she performed this familiar motion. Her *yiayia* had been in her thoughts all afternoon – in her mind, the old woman was inseparable from this part of the world. There was a slight wildness, a touch of magic, about them both. Her grandmother had been rumoured to be a witch. And Agathi could feel her presence here. She could sense her in the sunlight, and in the sound of the sea – and in gutting a fish.

She turned off the tap, dried the sea bream with kitchen paper, and placed it with the others on a plate.

Agathi was forty-five years old. She had a strong face, black eyes, sharp cheekbones – very Hellenic-looking, to my mind. A handsome woman, who rarely bothered with make-up. Her hair was always pulled back and pinned up. A severe look, perhaps – but Agathi had precious little vanity, and even less free time, which she didn't waste on her appearance. She left that to others.

She considered the fish. They were on the large side.

Three should be enough, she thought. But she'd check with Lana, just in case.

Lana seems happier, she thought. *Good.*

Lana had been in an odd mood recently. Distant, unreachable. Something was obviously bothering her. Agathi knew better than to ask. She was the soul of discretion and never gave her opinion unless asked – even then, only under duress.

Agathi was the only member of the household observant enough to notice this recent change in Lana. The others – the two men in the house – spent very little time contemplating Lana's mood. Leo's selfishness, Agathi excused on account of his youth. Jason, she found harder to forgive.

Agathi felt determined that Lana should have a restful and enjoyable few days on the island. No reason to think she wouldn't.

So far, they were lucky with the weather. No sign of any disturbing wind. The sea couldn't have been flatter on their crossing. There was barely a ripple on the surface.

Their arrival had been bumpier – in a logistical sense. Agathi was a formidable housekeeper and made everything run like clockwork. But today, things were running late. They had arrived to find Babis in the kitchen, the groceries yet to be unpacked and the cleaners still at work in the house, mopping floors and making beds. Babis was visibly embarrassed, and very apologetic. Lana was gracious, of course, insisting it was her fault for giving them such short notice. She thanked all the cleaners individually, and the old ladies beamed at her, adoring, starstruck. Lana and Leo went for a swim and Jason retired moodily to his study, armed with his laptop and phone.

Agathi was left alone with Babis – which was uncomfortable, of course. But she stood her ground. What a pompous arse that man was! Obsequious to Lana, grovelling, practically crawling on the floor. And, in the same breath, he'd hiss at his staff in Greek, dictatorial and contemptuous, as if they were dirt.

Agathi, he loathed above all. To him, she would always be the waitress at his restaurant. He never forgave her for what happened that summer – the first time Otto and Lana appeared for lunch at Yialos, on the hunt for a babysitter, and fate decreed Agathi serve their table. Lana took an instant shine to Agathi. They hired her on the spot, and she became indispensable to them. When their visit came to an end, they asked if she would like to live with them, as a nanny, in Los Angeles. She said 'yes' without even a second thought.

You might think it was the allure of Hollywood that made Agathi so quick to accept – but you'd be wrong. She didn't care where she went, as long as she was with Lana. She was so completely under Lana's spell, in those days. She would have gone to Timbuktu if Lana asked her.

So, Agathi moved to LA with the family, and then London. And she graduated, as Leo grew older, from nanny to cook, housekeeper, assistant, and – was she flattering herself here? – Lana's confidante and best friend? Perhaps this was overstepping the mark slightly;

but not much. In a practical, day-to-day sense, Agathi was closer to her than anyone else.

Alone in the kitchen with Babis, Agathi took wicked pleasure in slowly, painstakingly going through the long grocery list, item by item by item – insisting he check everything was there. He found this excruciating, of course, and there was much heavy sighing and tapping of feet.

When Agathi felt she had tortured him enough, she released him. Then she began to put away all the groceries, and plan the next few meals.

As she poured herself a cup of tea, the back door opened.

Nikos was standing there, in the shadow of the doorway. He held a dagger and a fierce-looking hook in one hand. In his other hand, he had a bag of wet, black, spiky sea urchins.

Agathi glared at him. 'What do you want?' she said in Greek.

'Here.' Nikos held out the sea urchins. 'For her.'

'Oh.' Agathi took the bag.

'You know how to clean them?'

'I know.'

Nikos lingered for a moment. He seemed to be trying to peer over her shoulder, to see who else might be in the kitchen.

Agathi frowned. 'Want anything else?'

Nikos shook his head.

'Then I have work to do,' she said.

She firmly shut the door in his face.

She dumped the bag of urchins on the counter. She

looked at them for a moment. Eaten raw, they were a local delicacy, and Lana loved them. It was kind enough of Nikos, yes; and Agathi didn't begrudge the extra effort it would take to prepare them. But this gesture of his bothered her. Something about it made her nervous.

There was something odd, she thought, about the way he looked at Lana. Agathi had noticed it earlier, when Nikos greeted them at the jetty. Lana hadn't noticed.

But Agathi had. And she didn't like it one bit.

9

Nikos walked away from the back door.

He was thinking how strange it felt, after months of solitude, to be around other people again.

It felt, in some ways, almost like an invasion – as if his island were under siege.

'His island'. How absurd to think of this island as his own. But he couldn't help it.

Nikos had lived a solitary existence on Aura for almost twenty-five years now. He was practically self-sufficient, hunting and growing whatever he needed. He had a vegetable plot at the back of his cottage, some chickens – and an abundance of fish in the sea. He only went back to Mykonos for essentials these days, like tobacco, beer, ouzo. Sex, he did without.

If occasionally he felt lonely, in need of human company – for other voices and laughter – he'd visit the tavern frequented by the locals. It was on the other side of town from Mykonos port, away from the billionaires and their yachts. Nikos would sit alone at the bar, drinking a beer. He wouldn't talk but he'd listen, keeping one ear on local gossip. The other drinkers, apart from acknowledging him with a nod, mainly left him alone. They sensed Nikos was different now – his decades of isolation had turned him into an outsider.

He would listen to them gossiping about Lana, the

old men, sitting at their small tables with their back-gammon sets and dainty glasses of ouzo. Many of them remembered Otto, and, rather quaintly, referred to Lana, in Greek, as 'the screen siren'. They were intrigued by this reclusive American movie star who owned that haunted island – a property, it must be said, that had brought her precious little happiness, and much grief.

That island is cursed, someone said. *Mark my words, it will happen again. Before long, this new husband will go the way of the old one.*

He has no money, said someone else – *the husband is a kept man, paid for by his wife.*

Well, she's rich enough, said another. *I wish mine paid for me.*

This got a laugh.

How true this was about Jason, Nikos didn't know – nor care. He appreciated Jason's predicament. Who could compete with such wealth as Lana possessed? All Nikos had to offer her was his bare hands. But at least he was a real man – not a fake one, like Jason.

Nikos had disliked Jason on sight. He remembered the first time Jason visited Aura, bad-tempered, in a suit and sunglasses, inspecting the island with a proprietorial air.

Nikos continued to observe him at close quarters, over several years, often when Jason had no idea he was being observed. And Nikos had come to the conclusion Jason was a fraud. His latest 'hobby', for instance, pretending to be a hunter – this was the biggest joke so far. Nikos had to make an effort not to laugh, watching Jason handle the guns so clumsily, aiming so badly; yet so full of bravado, like a puffed-up boy pretending to be a man.

As for his kill – pathetic, measly birds that weren't worth the effort of Agathi plucking them. Not to mention a waste of bullets.

A man like that didn't deserve Lana.

She was the only one of them Nikos didn't mind being here. It was her island, after all. She belonged here; she came alive here. She was always deathly pale on arrival, in desperate need of sun. And then, in a few days, the island would work its magic on her – she'd swim in its sea, eat its fish and the fruits of its earth. And bloom like a flower. The most beautiful thing he'd ever seen. A visceral reminder that nature – while glorious and sustaining – was not the same thing as a woman.

Nikos couldn't remember the last time he had been touched. Let alone kissed.

He spent too much time alone. Sometimes he wondered if he were going mad. They said, in the tavern, that the wind drove you mad. But it wasn't the wind.

It was the solitude.

If he left Aura, where could he go? He could no longer be around other people for any extended period of time. His only option was the sea – to live on a boat, sail the islands. But he didn't own a boat large enough and could never afford one fit for more than a fishing trip.

No, he must resign himself to never leaving the island, until he was dead. And probably not even then.

It would be several months, after all, before his body was discovered. By then, in all likelihood, he would be torn apart, eaten, devoured by the other inhabitants of the island – like that dead beetle outside his kitchen door, dismembered and carried away by a long line of industrious ants.

His mind seemed to revolve around death, these days. Death was everywhere on Aura, he knew that.

As he walked away from the house, taking the shortcut through the trees, Nikos saw something that made him stop in his tracks.

A huge wasps' nest.

He stared at it. The nest was massive, the biggest he'd ever seen. It was at the base of an olive tree, in a hollow that was formed by the roots. A large mass of swirling wasps – like a billowing ball of black smoke, turning in on itself. In a way, it was beautiful.

Be crazy to disturb a nest that size. Besides, he didn't want to destroy it. It wasn't right to kill them. The wasps had as much right to be here as anyone else. They were a blessing, really – they ate the mosquitoes. He hoped the family wouldn't see it and demand it be destroyed.

The thing to do, he decided, was to guide the wasps away from the main house – and hopefully not get stung in the process. A plate of meat outside his cottage should do it: beef, chopped up, or a skinned rabbit. The wasps had a particular fondness for rabbit.

Just then, he heard a splash. He stopped. He looked over, through the trees, and saw that Kate had jumped in the swimming pool.

Nikos stood there, invisible in the darkness, watching her swim about.

After a while, Kate seemed to sense his presence. She stopped swimming. She looked around, trying to see beyond the lights, into the dark.

'Who is it?' Kate said. 'Who's there?'

Nikos was about to keep walking, when he heard some footsteps. Then someone else emerged from the shadows – it was Jason, descending the steps. He walked over to the edge of the pool.

Jason stood there, staring at Kate in the water. His face was expressionless, like a mask. Kate swam up to him.

She smiled. 'You should jump in, the water's lovely.'

Jason didn't smile back. 'What are you doing here?'

'What do you mean?'

'You know what I mean. Why are you here?'

Kate laughed. 'You're obviously not pleased to see me.'

'I'm not.'

'That's not very nice.'

'Kate –'

Kate stuck her tongue out at him, and submerged herself with a splash. She swam off underwater, ending the conversation.

Jason turned and walked back to the house.

Nikos hesitated for a moment, pondering what he had just seen. He went to leave – then had a sudden, strange feeling. He froze.

He wasn't alone. Someone else was here, too, in the dark, watching Kate.

Nikos looked around, squinting, trying to see in the darkness. He couldn't see anyone. He listened hard – and there was only silence. But he could swear someone was hiding there.

He hesitated a moment. Then, feeling unnerved, he turned and hurried back to his cottage.

10

I took a couple of glasses of champagne to Lana in her bedroom. She was alone. She was sitting at her dressing table, in a bathrobe. Lana looked even more beautiful, I thought, without make-up.

We chatted for a while, before the door was thrown open. Jason charged into the room. He noticed me and stopped.

'Oh,' Jason said. 'You're here. Who are you two gossiping about?'

Lana smiled. 'No one you know.'

'As long as it's not me.'

'Why?' I said. 'Guilty conscience?'

He glared at me. 'What the fuck's that supposed to mean?'

Lana laughed – but I could tell she was annoyed. 'Jason. He's joking.'

'Well, he's not funny,' he said – adding, with a Herculean effort at wit: 'Ever.'

I smiled. 'Thankfully, thousands of theatre-goers around the world disagree with you.'

'Uh-huh.' He didn't smile back.

These days, Jason's goodwill towards me was entirely depleted – the best I could hope for was that he remain civil and not actually become violent.

He was jealous of me, of course – because I provided

Lana with something he couldn't understand, and was incapable of supplying himself. What was that? Well, for want of a better word, let's call it friendship. Jason couldn't comprehend a world in which a man and a woman could be such close friends.

Although Lana and I weren't just friends – we were soulmates.

But Jason couldn't understand that either.

'Elliot had a bright idea,' Lana said. 'Let's go to Mykonos tomorrow for dinner. What do you think?'

Jason grimaced. 'No, thanks.'

'Why not? It'll be fun.'

'Where? Just don't say Yialos.'

'Why not?'

'Oh, for Christ's sake.' Jason sighed. 'Yialos is a whole production. I thought we came here to relax.'

I couldn't resist intervening. 'Oh, go on, Jason. Think how good the food is at Yialos. Yum, yum.'

Jason ignored me. But he didn't object further, knowing he had little choice. 'Whatever. I need a shower.'

'That's my cue, then. I'll be off. See you both downstairs.'

I went to the door and walked out. I closed it behind me.

Then – and I wouldn't normally admit this, but seeing as it's you, I'll be honest – I pressed my ear to the door. Wouldn't you do the same? They were bound to be talking about me. I was curious to hear what Jason said the moment my back was turned.

Their conversation was faint but audible through the door. Lana sounded irritated.

'I don't understand why you can't be polite to him.'

'Because he's always in your fucking bedroom, that's why.'

'He's one of my best friends.'

'He's in love with you.'

'No, he isn't.'

'Of course he is. Why else has he never had a girl-friend, since that old woman he murdered?'

A pause. 'That's not funny, Jason.'

'Who said I was joking?'

'Darling, did you want something? Or just to start a fight?'

There was another pause, as Jason calmed himself. He continued in a gentler tone. 'I need to talk to you.'

'Okay. But lay off Elliot. I mean it.'

'Fine.' Jason spoke in a low voice. I had to press my ear hard against the door to catch his words. 'It's nothing serious . . . I need you to sign something.'

'Now? Can't it wait?'

'I need to send it out tonight. It'll just take a second.'

Lana paused. 'I thought it wasn't serious.'

'It isn't.'

'So what's the rush?'

'No rush.'

'Then I'll read it tomorrow.'

'You don't need to read it,' Jason said. 'I'm just moving things around. I'll give you the gist.'

'I still need to read it. Let's email it to Rupert, and he can take a look – then I'll sign later. How's that?'

'Forget it.' He sounded furious.

Jason didn't explain – but I had no need of an explanation. Even from several feet away, through solid oak, I knew exactly what he was up to. I could tell by his hesitation and the change in his voice, that the mere mention of her lawyer's name had put him off. Jason realized that his little scheme, whatever it was, wasn't going to work.

'It's fine,' he said. 'It doesn't matter. It can wait.'

'You're sure?'

'Yeah. No worries. I'm going to have a shower.'

At that, I slipped away from the door. I could imagine what happened next.

I imagined Jason going into the bathroom – and the moment he was alone, his smiling mask falling from his face. He stared at himself in the mirror. There was desperation in his eyes. Was it a mistake, he wondered, talking to Lana like that? Had he aroused her suspicions?

He should have waited until she'd had a few drinks – then slid the papers in front of her, and got her to sign them. *Yes, in fact that might still work.*

Later on, after dinner, he'd try again – when she was more relaxed. He had to keep refilling her glass. Be extra nice to her. And knowing Lana, she might have a change of heart, and suggest signing the papers herself – to please him. That was just the kind of thing she might do.

Yes – it might all still work out. *Breathe,* Jason told himself, *breathe and stay calm.*

He turned on the shower. The water was too hot and it lashed against his face, his skin, burning him.

What a relief – to feel that pain, a welcome distraction from all his thinking . . . from everything that he had to do . . . everything that lay ahead.

He closed his eyes and burned.

A little while later, Kate wandered into the kitchen. She was out of breath, and a little high. She hoped the others wouldn't notice.

Perching on a stool, she watched Lana and Agathi prepare dinner. Lana was making a green salad with the spicy green rocket leaves that grew plentifully all over the island. Agathi showed Lana the plate of sea bream she had cleaned.

'I think three's enough, don't you?'

Lana nodded. 'Three's plenty.'

Kate reached for a bottle of wine and poured a glass for her and Lana.

They were soon joined by Leo, fresh from the shower. He looked flushed, and his hair was wet, dripping on to his T-shirt.

Leo was seventeen now, almost eighteen. He looked like a younger, male version of Lana – like a young Greek god. The teenage son of Aphrodite – what was his name? – Eros. He looked as Eros must have looked. Blond hair, blue eyes, athletic and lean. And a gentle soul, too, like his mother.

Lana glanced at him. 'Darling, dry your hair. You'll catch cold.'

'It'll dry in a second. There's like zero humidity outside. Do you need any help?'

'Can you set the table?'

'Where are we eating? In or out?'

'How about outside? Thank you.'

Kate watched Leo with approval. 'Aren't you *gorgeous*, Leo? When did you get so handsome? Fancy some wine?'

Leo shook his head as he collected place mats and napkins. 'I don't drink.'

'Come on, then, sit down, spill the beans.' Kate patted the stool next to hers and beckoned him over. 'Who's the lucky girl? What's her name?'

'Who?'

'Your girlfriend.'

'I don't have a girlfriend.'

'But you *must* be seeing someone. Go on . . . tell us. What's her name?'

Leo looked mortified, muttered something unintelligible and hurried out of the kitchen.

'What's wrong?' Kate turned to Lana, mystified. 'Don't tell me he's single? He can't be. He's *gorgeous*.'

'So you said.'

'Well, he is. Should be shagging away like mad, at his age. What's wrong with him? Do you worry he's a bit . . . ?' Kate trailed off and gave Lana a meaningful look. '*You know*.'

'No.' Lana gave her a quizzical smile. 'What?'

'I don't know . . . *Attached —*'

'Attached? To whom?'

'To *whom*?' Kate laughed. 'To you, my love.'

'Me?' Lana looked genuinely surprised. 'I don't think Leo's particularly attached to me.'

Kate rolled her eyes. 'Lana. Leo is besotted with you. He always has been.'

Lana brushed this aside. 'If he is, he'll grow out of it. I'll be sorry when he does.'

'Do you think he might be gay?'

Lana shrugged. 'I have no idea, Kate. What if he is?'

'Maybe I should ask him.' Kate smiled and poured herself another glass, warming to the idea. 'In a "big sister" kind of way – you know? I'll talk to him for you.'

Lana shook her head. 'Please don't.'

'Why not?'

'I don't think you're the big sister type.'

Kate considered this. 'No, I don't think I am either.' They both laughed.

'What's so funny?' I said, as I walked into the kitchen.

'Never mind,' said Kate, still laughing.

She raised her glass to Lana. 'Cheers.'

There was a lot of laughter that night. We were a merry bunch – you'd never guess it was the last time we would be together like this.

What could possibly happen in the space of a few hours, you might ask; what could go so badly wrong as to end in murder?

It's hard to say. Can anyone pinpoint that precise moment when love turns to hate? Everything ends, I know that. Especially happiness. Especially love.

Forgive me, I've become such a cynic. I used to be so idealistic when young – romantic, even. I used to believe that love lasted forever. Now, I don't. Now, I know only this for sure – the first half of life is pure selfishness; the second half, all grief.

Indulge me for a moment, if you will – let me linger there, and enjoy this last happy memory.

We ate dinner outside under the stars. We sat beneath the pergola, lit by candlelight and surrounded by sweet-smelling climbing jasmine.

We began with the salty sea urchins, freshly pre-pared by Agathi. Eaten raw with a sharp squeeze of lemon, they've never been to my taste, personally – but if you close your eyes and swallow fast, you can pretend they're oysters. Then the grilled sea bream, and sliced steak, various salads and garlic-tossed vegetables – and the pièce de résistance: Agathi's deep-fried potatoes.

Kate didn't have much of an appetite – so I ate for two, piling my plate high. I eulogized Agathi's cooking, careful to tactfully praise Lana's efforts also. But her healthy salads couldn't compare to those decadent potatoes, grown in the red earth of Aura itself, golden, and oozing oil. It was a perfect meal, that last supper.

Afterwards, we sat by the fire pit. I chatted to Lana, while Leo played a game of backgammon with Jason.

Then Kate suddenly demanded Agathi's crystal. She went into the house to fetch it.

I must tell you about the crystal. It held near-mythical status within the family. A crude fortune-telling device, it had belonged to Agathi's grandmother, and sup-posedly had magical qualities.

It was a pendant – a white opaque crystal, in the

shape of a small cone, like a baby pine cone, attached to a silver chain. You held the chain in your right hand, dangling the crystal over the open palm of your left hand. You asked a question – phrasing it so it could be answered with a 'yes' or a 'no'.

The crystal would swing in response. If it moved like a pendulum, in a straight line, the answer was 'no'. If it swung in a circle, the answer was 'yes'. Absurd in its simplicity – but with an unnerving tendency to give accurate results. People would consult it about their future plans, their intentions – *should I accept this job, should I move to New York, should I marry this man?* The majority would unfailingly report back – months, sometimes years, later – that the crystal had been right in its prediction.

Kate believed in the magic of the crystal passionately, in that naive way she sometimes had, with a childlike faith. She was convinced it was the genuine article – a Greek oracle.

We all took turns on it that night – asking it our secret questions – apart from Jason, who wasn't interested. He didn't stay long in any case. He lost his temper when Leo beat him at backgammon – and stormed into the house, in a sulk.

Once the four of us were alone, the atmosphere became more convivial. I rolled a joint. Lana never smoked weed, but tonight she broke a cardinal rule and had a drag; so did Kate.

Leo took out his guitar, and played something he had written. A duet, for him and Lana. It was a pretty song; mother and son had sweet voices that complemented each other. But Lana was stoned, and she kept forgetting the words. Then she got the giggles, which Kate and I found hilarious – much to Leo's irritation.

How annoying we must have been to him, this earnest seventeen-year-old boy; these silly, stoned adults behaving like teenagers. We couldn't stop laughing, the three of us, clinging on to each other, rocking back and forth with laughter.

I'm glad I have that memory. The three of us, laughing. I'm glad it's untainted.

It's hard to believe, in twenty-four hours, one of us would be dead.

Before I tell you about the murder, I have a question for you.

Which comes first – character or fate?

This is the central question in any tragedy. What takes precedence – free will or destiny? Were the terrible events of the next day inevitable, ordained by some malevolent god? Were we doomed – or was there hope of escape?

This question has haunted me over the years. *Character or fate?* What do you think? I'll tell you what I think. Having deliberated long and hard, I believe that they are one and the same thing.

But don't take my word for it. The Greek philosopher Heraclitus said:

Character is *fate.*

And if Heraclitus is right, then the tragedy that awaited us in a few hours was a direct consequence of our characters – of who we were. Correct? So, if *who you are* determines what happens to you, then the real question becomes:

What determines *who you are*?

What determines your *character*?

The answer, it seems to me, is that my entire personality – all my values, and opinions about how to get on in the world, succeed, or be happy – can be traced directly back to the shadowy, forgotten world of my childhood, where my character was forged – and ultimately defined – by all the things I learned to conform to, or even rebel against, but was nonetheless defined by.

It took me a long time to come to this realization. When I was young, I resisted thinking about my childhood, or my character, for that matter. Perhaps that's not surprising. My therapist once told me that all traumatized children, and the adults they become, tend to focus exclusively on the outside world. A kind of hyper-vigilance, I suppose. We look *outwards*, not inwards – scanning the world for danger signs – is it safe or not? We grow up so terrified of incurring anger, for instance, or contempt, that now, as adults, if we glimpse a stifled yawn while talking to someone, a look of boredom or irritation in their eyes, we feel a horrible, frightening disintegration inside – like a frayed fabric being ripped apart – and swiftly redouble our efforts to entertain and please.

The real tragedy is, of course, by always looking outwards, by focusing so intently on the other person's experience, we lose touch with our own. It's as if we live our entire life pretending to be ourselves, as imposters impersonating ourselves; rather than feeling *this is really me, this is who I am.*

That's why, these days, I repeatedly force myself to return to my own experience: not *are they enjoying themselves?* – but *am I?* Not *do they like me?* But *do I like them?*

So in that spirit, I ask the question:

Do I like you?

Of course I do. You're a little quiet – but a great listener. And we all love a good listener, don't we? God knows, we spend our whole lives not being heard.

I started having therapy in my mid-thirties. By then, I felt that I had enough distance from my past for me to begin to safely glance at it; to squint at it through my fingers. I chose group therapy not just because it was cheaper but, truthfully, because I like watching people. I've been so bloody lonely my whole life; I enjoy watching others and seeing them interact – in a safe space, I hasten to add.

My therapist was called Mariana. She had dark inquisitive eyes, long, wavy dark hair – I think she might have been Greek, or half Greek. She was wise and very kind, for the most part. But she could be brutal too.

I remember once, she said something chilling – it messed up my head for a long time. Looking back, I think it changed my entire life.

'When we are young,' Mariana said, 'and afraid – when we are shamed and humiliated – something happens. Time *stops*. It freezes, in that moment. A version of us is trapped, at that age – forever.'

'Trapped where?' asked Liz, one of the group.

'Trapped *here*.' Mariana tapped the side of her head. 'A frightened child is hiding in your mind – still unsafe; still unheard and unloved. And the sooner you get in touch with that child and learn to communicate with them, the more harmonious your life will be.'

I must have looked dubious, because Mariana delivered the killer blow directly to me:

'After all, that's what he grew you for, isn't it, Elliot? A strong adult body, to look after him and his interests? To take care of him, protect him? You were meant to liberate him – but ended up becoming his jailer.'

Strange, that. Hearing a truth you've always known, in your heart, but never put into words. Then one day, someone comes along and spells it out for you – *this is your life – here it is, take a look.* Whether you hear it or not is up to you.

But I heard it. I heard it loud and clear.

A terrified child trapped inside my mind. A child who won't go away.

Suddenly it all made sense. All the uneasy feelings I experienced on the street or in social situations, or if I had to disagree with someone, or assert myself – the queasiness in my stomach, fear of eye contact – this had nothing to do with me, nothing to do with the here and now. They were old feelings that were displaced in time. They belonged to a little boy long ago, who was once so afraid, under attack, and unable to defend himself.

I thought I had left him behind me, years ago. I thought *I* was running my life. But I was wrong. I was still being run by a frightened child. A child who couldn't tell the difference between the present and the past – and, like an unwitting time traveller, was forever stumbling between them.

Mariana was right: I had better take the kid out of my head – and sit him on my lap, instead.

It would be much safer for both of us.

Character *is* fate. Remember that, for later.

Remember the kid, too.

And I don't just mean the kid in me, but the kid in *you*.

'I know telling you to love yourself is a big ask,' Mariana used to say. 'But learning to love, or, at least, have compassion for, the child you once were, is a step in the right direction.'

You might laugh at that. You might roll your eyes. You might think it sounds Californian and self-indulgent, full of self-pity. You may say you're made of stronger stuff. Possibly, you are. But let me tell you something, my friend: self-derision is merely a defence against feeling pain. If you laugh at yourself, how will you ever take yourself seriously? How will you ever feel everything you went through?

Once I saw the kid in me, I started seeing kids in other people – all dressed as adults, play-acting at being grown-up. But I saw through the performances now, to the frightened children beneath. And when you think of someone as a child, it's impossible for you to feel hatred. Compassion arises, and –

You're such a hypocrite, Elliot. Such a damn liar.

That's what Lana would say, right now – if she were looking over my shoulder, reading this. She'd laugh, and call me out on my bullshit:

What about Jason? Lana would say. *Where's your compassion for him?*

Good point. Where is my compassion for Jason?

Have I been unfair? Misrepresenting him? Twisting the truth, deliberately making him unlikeable?

Possibly. I suspect my empathy for Jason will

forever be limited. I can't see beyond his terrible actions. I can't see into the heart of the man – all the things he endured as a kid: the bad things, the indignities; the cruelties that made him believe the only way to succeed in life was to be selfish, ruthless, a liar and a cheat.

That's what Jason thought being a man was. But Jason wasn't a man.

He was just a kid, playing make-believe.

And kids shouldn't play with guns.

13

Bang, bang, bang.

I woke up with a fright. What the hell was that noise?

It sounded like gunfire. What time was it? I checked my watch. Ten a.m.

Another gunshot.

I sat up in bed, alarmed. Then I heard Jason outside, swearing with annoyance as he missed yet another bird.

It was Jason hunting, that's all. I sank back in bed with a groan.

Jesus, I thought. *What a way to wake up.*

And so, we come to the day of the murder.

What can I say about that terrible day? Truthfully, if I had known how it would end, and the horrors it would bring, I never would have got out of bed. As it was, I must confess that I slept soundly, troubled by no bad dreams, no premonitions of what lay in wait.

I always slept well on Aura. The island was so quiet. So peaceful. No drunks or garbage trucks to disturb your sleep. No, it took Jason, with a gun, to do that.

I got out of bed, the cold stone slabs on the floor waking up my feet. I made my way to the window and threw open the curtains. Sunlight flooded in. And I looked out at the clear blue sky, the orderly rows of tall green pine trees, and the blue-and-silver olive trees, pink spring flowers, and clouds of yellow butterflies. I listened for a moment to a chorus of cicadas and bird-song, breathing in the heavy scents of earth, sand and sea. It was glorious – I couldn't help but smile.

I decided to do a little work before going down-stairs. I always felt inspired when I was on the island. So I sat at the desk and opened my notebook. I sketched out some ideas for a drama I was working on.

Then I had a quick shower, and went downstairs. The strong smell of coffee beckoned me to the kit-chen, where a fresh pot was on the stove. I poured myself a cup.

No sign of the others. I wondered where they were.

Then, looking out of the window, I noticed Leo and Lana outside. They were hard at work in the garden.

Aided by Nikos, Leo was digging up a plot of earth in an old flower bed. Nikos was doing most of the work, exerting himself. His vest was drenched with sweat. Lana was crouched nearby, picking cherry tomatoes, collecting them in a wicker basket.

I poured myself another cup of coffee. Then I went to join them.

I left the house and made my way down the uneven stone steps to the lower level. As I walked past the walled orchard, I glanced inside, at the rows of peach and apple trees. They had white and pink blossoms on their branches, and tiny yellow flowers growing among the roots.

Spring, it seemed, yet to arrive in England, was in full bloom on Aura.

'Good morning,' I said, as I reached Leo and Lana.

'Elliot, darling. Here –' Lana popped a cherry tomato into my mouth. 'Something sweet to start the day off.'

'Am I not sweet enough?' I said, chuckling, my mouth full.

'Almost. Not quite.'

'Mmm.' The tomato was indeed sweet and delicious. I took another from Lana's basket. 'What's going on?'

'We're planting a new vegetable garden. Our new project.'

'What's wrong with the old one?'

'This is for Leo. He needs his own plot.' Lana smiled at me with a hint of amusement. 'He's vegan now, you know.'

'Ah,' I said, smiling back. 'You did mention it, yes.'

'We're going to grow *everything*,' Leo said, gesturing enthusiastically at the dug-up earth.

'Almost everything,' Lana said, smiling.

'Kale and cauliflower, broccoli, spinach, carrots and radishes . . . what else?'

'Potatoes,' Lana said. 'So we stop stealing Nikos's. They were so delicious last night, by the way. Thank you.'

She directed this at Nikos with a smile. He waved away the compliment, embarrassed.

'Room for a little marijuana?' I asked.

'No.' Leo shook his head. 'I don't think so.'

Lana winked at me. 'We'll see.'

I glanced in the direction of the summerhouse. 'Where's madam?'

'Still asleep.'

'And Jason?'

Before she could reply, the answer came – a loud gunshot. And then another shot – from just behind the house.

I jumped out of my skin. 'Jesus.'

'Sorry,' Lana said. 'It's Jason.'

'Shooting people?'

'Just pigeons, so far.'

'It's murder.' Leo pulled a face. 'It's an act of violence. It's disgusting and offensive. It's *gross*.'

Lana's voice took on a patient but strained quality, making me think they'd had this discussion before. 'Well, darling, I know that, but he enjoys it – and we do eat everything he kills, so it doesn't go to waste.'

'*I* don't eat it. I'd rather starve.'

Wisely, Lana changed the subject. She touched Leo's arm and gave him a pleading look.

'Leo, can you perform a miracle and raise the dead? Remind Kate the picnic was all her idea, will you? Agathi has put so much work into it. She's been cooking all morning.'

Leo sighed. He stabbed his spade in the earth. He didn't look thrilled about the assignment.

'Nikos,' he said, 'we'll finish up later, all right?'

Nikos nodded.

While Lana showed me where the bulbs were going to go, I glanced at Nikos, over her shoulder. He took a break from digging for a moment. He caught his breath and wiped his brow.

How old was Nikos then, I wonder? He must have been in his late forties, and I noticed that his once jet-black hair was streaked with white, his face tanned and deeply lined.

He was an odd man. He only spoke directly to Agathi and Lana or occasionally to Leo. He never spoke to me, even though I had been to the island several times. He seemed wary of me, somehow, as if I were untamed.

And as I looked at him, I noticed something strange. He was staring at Lana with the oddest expression. It was quite intense, and completely unselfconscious.

He was looking at her with adoration, fascination – with a faint half-smile on his lips. He looked younger, somehow, almost boyish.

Gosh, I thought, as I watched him gaze at her. *He's in love with her.*

I don't know why I was surprised. It made perfect sense, on reflection. Put yourself in his place – imagine being stranded on a tiny island all year round, deprived of any company, male or female, only to have a goddess wash up on your shore every few months. Of course he was in love with her.

We all were. All of us – Otto, Agathi, me, Jason. Half the world. Even Kate, at one time, was entirely besotted. And now Nikos was, too. He stood no chance against Lana's charms, poor bastard. He was bewitched, like the rest of us.

But spells don't last forever, you know. One day, the spell breaks, the enchantment ends; the illusion is over.

And nothing is left but thin air.

14

Kate woke up to someone banging on the door.

She rubbed her eyes, disorientated. It took her a second to work out where she was – on the island, in the summerhouse. Her head was throbbing. Another bang at the door made her groan.

'Stop it, for Christ's sake,' she cried out. 'Who is it?'

'It's Leo. Wake up.'

'Go away.'

'It's after eleven. Get up – you're late for the picnic.'

'What picnic?'

Leo laughed. 'Don't you remember? It was your idea. Mum says hurry up.'

Kate had no idea what he was talking about. And then, vaguely, hazily, it started coming back to her – a recollection of overexcited drunken plans, hatched last night, to have a picnic on the beach. The thought of food right now made her feel physically sick.

Leo banged again. And Kate lost her temper.

'Give me a fucking minute!' she yelled.

'How many minutes do you need?'

'Five hundred thousand.'

'You can have five. Then we're going without you.'

'Go, *now. Please leave.*'

Leo sighed heavily. His footsteps retreated.

Swearing under her breath, Kate sat up, wearily swinging her feet over the bed. Her head was heavy and she felt woozy. Christ, she felt rough. The latter part of the evening was a total blur. Had she said anything she shouldn't? Done something stupid? It would be just like her to betray herself in a drunken slip. That mustn't happen. She must keep focused.

Idiot, she thought, *be more careful.*

She had a quick shower to wake herself up. Her head was aching, but she didn't have any paracetamol. So she took half a Xanax instead. There was nothing to wash it down with, except the dregs of a bottle of champagne from last night. Feeling rather sordid, she popped a cigarette in her mouth. Then she grabbed her sunglasses, and, as a sudden afterthought, the script for *Agamemnon*.

Thus armed, Kate left the summerhouse.

As she walked to the beach, Kate passed Nikos's cottage.

The cottage was very much in harmony with its surroundings. Built from stone and wood, it had a huge green cactus growing outside the front door, partly covering one wall. Huge, thorny cactus leaves spread out along the path. There was ivy growing up another wall, in a tangle of leaves and stems. An old rope hammock was suspended between two gnarled, bent olive trees.

Kate slowed down as she walked by, and peered at the cottage. Something had attracted her attention. What was it?

The smell, or that sound? *What was that noise?*

A loud buzzing, like a beehive – but the smell wasn't honey. It was a disgusting, creeping stench – so revolting, in fact, that Kate's hand flew to cover her nose. It stank of flesh gone bad; rotting meat, putrefying in the sun.

And then she saw the source – both of the sound and the stink.

A black cloud of wasps, buzzing around a stump of wood. And there, on the wood, the remains of the bloodied carcass of a small animal. A rabbit, perhaps. It was crawling with ants and wasps, fighting over it, devouring it.

Kate felt sick to look at it. She was about to walk off, when she noticed a figure at the window, staring at her.

Nikos was standing there. He was shirtless. He was looking right at Kate. Expressionless, his blue eyes fixed on her.

Kate felt an involuntary shiver. She kept walking, and didn't look back.

15

Leo advised us to give up waiting for Kate, so we made our way to the beach without her. Lana walked slightly ahead, laden with towels. Leo and I followed, carrying the heavy picnic hamper, each of us holding a handle.

Of the several beaches on Aura, this was my favourite. It was the smallest; Agathi called it '*to diamánti*' – 'the diamond' – and it was a jewel, a perfect beach in miniature.

The sand was soft, thick and white, like sugar. Pine trees grew almost all the way to the water's edge, dropping a fine carpet of green needles on the sand that crunched under your feet. The sea was crystal-clear, where it was shallow; further off, it became green, aquamarine, turquoise; and finally, a deep, dark blue.

Years ago, Otto had had a wooden raft built, a little way out – a raised platform, bobbing in the waves, accessible by a rope ladder. I would often swim out to the raft, keeping my head above water, a book clenched between my teeth; climb up, lie in the sun and read.

That morning, we parked the picnic hamper in the shade of a tree, then Lana and I went for a swim. The water temperature was fairly bracing, but not too chilly for the time of year. Lana swam to the raft, and I followed her.

Alone on the beach, Leo opened the lid of the hamper and investigated its contents.

It was indeed a feast, prepared by Agathi – baked vegetables, stuffed with rice and mincemeat, stuffed vine leaves, different kinds of local cheese, smoked salmon sandwiches, sweet melons and cherries.

Apart from fruit, there wasn't much vegan fare for Leo. He searched dispiritedly through the hamper – until, at the bottom, he found it. Wrapped in clingfilm, labelled 'L', was a small stack of tomato and cucumber sandwiches in brown bread, with no butter.

Not very appetizing, he thought. Obviously a passive-aggressive attack on his dietary requirements by Agathi. But better than nothing, so he took a sandwich.

Then Leo sat in the shade of a pine tree. He ate his lunch while reading his book – *An Actor Prepares*. He was finding it dull, admittedly. Stanislavski was a lot more heavy-going than he expected – but he was determined to persevere.

Lana didn't know this yet, but Leo had just sent off his applications to drama schools in the UK and the US. He hoped she wouldn't mind – but truthfully, given their talk the other day in London, he wasn't so sure. He planned to speak to her about it further this weekend.

If I ever get the chance, he thought, *with Kate and Elliot here, monopolizing her every second.*

A distant gunshot suddenly distracted him. Then another.

Leo scowled. Those poor birds, shot for that psycho's amusement. It angered Leo so much, he was afraid he'd do something drastic.

Maybe he should.

Maybe it was time to make a stand – make a deliberate point. Nothing excessive – something subtle, but effective. But what?

The answer came to him at once.

The guns.

What if Jason found his guns missing – and no one knew where they were? He'd blow a fuse. He'd lose his mind.

Yes, Leo thought, smiling, *that's it. When we get back to the house, I'll hide the guns somewhere he'll never find them. That'll serve him right.*

Pleased with his decision, Leo finished his sandwich. Then he padded through the sand, back to the hamper, in search of cherries.

16

Jason was alone at the ruin. He had gone there with a rifle, to practise his aim.

His target was a tin can. It was balanced on one of the ruined columns, and, so far, had remained unscathed.

He was relieved to be alone. The mindless chatter of Lana's friends irritated him at the best of times. And now, when he had so much on his mind, it was almost unbearable.

Just then, a small bird, a wood pigeon, settled on one of the broken columns. It seemed oblivious to Jason standing there. He gripped the gun in his hands. *Okay*, he said to himself. *Focus.*

He carefully took aim, and –

'Jason.'

Distracted, he fired – but his aim was off. The bird flew away, unhurt. He turned around, furious.

'I have a gun in my hand, for Christ's sake! Do not creep up on me like that.'

Kate smiled. 'You won't shoot me, love.'

'Don't bet on it.' Jason glanced over her shoulder. 'Where are the others?'

'We just left the beach. They're back at the house, showering. No one saw me – if that's what you mean.'

'What are you doing? Why are you here?'

'Lana invited me,' Kate said with a shrug.

'You should have said no.'

'I didn't want to say no. I wanted to see her.'

'Why?'

'She's my friend.'

'Is she?'

'Yes. You seem to forget that at times.' Kate sat down on a low slab of marble, then lit a cigarette. 'We need to talk.'

'What about?'

'Lana.'

'I don't want to talk about Lana.'

'She knows, Jason.'

'What?' He stared at her for a second. 'You told her?'

Kate shook her head. 'No. But she knows. I can tell.'

Jason studied Kate's face for a second. To his relief, he decided he didn't believe her. She was being dramatic, as usual.

'You're imagining it.'

'I'm not.'

There was silence for a second. Jason looked away, playing with the gun in his hands. When he spoke again, there was a suspicious tone to his voice.

'You better not say anything, Kate. I mean it.'

'Is that a threat?' Kate dropped her cigarette and ground it into the earth with her foot. 'Darling, how romantic.'

Jason looked into her dark, brilliant, hurt eyes – they had a slight shine to them to indicate she'd been drinking. But she wasn't drunk – not the way she had been last night.

He could also see his own face reflected in Kate's eyes. His own unhappy face. And, for a second, did Jason consider abandoning his defences? Did he nearly fall to his knees, bury his head in Kate's lap – and unburden himself, telling her the truth about the terrible trouble he was in? How his juggling act with other people's money had collapsed, all the balls tumbling through his fingers – how he needed a massive financial injection, money he didn't have, but crucially Lana did; and, without it, he would almost certainly be going to jail?

The thought of this, of jail, being caged like a bird, made Jason's heart thud in his chest. He'd do anything to prevent it. He felt so afraid, like a little boy – he wanted to cry his eyes out. But he didn't.

Instead, he propped up the gun against a column. He bent down, reached around Kate's waist – and pulled her to her feet.

He leaned forward and kissed her on the lips.

'Don't,' Kate whispered. 'Don't.'

She tried to pull away but he didn't let her. Jason kissed her again.

This time, Kate let him.

While they kissed, Jason had a funny feeling – a kind of sixth sense, perhaps? – that they were being observed.

Is it Nikos? he thought. *Is he watching us?*

Jason pulled away for a second, and looked around. But there was no one there. Just the trees, and the earth. And the sun, of course – white, dazzling, burning in the sky.

It blinded him to look at it.

17

Almost immediately, the weather began to change.

The sun disappeared behind a cloud, casting us into a gloomy half-light. And the wind, which had been picking up all day, first as a whisper, and now as a wail, began rushing at us, in a rage, across the water; tearing along the ground, shaking bushes and shrubs, rattling spiky cactus leaves, making the branches of the trees sway and creak.

We had planned to venture out to Mykonos, for dinner at Yialos restaurant. Agathi warned against it, on account of the wind, but we decided to go anyway. Jason insisted he'd taken the speedboat out in worse weather than this. Even so, I was feeling a little uneasy, and before we headed out into that dark and windy night, I thought I'd have a stiff drink – for Dutch courage, you could say.

I went into the living room. I examined the drinks cabinet, although calling it a 'cabinet' was an exercise in understatement.

What a beautiful, perfectly stocked bar. It had everything you needed – shakers, spoons, whisks and all kinds of paraphernalia; expensive spirits and mixers; limes, lemons, olives; a fridge for wine and a little freezer for ice. With such perfect ingredients, how could I resist making a martini?

I have very strict ideas, you know, about how a martini should be made. Controversially, I prefer vodka, not gin. It must be ice-cold, and *extremely* dry. Vermouth originated in Milan; and Noël Coward once famously quipped that the nearest a martini should ever get to vermouth was a wave of the glass in the general direction of Italy. I agree, and I was careful to add only a drop or two, for the merest *whisper* of vermouth. This was an excellent vermouth, fortunately – French, not Italian – and kept chilled in the fridge, as it should be.

Then I opened a bottle of vodka. I threw some ice into the cocktail shaker and got to work. A few moments later, I poured out the thick, white, icy liquid into a small triangular glass. I plunged a silver cocktail stick into an olive, delicately placed it in the drink; then I held it up to the light and admired it.

It was indeed the *perfect martini*. I congratulated myself. I was about to bring it to my lips – when I stopped, distracted by the oddest sight.

Behind me, reflected in the mirrored door of the cocktail cabinet, I saw Leo, creeping past the living room door, holding an armful of guns.

I put down my drink and went to the door. I peered out.

Leo was carrying the guns to the end of the passage. He went up to the large wooden chest, on the floor by the kitchen door. With one hand, he opened the chest. Then he carefully lowered the guns into the chest. He handled them distastefully, as if they stank. He closed the lid.

Leo stood there for a moment, contemplating his efforts. He looked pleased. Then he sauntered off, whistling to himself.

I hesitated. Then I left the living room. I went along the passage, to check the room that Jason called his 'gun room'. It was a fairly useless room, near the back door; previously a boot room, for muddy shoes and umbrellas – which, in this dry climate, were rarely used. Jason had cleared it out, installing gun racks, and kept his hunting paraphernalia there. He had three or four guns – including a rifle, a semi-automatic shotgun and a couple of handguns.

All the gun racks were empty.

I let out a silent laugh. Jason wouldn't like that *at all.* He would flip out, in fact. As much as I relished the prospect, I knew I couldn't leave it like this. I wondered whether I should tell Lana or not. I decided to mull it over, while I had my cocktail.

I went back to the living room – and returned to my perfect martini. But, having lost its chill, the martini was disappointingly warm.

Rather a letdown, in fact.

18

There was a strained atmosphere in the boat, on the way to the restaurant.

Jason had a fixed, determined scowl on his face, as he attempted to steer the speedboat through the large black waves. Lana was silent, and she didn't look happy. I wondered if they'd had a fight. Kate was sitting next to her, also looking morose, chain-smoking, staring at the waves.

I was the only one in jolly spirits. I'd had a couple of martinis by then, and was looking forward to dinner immensely. Rather than travel in miserable silence, I turned to Leo, who was sitting next to me. I had to shout to be heard over the wind:

'So, Leo. What's all this I hear about you wanting to be an actor?'

Leo threw me a startled look. 'Who told you that?'

'Your mother, of course. I can't say I'm surprised.'

'You're not?' Leo looked suspicious. 'How come?'

'Well, you know the old saying,' I said, winking at him. '*The apple never rots far from the tree.*'

I laughed, but Leo frowned.

'Is that a joke? I don't get it.'

He gave me a suspicious look, then turned to look at the glowing island in the distance.

'We're almost there,' I said. 'Beautiful, isn't it?'

Beautiful is the word. Arriving at Mykonos at night

is an enchanting, almost hallucinatory experience. As you approach, the island sparkles with shimmering white lights, illuminating the white domed buildings that rise and fall on the curves of the hills.

Yialos means 'waterfront' in English. Appropriately enough, the restaurant was along the harbour wall. We disembarked at the private jetty. I was relieved to be out of the lurching boat and on dry land. Then we made our way up the stone steps, to the restaurant.

It was a picturesque spot: the tables were along the water's edge, with white linen tablecloths, and illumin- ated by lanterns hanging from the branches of the olive trees. The sound of the tide could be heard, slap- ping at the stone sea-wall.

As soon as Babis saw us, he hurried over. He snapped his fingers at his flock of waiters, all of them in gloves and bow ties and gleaming white jackets. At the other tables, people turned and stared. I felt Leo squirm by my side; even after a lifetime of it, he still disliked the attention – who could blame him? – and tonight there was a lot of it.

Yialos was an over-priced and pretentious restaur- ant, catering to an extremely wealthy, sophisticated clientele. Even so, Lana's unexpected appearance from the water, like the birth of a modern-day Aphrodite, rendered everyone agog. Everyone stopped and stared.

Lana was luminous that night – diamonds glittering in her hair, in her ears and around her neck. She was wearing a white dress, a simple but expensive gown, perfectly fitted to her figure, which reflected the light and made her glow, like some kind of beautiful apparition. You had to marvel at the spectacle, really. And then, to cap it all, a little kid, about seven or eight years old, tottered up to her. He had been sent over by his parents. The boy timidly held up his napkin, and asked Lana for her autograph.

Lana smiled and graciously complied – signing her name on his napkin with Babis's pen. Then she bent down and kissed the boy's cheek. He went bright red. The entire restaurant burst into delighted, spontaneous applause.

All the while, Kate was standing next to me. I could sense her mounting irritation. Anger was radiating from her like body heat.

That's something you should know about Kate – she had quite a temper. This was well known among her colleagues in the theatre, all of whom had borne the brunt of one of her rages at some point. Once provoked, her fury was fearsome, white-hot and incendiary – until it burned itself out. Whereupon she would be stricken with remorse, and desperate to repair what damage she had done – which, sadly, wasn't always possible.

And now, I sensed Kate getting madder by the second. Her temper was getting the better of her, I could tell. When she caught my eye, she looked positively murderous.

Then she said loudly, in a stage whisper, audible to most of the restaurant:

'Does no one want *my* autograph? Fine. *Fuck off, then.*'

Babis looked horrified and quickly decided she was joking. He laughed long and hard. He guided us to our table, cooing and fawning all over Lana – bowing so low, he was in danger of toppling over.

At the table, Kate made a show of pulling out her own chair and sitting down – before a waiter could assist her.

'No, thanks, mate,' Kate said to the waiter. 'I don't need any help. No special treatment for me. I'm not a *movie star*. Just a normal person.'

Lana also refused assistance being seated. She smiled.

'I'm a person too, Kate,' she said.

'No, you're not.' Kate lit a cigarette and gave a long, theatrical sigh. '*Jesus*. Don't you *ever* get sick of it?'

'Sick of what?'

'Sick of *this*.' Kate gestured at the other tables. 'Is it not possible for you to have dinner without five hundred people applauding?'

Lana opened the menu and studied it. 'Hardly five hundred. Just a few tables. It made them happy. It didn't cost me much to oblige.'

'Well, it cost me.'

'Did it?' Lana looked up. Her smile was wavering. 'Did it cost you so very much, Kate?'

Kate ignored her and turned to Babis:

'I need a drink. Champagne?'

'But of course.' Babis bowed and looked at Lana. 'And for Madame?'

Lana didn't reply; she seemed not to hear him. She kept staring at Kate with a strange, puzzled expression.

Leo nudged her. 'Mum? Can we order, please?'

'Yes,' said Jason. 'For Christ's sake, let's get this charade over with.'

'Wait a second,' I said, poring over the menu. 'I don't know what I want yet. I love ordering in Greek restaurants, don't you? I want it *all* – all seventy-five courses.'

That made Lana smile, and she snapped out of it. She proceeded to order for the table.

It must be said that one of Lana's most endearing skills was ordering well – over-generously, usually far too much; and she always insisted on picking up the bill, which made her the perfect host, in my book. She chose a selection of dips and salads, local squid and lobsters, meatballs and mashed potato; and the house speciality, a large sea bass, baked in a flaming salt crust, smashed open by Babis at the table: very theatrical and delicious.

Having taken the order, Babis departed, bowing low as he went, dispatching waiters to fetch our food and drinks. Champagne appeared, a glass poured for everyone except Leo.

'I'd like to make a toast.' I raised my glass. 'To Lana. To thank her, for her incredible generosity and for –'

Kate snorted, rolling her eyes. 'I'm not participating in this performance.'

'Sorry?' I frowned. 'I don't understand.'

'Work it out.' Kate knocked back her champagne. 'Having a good time, are you? Enjoying yourself?'

To my surprise, I realized Kate was directing this at me. There was a sarcastic tone to her voice. When I looked into her eyes, I saw the burning anger there.

Apparently, I had accidentally stumbled into her firing line. A quick glance at Lana told me that she saw this too. I gave Lana a reassuring smile – to show I could take care of myself. Then I turned back to Kate.

'Yes,' I said. 'I am, thanks, Kate. I'm having a lovely time.'

'Oh, good.' Kate lit a cigarette. 'Enjoying the show?'

'Very much so. After a slow start, it's picking up enormously. I can't wait to see the finale. I bet you have something really spectacular planned.'

'I'll do my best. You're such a good audience.' Kate smiled dangerously. 'Always watching — aren't you, Elliot? Always scheming. What's going on in your little mind? Hmm? What plots are you hatching?'

I didn't know why Kate was attacking me like this. I doubted she knew herself. She had no reason to be angry with me, I thought — she must be lashing out because she assumed I wouldn't fight back. Well, she was wrong. If there's one thing I've learned, it's that you must stand up for yourself.

Nobody loves a doormat, Barbara West used to say. *They just wipe their feet on it.* God knows, Barbara trampled all over me for years. I learned that lesson the hard way.

'You're in a foul mood tonight, Kate,' I said, sipping my champagne. 'What's going on? Why are you determined to ruin this?'

'Do you really want me to answer that? I can if you like.'

'Kate,' Lana said in a low voice. 'Stop this. Now.'

The two women stared at each other for a moment. Lana's eyes said that she'd had enough. To my surprise, the intervention succeeded; Kate unwillingly backed down.

Then Kate made a sudden movement — and for a split second, I thought she was about to lunge at me or

Lana across the table, or something crazy like that —
but she didn't.

She stood up jerkily, unsteady on her feet.

'I'm — I need the bathroom.'

'Going to powder your nose?' I asked.

Kate didn't reply. She stalked off. I glanced at Lana.

'What the hell's the matter with her?'

'I don't know,' Lana said with a shrug. 'She's drunk.'

'That's not all she is. Don't worry, I have a feeling
she'll come back from the bathroom in a much better
mood.'

But I was wrong. Kate returned to the table in a
much worse state. She was high, clearly, agitated, spoiling for a fight — not just with me — any of us would do,
at this point.

Leo and Jason wisely kept their heads low and ate
fast. They wanted to go as soon as possible. But the
courses kept coming, a seemingly endless number, so
I concentrated on the food.

I suspect I was the only one who enjoyed the meal.
Lana just picked at her plate. Kate didn't touch a
thing — she smoked and drank, glowering around the
table malevolently. After a long, uncomfortable silence,
Lana tried deflecting Kate with a compliment:

'I love that scarf you're wearing,' Lana said. 'Such a
deep red.'

'It's a *shawl.*' Kate threw it over her shoulder. She
proceeded to tell a long, grandiose story about how
the shawl was made for her by an orphan she spon-
sored in Bangladesh, as a gesture, to thank Kate for
putting her through school.

'It's not *fashion*,' said Kate, 'so I know you'd never touch it – but I love it.'

'Actually, I think it's rather beautiful.' Lana reached out and fingered the end of it. 'Such delicate work. She's very talented.'

'She's *clever*, more importantly. She's going to be a doctor.'

'Thanks to *you*. You are wonderful, Kate.'

This attempt to pacify Kate was like buttering up a grumpy child – *oh, you are clever, well done* – and it was clumsy of Lana. But I could tell she was rattled by this sudden change in Kate. We all were.

If I had to select one moment that weekend when it all went wrong, it was there, at the restaurant. An indefinable line was crossed, somehow – and we sailed from a place of normality into uncharted territory: into a dark, friendless no-man's land, from which there was no safe return.

The whole time we were sitting there, I could hear the wind, wailing on the water. It was picking up speed; tablecloths were flapping; candles blowing out. And below us, large black waves were slapping hard against the sea wall.

We'd better go soon, I thought. *Or we'll have trouble getting back*.

I took hold of my white linen napkin with my right hand and dangled it over the edge of the wall, above the water. I opened my fingers and let it go –

The napkin was snatched from my fingers by the wind. It danced in the night sky for a moment.

Then it was swallowed by the dark.

19

As Agathi had predicted, the wind was worse on the way back.

The speedboat lurched over huge black waves, while the wind spat salty sea-spray at us. The journey seemed to take forever. When we finally got back to the house, we were drenched and badly shaken up.

Ever the gentleman, Leo went and found towels for everyone. As we dried ourselves off, Jason made a feeble attempt to end the evening. A pre-emptive strike, you might say. Honestly, he should have known better. Any attempts to 'manage' Kate, to send her to bed like a naughty child, were doomed to failure. Kate wasn't the type of person to be managed.

'How about we call it a night?' Jason said. 'I'm knackered.'

'Not yet,' Kate said. 'I'm having a nightcap first.'

'Haven't you had enough?'

'No. That boat ride completely sobered me up. I need another drink.'

'Good idea,' I said. 'Me too. A double anything, please.'

I wandered outside through the French windows, on to the veranda. It was shielded from the worst of the wind, by the stone wall surrounding it.

We used the veranda a lot: it had various couches,

coffee tables, a fire pit and a barbecue. I flicked on the fire pit and used the flame to spark the end of my joint – which I had rolled in the hope of repeating last night's merriment. Alas, how far away that seemed now. Like a different lifetime.

Leo followed me outside. He nodded at the joint.

'Can I have some?'

I was a little surprised at the request. He didn't drink alcohol and I assumed he didn't approve of marijuana. I considered it.

'Hmm. I suppose you're old enough.'

'I'm nearly eighteen. *All* my friends smoke. It's no big deal.'

'Don't tell your mother.' I handed him the joint. I nodded at Kate in the living room. 'I wouldn't stick around if I were you. Unless you fancy a ringside seat.'

Leo nodded. He brought the end of the joint to his lips and inhaled deeply. He held the smoke in his lungs for a moment. Then he slowly exhaled, managing not to cough, which impressed me. He handed me the joint.

Then, without another word, Leo turned and walked down the stone steps, away from the house.

Sensible chap, I thought. Braving the gale was infinitely safer than putting up with Kate's current mood. Even so, he should watch his step.

'Be careful,' I yelled after him. 'The wind is really picking up.'

Leo didn't reply. He just kept walking.

20

Leo walked towards the water, to watch the waves, as the wind attacked the coastline. He followed the winding path down to the beach.

The joint was hitting him now. He could feel his senses heighten. A delicious tingling feeling. Although Leo disapproved of alcohol – after all, he had spent his childhood witnessing its worst effects on his mother's friends – weed, on the other hand, he had become curious about. His drama teacher at school, Jeff, whom he deeply admired, said that getting stoned was good for an actor.

'It unlocks chambers in the mind,' Jeff said. 'Weed opens doors into rooms that should be explored.'

This sounded intriguing – creative, and inspiring. He'd hadn't tried it, only because he hadn't had the opportunity. He was lying when he said all his friends smoked. Leo didn't have that many friends, and the ones he did have were as responsible and rule-abiding as he was. I was the only reprobate in his life.

Wicked Uncle Elliot. Jolly good, glad to oblige.

Sadly, what he was experiencing now, after a drag on the joint, he couldn't describe as revelatory. He felt mellow, and enjoyed the sensation of the wind rushing between his fingers and through his hair. But nothing else, nothing profound or spiritual.

Leo took his shoes off, and left them on the sand. He walked barefoot in the swirling surf, with the wind whistling in his ears.

He lost track of time as he walked – it seemed to disappear, as if blown away by the gale. He felt oddly peaceful; at one with the wind, and the waves churning up the water.

Then, suddenly, a dark cloud blew in front of the moon, lingering there. Everything was thrown into shadow. As if the lights had been turned off.

Leo sensed something behind him. A pair of eyes, on the back of his head – and a creeping, crawling sensation on the back of his neck, making him shudder.

He spun around but couldn't see anyone. Only the empty beach and the black trees, shivering in the wind. No one was there. He was about to turn away – when he saw it.

It was straight ahead, at the back of the beach, in the shadows of the trees. What was it? It didn't look entirely human. Leo peered, trying to make sense of what he was seeing. Was it an animal of some kind? – the legs were the legs of goat, or something like that – but it was standing upright. And on its head . . . were they horns?

Leo remembered the island's legendary ghost. Was this what he was witnessing? Or something more sinister? Something evil . . . A kind of *devil*?

In that instant, he felt a terrifying premonition – he knew, with complete and utter certainty, that something terrible was about to happen, very, very soon – something horrific and deadly; and he would be powerless to prevent it.

Stop it. You're stoned and paranoid, he told himself. *That's all.*

Leo shut his eyes and rubbed them, trying to un-see what he was seeing. Then, mercifully, the wind came to his aid, blowing the clouds from the moon. Moonlight illuminated the scene like a floodlight, instantly dissolving Leo's fantasy.

The monster was revealed to be nothing but a collection of various interconnecting branches and foliage. Leo's overactive imagination had drawn the dots together and assembled a devil. It wasn't real, just a trick of the light. Even so, he was thoroughly spooked.

And then – Leo grabbed his stomach. He groaned.

Suddenly, he was feeling sick.

While we had been at the restaurant, Agathi had taken the opportunity of dealing with the two measly-looking wood pigeons Jason had managed to shoot that afternoon.

She had sat at the kitchen table and begun the slow, patient process of plucking the birds. This was something she had been doing since she was a girl, when her grandmother taught her. She had been reluctant to learn at first – it looked unpleasant, even gruesome.

Don't be silly, girl, her grandmother said, taking her hands and placing them firmly on the bird. *Doesn't it feel nice, soft under the fingers?*

She was right, it did – and plucking these feathers, enjoying the sensation, the rhythmical movement, comforted by the memory of her *yiayia*, Agathi went into a kind of meditative trance, listening to the wind.

That wind, it was like the wrath of God. Appearing from nowhere – a lightning bolt from a clear blue sky. No warning. *The fury* – that's what her grandmother called it. And she was right.

Agathi remembered how the old woman would watch the gales from the kitchen window. She would clap in delight, applauding, as branches were ripped from trees, and hurled through the air. As a child, Agathi used to believe her grandmother was somehow responsible for the violent gales; that she had conjured them up by one of her spells, by one of her magic potions bubbling on the stove.

Agathi's eyes were suddenly wet with tears. She missed her, terribly – she'd give anything to have the old witch back again, bury herself in those bony arms.

Stop it, she thought. *Stop thinking about the past so much.*

What was the matter with her? She pulled herself together and wiped the tears from her eyes, leaving fluff and traces of feathers on her cheeks. She was tired, she thought, that's all.

Once she'd plucked the birds, she made herself a cup of mint tea, and went upstairs.

She wanted to be asleep before the family returned from the restaurant. Years of experience had given Agathi a nose for trouble – she sensed something was in the air. If there were to be any drama, she wanted no part of it.

In the end, Agathi fell asleep as soon as her head hit the pillow. Her mint tea remained on the bedside table, untouched.

She wasn't sure what woke her up.

At first, while asleep, she became aware of voices downstairs – muffled voices, raised in argument. Then she dreamed Jason was looking for Lana, calling her name.

Suddenly, Agathi realized it wasn't a dream. It was real.

'Lana!' Jason yelled.

Agathi opened her eyes. She was instantly awake.

She listened. There was no further shouting. Only silence.

She got out of bed. She crept to the door – and opened it a crack. She peered out.

And, sure enough, at the end of the corridor, she saw Jason. He was emerging from Lana's bedroom.

Then Kate climbed up the stairs. She and Jason spoke to each other in low voices, barely audible. Agathi strained to hear.

'I can't find Lana,' said Jason. 'I'm worried about her.'

'What about *me*?'

'Haven't you had enough attention for one night?' Jason gave her a look of contempt. 'Go to bed –'

He tried to pass by her and they tussled for a second. He threw her aside with more force than he possibly intended. Kate lost her balance, clutching on to the banister for support.

'You're pathetic,' Jason said.

Agathi silently shut the door. She stood there for a moment, feeling uneasy. Her instinct was to pull on her dressing gown and go in search of Lana. Yet something held her back. Better not get involved. *Go back to sleep*, Agathi told herself.

There had been similar evenings to this over the years, many dramatic scenes, often involving Kate, and they were always resolved amicably the following morning. No doubt Kate would sober up, apologize for whatever she had done. And Lana would forgive her.

Everything would go on as before.

Yes, Agathi thought, yawning. *Just go to bed.*

She lay down and tried to sleep. But the wind kept slamming her window shutters against the wall outside. It kept her from entering a deep sleep.

Eventually, she got out of bed, and closed the shutters. After that, she slept soundly for about an hour or so – perhaps longer – until once again her sleep was interrupted.

The shutters were banging against the wall:

Bang, bang, bang.

Opening her eyes, Agathi suddenly realized it couldn't be the shutters banging. She had locked them. It took her a second to work out what she had just heard.

It was gunfire.

Agathi's heart was racing as she hurried out of her bedroom, and she rushed downstairs. She ran out the back door.

The wind was fierce but she barely noticed it. She heard other footsteps nearby, bare feet thudding on the earth, but she didn't look around. She focused on running, racing in the direction of the sound.

She had to get there, she had to prove to herself she was imagining it, that she was wrong, that nothing terrible had happened.

Finally, she reached the clearing beyond the olive grove. She reached the ruin.

And on the ground was a body.

A woman's body – in a pool of blood. The face was in shadow. Three bullet wounds on the front of the dress. A deep red shawl around her shoulders; red turning black, as it soaked up blood.

Leo got there just before Agathi. He peered at the body, as if he needed to make sure who it was. Then he let out a horrible, strangled scream.

I arrived then – the same time as Jason. I ran over and knelt by the body, grabbing the wrist, desperately feeling for a pulse. It was difficult – Leo was in my way, cradling her; he wouldn't let go. He was covered in blood, burying his face in her hair, clinging on to her, sobbing. I tried and failed to disentangle her from him.

Jason attempted to take charge. But he sounded lost, and afraid.

'What happened? *What the fuck happened* –? Elliot?'

'She's gone,' I said, shaking my head. 'She's – gone . . .'

'*What?*'

'She's dead.' I lowered her wrist, fighting tears. 'Lana's dead.'

Act Two

Every murderer is probably somebody's old friend.

—Agatha Christie, *The Mysterious Affair at Styles*

I

I still can't believe she's gone.

Even now, after all this time, it doesn't feel real. Sometimes I think if I were to shut my eyes, I could reach out and touch her – as if she were sitting right next to me. But Lana's not here. She's in a different galaxy, light years out of reach, getting further away by the second.

I read somewhere that Hell has always been misrepresented. It is not a burning pit, full of torments. In fact, Hell is just an *absence*, a banishment from God's presence. To be removed from Him is Hell itself. And so I'm in Hell. Condemned to dwell forever in some empty place – away from Lana's radiance, away from her light.

I know, I know – I must cease this maudlin self-pity. It does no one any good – Lana least of all. It's *me* I'm feeling sorry for, really – this poor wretch who must live without her.

In one sense, of course, I still possess her. She lives on forever, immortalized in her movies; eternally young, eternally beautiful – while we mortals grow older, uglier and sadder every day. But that's the difference between two and three dimensions, isn't it?

As Lana exists now, preserved in celluloid, she's only to be gazed at. Not touched. Not held, not kissed.

So, it seems Barbara West was right in the end (though in an entirely different way from how she meant, of course) when she said to me spitefully one day: 'Darling, I do hope you're not falling in love with Lana Farrar. Actors simply aren't capable of love. You're much better off hanging a picture of her on your wall, and having a wank over it.'

Funnily enough, I have a photograph of Lana here with me, on my desk, as I write. It's an old publicity still – slightly aged, curling at the edges, faded and yellowed. It was taken a few years before I met Lana. Before I ruined her life, and my own.

But no – that's not fair.

My life was ruined already.

2

Okay, I have something to tell you.

Before we go any further, before I can reveal who committed the murder – and, more importantly, *why* – I have a confession of my own to make.

It's about Lana.

There is so much I could say about her. I could tell you how much I loved her. I could reminisce about our friendship, regaling you with stories and anecdotes. I could romanticize her, mythologize her – paint you an artist's flattering impression, idealized beyond recognition.

But that would be a disservice to you – and to Lana. What's required, if I have the stomach for it, is a 'warts and all' portrait, like the one Oliver Cromwell famously demanded. What's needed is the truth.

And the truth is, much as I loved her, Lana wasn't quite the person I believed she was. She had many secrets, it seems, even from those closest to her. Even from me.

But let's not judge her too harshly for that. We all keep secrets from our friends, don't we? I know I do.

Which brings me to my confession.

Believe me, it's not easy. I hate pulling the rug out from under you like this. All I ask is that you hear me out. Here, in the imaginary bar in my mind, where I'm talking to you, I'll order you another drink – and tell you to brace yourself. I'll have one, too – not a perfect martini like in the old days; just a quick slug of vodka, cheap stuff that burns the throat. I need it, you see, to steady my nerves.

Why am I nervous? It sounds ridiculous, I know – but after telling you my story, and spending this time with you, I find myself growing attached. I don't want to lose you, or your good opinion.

Not yet – when I have so much more to tell.

The thing is, when I first began writing this account, I promised you I would tell only the truth. But looking back over what I have written, it occurs to me that I may have misled you over a few points, here and there.

I have told you no actual lies, I assure you – it's a sin of *omission*, that's all.

I've told you nothing but the truth.

Just not all of it.

I did this from an honourable motive: the desire to protect my friend; not to betray her confidence. But unless I do, you will never understand what happened on the island.

So, I must rectify this error. I must tell you things you need to know, fill in certain gaps. I must reveal all Lana's secrets.

And mine too, for that matter.

That's the tricky thing about honesty. It cuts both ways, that sword; which is why I am so wary of wielding it.

Here goes.

*

To begin with, I must turn back time.

Do you remember when you first encountered Lana, on the street in London?

Let us return there, for a moment. Let us go back to that miserable day in Soho – and the rainfall that prompted Lana to make the spontaneous decision to flee the English weather, for a few days in sunny Greece.

I suppose my first and most grievous omission, when I began telling this story, was in allowing you to assume that once she made this decision, Lana immediately phoned Kate at the Old Vic – to invite her to the island.

But, in fact, twenty-four hours elapsed before Lana made that call.

Twenty-four hours, during which, as you shall see, a great deal happened.

3

Lana was walking on Greek Street, appropriately enough, when she had the idea about going to the island. But the moment she pulled out her phone to call Kate, to invite her to the island, the rain started coming down heavily. A sudden deluge.

Lana quickly returned the phone to her pocket, and hurried home.

No one was in the house when she let herself in. She dried herself off as best she could. She'd have a bath, she decided, once she'd had a cup of tea.

Tea-drinking was a habit Lana had only picked up since moving to London. Endless comforting cups of hot tea in this damp, depressing climate made perfect sense. She brewed a pot of Earl Grey and perched on the window-seat, watching the rain fall outside.

As she sat there, Lana's mind went back on the same track it had been on earlier. Back to what was bothering her. She was determined to work it out. If she kept puzzling over it, she felt sure the answer would unearth itself.

Once again, Leo popped into her mind. Why? Did this anxious feeling have something to do with him? With that awkward conversation they'd had, a few days earlier, here, in this kitchen?

'Mum, I've got something to tell you,' Leo said.

Lana braced herself. 'Go on.'

She didn't know what she was expecting – some typical teenage confession involving sexuality, addiction or religion? None of these possibilities bothered her. They'd work it out together, the way they always had. Lana had never given her son anything other than one hundred per cent support in anything he did.

'I want to be an actor,' Leo said.

Lana was taken aback. This was a shock. Not just the words that had come out of Leo's mouth – which she hadn't anticipated – but also her reaction, which was instantly, violently hostile. She suddenly felt very angry.

'What the hell are you talking about?'

Leo stared at her blankly. He didn't know how to respond. He looked like he might burst into tears. The conversation went downhill from there. Lana's response had surprised and hurt him. Leo wasted no breath in telling her so: she was being 'toxic' – and he didn't understand why.

Lana tried to explain that it was her duty as a parent to try and dissuade him. Acting was a waste of all the advantages and opportunities he had been given. An extraordinary education, a natural scholarly aptitude and intelligence, as well as his mother's contacts – many of the world's most influential people's numbers were on her phone, just a call away. Wouldn't Leo be much better off going to university – here in Britain, or in America – and qualifying as something more substantial? Last year he had expressed an interest in human rights law – surely something like that would suit him better? – or medicine? – or psychology, or philosophy – anything . . . but an *actor*.

Lana was clutching at straws here, and she knew it. And so did Leo. He gave her a cold look of contempt.

'What are you talking about? You're such a *hypocrite*. You're an actor. And Dad was in the business too.'

'Leo, your father was a producer. A businessman. If you said you wanted to move to LA and work in production, that would be entirely different –'

'Oh, really? You'd be over the moon?'

'I wouldn't be over the moon, but I'd be happier.'

'I can't believe you're saying this –' Leo rolled his eyes, breathing heavily. He was getting angry now, Lana knew. She didn't want this to get out of hand. She lowered her voice and tried to placate him.

'Darling, listen. What happened to me just doesn't happen. I was incredibly lucky. Do you know how many unemployed actors there are in LA? Your odds are one in a million. One in *ten* million.'

'Oh, I get it. I'm not talented enough? That's what you think?'

Lana nearly lost her patience. 'Leo. I have absolutely no idea if you are talented or not. Until this very moment you have expressed no interest in acting. You've never even been in a *play* –'

'A play?' Leo blinked, mystified. 'What's that got to do with it?'

Lana nearly laughed. 'Well, quite a lot, I should imagine –'

'I'm not interested in plays! Who said anything about plays? I want to be a *movie star* – like you.'

Oh my God, Lana thought. *This is a disaster.*

Realizing the situation was far more serious than she'd initially thought, Lana sought my advice. She called me as soon as she was alone.

I remember how tense and anxious she sounded on the phone.

Looking back, I probably could have been more sympathetic. I could see why Lana was disappointed – as Barbara West used to put it: 'An actress is a little bit more than a woman. An actor, a little bit less than a man.'

I figured, wisely, Lana wouldn't find that quip funny at the moment.

'Well, Leo's found his calling,' I said. 'That's good. You should be pleased.'

'Don't be sarcastic.'

'I'm not. Isn't that just what the world needs – another actor?'

'*Movie star*,' Lana corrected, miserably.

'Sorry – movie star.' I chuckled. 'Lana, my love – if Leo wants to be a movie star, let him. He'll be fine.'

'How can you say that?'

'He's your son, isn't he?'

'What's that got to do with it?'

I searched for the right analogy. 'Well, you don't buy a horse without looking the mare in the mouth, do you?'

'Meaning what? Is that a joke?' Lana sounded annoyed. 'I don't get it.'

'Meaning every agent in London and LA will be falling over themselves to have him, once they know whose son he is. Anyway,' I went on, before she could object, 'he's *seventeen*. He'll change his mind in approximately twenty-five minutes.'

'No. Not Leo. He's not like that.'

'Well, he won't starve, anyway. Not with Otto's billions in the bank.'

I shouldn't have said that. Lana's voice tightened.

'Not billions. That's a dumb thing to say, Elliot. And any money his father set aside for him has nothing to do with this.'

Lana ended the phone call soon after that. She was cool with me for the next few days. I could tell I'd touched a nerve.

She didn't want Leo to depend upon his inheritance. Fair enough. He must work.

Work was important, Lana believed, for all kinds of reasons. For years, she had defined herself solely through it, deriving intense satisfaction from it: a feeling of self-worth, a sense of purpose – not to mention the fortune that she made for herself and others.

One day, Leo would inherit all of it, as well as his father's money. He would be an extremely wealthy man. But not until she was dead.

In her mind, Lana kept coming back to the last thing Leo had said to her – his parting shot, as he left the kitchen. It was like a knife, slid between her ribs.

Leo paused at the door, and threw her a sideways look.

'Why did you do it?'

'Do what?'

'Give up acting. Why did you quit?'

'I've told you.' Lana smiled. 'I wanted a real life, not a pretend one.'

'That doesn't mean anything.'

'It means I'm happier now.'

'You miss it,' Leo said. This was not a question but a statement.

'No, I don't.' Lana kept smiling. 'Not at all.'

'Liar.'

Leo turned and walked out. Lana stopped smiling.

Liar.

Leo was right. Lana was a liar. She was lying to Leo – and to herself.

Finally she understood why this conversation had bothered her so much. This was the secret that had been chasing her around Soho. It had caught up with her at last.

I do miss it, she thought. *Of course I miss it. I miss it every day.*

The irony was that Leo had no idea that he himself was the cause of Lana's retirement. She never told him that. Lana told very few people why she quit. I was one of them.

When Otto died, Leo was six years old. And Lana's entire world fell apart. But she had to keep going, for Leo's sake. So, she put herself back together the only way she knew how: through work. She threw herself into it. And even though her career went from strength to strength – and she made one of her most successful movies, *The Loved One*, that finally won her an Oscar – Lana wasn't happy. She had the horrible feeling she was screwing up as a parent. Just as her own mother had screwed up.

Lana knew she was in the privileged position of not needing to work, so why not retire, and dedicate herself to raising her son? Why not put him first – as she had never been put first?

So that's what she did. She quit.

Does that sound flippant? As if Lana made life-changing decisions on the toss of a coin? I assure you she didn't. This was something I suspect she had been mulling over for years. Otto's sudden and unexpected death forced Lana's hand. You only had to glance at Leo now to see that her gamble had paid off. Yes, Leo was an occasionally temperamental teenager, but he was good-natured, intelligent, kind and responsible. He cared about other people, and the planet he lived on.

Lana was proud of how Leo had turned out. She felt sure it was down to the fact she had the right priorities. Unlike Kate, who was unmarried, childless, lurching from one disastrous, self-destructive relationship to another.

Lana thought of Kate for a moment. She was currently rehearsing *Agamemnon* at the Old Vic. Kate was at the height of her profession, hugely creatively fulfilled, still cast in leading roles. Was Lana envious? Perhaps.

But there was no going back. What if she were to return to work now? Looking older; feeling older, inevitably inviting unfavourable comparison with her younger self? Any kind of comeback would involve compromise – and probably end in disappointment. Imagine a disastrous, or even mediocre, production. That would be devastating for her.

No, Lana had made her choice – and been rewarded with a happy, well-adjusted son; a husband she loved; a marriage that worked. All this mattered enormously.

Yes. She nodded to herself. *That's the end of the story, right here.*

It seemed poetic, somehow, after such a hectic and turbulent life, that Lana should end up here, quietly drinking tea, watching the rain fall. Lana Farrar was an old married lady – a mother, and one day, hopefully, a grandmother.

She felt calm. That horrible anxious feeling left her.

This is what it means to be content, she thought. *Everything is perfect, just as it is.*

It was particularly cruel of fate to select that precise moment – just as Lana reached this epiphany about her life – for Agathi to enter the room . . .

And Lana's world to fall apart.

4

Agathi's day began uneventfully enough.

Tuesday was always busy for her; the day she ran errands. She enjoyed being out and about, charging around Mayfair, a long list in her hand.

As she left the house that morning, it seemed like a lovely day to be outdoors. The sun was shining and the skies were clear. Later on, like Lana, Agathi was caught in the rainstorm. But unlike her employer, she had been wise enough to take an umbrella.

Agathi walked to the pharmacy, dropping off a prescription for Lana. Then she went to the local dry cleaner's.

It was run by a notoriously prickly man, in his sixties, named Sid. He was civil to Agathi, however, unlike to the rest of his clientele, on account of her association with Lana, whom he adored.

Sid beamed at Agathi as she entered, and beckoned her to the front of the queue. 'Excuse me, dear,' he said to the waiting customer. 'I'll just serve this lady first. She's in a hurry – she works for *Lana Farrar*, you know.'

Agathi winced slightly, embarrassed, as she made her way past the queue of waiting customers, none of whom dared to object. Sid gestured at the clothes hanging on the rail. They were wrapped in plastic, ready to go.

'Here you go,' he said, 'her majesty's garments. All nice and snug in case there's a change in the weather. Looks like rain.'

'You think so? Seems like a fine day to me.'

Sid frowned. He didn't like being contradicted. 'No. Take it from me. It'll be pissing down in half an hour.'

Agathi nodded. She paid him for the clothes and was about to leave, when Sid suddenly stopped her.

'Wait a sec. Nearly forgot. Head like a sieve. Hang on –'

Sid opened a little drawer. Then he carefully took out a small, sparkling piece of jewellery. An earring.

He slid it across the counter.

'Caught in Mr Farrar's suit, it was. Inside the lapel.'

It's Mr Miller, not Farrar, Agathi thought. But she didn't correct him.

She looked at the earring. A delicate silver thing, in the shape of a half-crescent moon, with a chain of three diamonds hanging from it.

She thanked him. She took the earring. Then she paid for the clothes, and left.

As she walked home, Agathi wondered if she should tell Lana about the earring, or not? Such a stupid dilemma; so small, so trivial. And yet . . .

What would have happened if she had dropped the earring in a rubbish bin, there on the street? Or put it in her bedside drawer, next to her grandmother's crystal and forgotten about it? What if she never mentioned it to Lana? What if she had kept her mouth shut?

Well, I wouldn't be sitting here now, talking to you, would I? Everything would be different. Which makes me think that the real hero of our story – or do I mean *villain*? – is Agathi. For it is her actions, and the decision she was about to make, that determined all our fates. She had no idea she was holding life and death in the palm of her hand.

Just then, the rain began to fall.

Agathi opened her umbrella, and hurried home. When she got back to the house, she let herself in and made her way along the passage. She was shaking raindrops from the plastic-wrapped clothes, muttering to herself in Greek, in annoyance, when she entered the kitchen.

Lana smiled. 'Were you caught in the rain, too? I was – I got drenched.'

Agathi didn't reply. She draped the dry cleaning over the back of a chair. She looked miserable.

Lana glanced at her. 'Darling, are you okay?'

'Huh? Oh – I'm fine.'

'What is it? Is something wrong?'

'No.' Agathi shrugged. 'It's nothing. Nothing. Just ... this.' She removed the earring from her pocket.

'What is it?'

Agathi went over to Lana. She unclenched her fist. She revealed the earring.

'The dry cleaner found it. It was stuck on Jason's jacket, inside the lapel. He thought it must be yours.'

Agathi didn't look at Lana as she said this. Nor did Lana look at her.

'Let me see.' Lana held out her palm.

Agathi dropped the earring on her hand. Lana went through the pretence of looking at it.

'I can't tell,' Lana said. She gave the slightest of yawns, as if the conversation was boring her. 'I'll check later.'

'I can check for you,' Agathi said quickly. 'Give it back to me.'

She held out her hand –

Lana, give it back to her. Give Agathi the earring – let her cover it up and take it away, out of your life. Put it out of your mind, Lana. Forget it, distract yourself, pick up your phone, give me a ring – let's go for dinner, or a walk, watch a movie – then this terrible tragedy will be averted . . .

But Lana didn't give the earring back to Agathi. She simply closed her fingers around it.

And Lana's fate was sealed.

But not just her fate. What was I doing, I wonder, at that exact moment? Lunching with a friend? Or visiting an art gallery, or reading a book? I had no sense that my whole life had been derailed. Nor had Jason, sweating away in his office – nor had Leo, emoting in drama class – nor Kate, forgetting her lines at rehearsal.

None of us had the slightest inkling that something so monstrous had occurred, rewriting all our destinies, setting into action a series of events that would ultimately end, four days later, in murder.

This is where it started.

This is where the countdown began.

5

Lana's reaction was extreme, I'll grant you that.

It only really makes sense if you happened to know her. And you do know her by now, don't you? A little bit, anyway. So what happens next might not surprise you.

Lana remained calm, at first – she went into her bedroom and sat at her dressing table. She stared at the earring in her hand. It wasn't hers, she could tell that at a glance. Even so, she thought she had seen it somewhere before. But where?

It's nothing, she thought. *It happened at the dry cleaner's. A mix-up. Forget it.*

But she couldn't forget it. She knew she was being irrational and paranoid – but she couldn't let it go. The earring signified something much bigger in her psyche, you see. A bad omen she had been dreading.

Her life had already fallen apart once before – when Otto died. Lana didn't think she would ever recover or find love. So when she met Jason, it felt like she was being given a second chance. She could scarcely believe it. She felt safe, and happy – and loved.

Lana was a deeply romantic person. She had been ever since she was a little girl; ever since that chilly, empty childhood, cursed with a mother who didn't give a damn whether she lived or died. Little Lana filled the vacant space with romantic dreams – fairytale visions of escape, and stardom; and, most importantly, love.

'All I've ever wanted was love,' she once admitted to me, with a shrug. 'Everything else was just . . . *incidental*.'

Lana had loved Otto, of course – but wasn't *in* love with him. When he died, it felt like losing a father, not a lover. What she experienced with Jason was ferociously physical, intense and exciting. Lana let herself be a girl again, a teenager, besotted, drunk on lust.

And it had happened so fast. One moment, she was being introduced to him by Kate – and the next, she was walking down the aisle.

How I wish I had grabbed Lana by the shoulders that first night – the night she met Jason – and shaken her hard. *Stop this*, I would have said. *Live in reality. Do not turn this stranger you don't know into a fairytale prince. Look closely at him – can't you see he isn't real? Don't be fooled by the bright eyes, the over-eager smile, the false laugh. Can't you see it's an act? Can't you see his desperate, mercenary mind?*

But I said none of this to Lana. Even if I had, I doubt she would have heard a word. Love, it seems, is deaf as well as blind.

And now, sitting at her dressing-table mirror, staring at the earring, Lana began to feel strangely dizzy – as though she were standing on the edge of a cliff, watching the ground crumble away in front of her, falling, falling, crashing to the rocks and the roaring sea below. It was all falling – all of it, her whole life, tumbling into the waves.

Was Jason sleeping with another woman? Was this

possible? Did he no longer desire her? Was their marriage a sham? Was she unwanted?

Unloved?

It was at this precise moment, it's fair to say, that Lana lost her mind. She raged, and trembled and shook – and so did the bedroom, as she tore it apart. She rifled through all Jason's things in a frenzy, drawers, cupboards, suits, pockets, underwear, socks, searching for anything concealed, any kind of clue. She nearly faltered when she looked through his washbag in the bathroom, convinced she'd find condoms. But no – nothing. Nor was there anything remotely shady or sinister in his study – no credit card receipts in the drawers, no incriminating bills. No second earring. Nothing. She knew she was driving herself mad. For the sake of her sanity, she must put this from her mind.

Jason loves you, Lana told herself, *you love him – and trust him. Calm down.*

But she couldn't calm down. Once again she found herself pacing – once again feeling pursued by something unknowable.

She glanced out of the window. It had stopped raining.

She grabbed her coat and went outside.

6

Lana walked for about an hour. She walked deter-
minedly, all the way to the Thames. She focused on the
physical sensation of walking, trying not to think, trying not to let her mind go crazy.

As Lana approached the river, she walked past a bus
stop – and saw a poster on a billboard. She stopped.
She stared at it. Kate's face stared back at her in black
and white – red blood spattered across it – and the title
of the play: *AGAMEMNON*.

Kate, she thought. Kate would counsel her. Kate
would know what to do.

Almost as a reflex, she hailed a passing black cab.

It pulled up with a screech of brakes. She spoke
through the open window to the driver.

'The Old Vic, please.'

Lana could feel herself calming down, as the taxi
raced over the bridge to the theatre on the South Bank.
In her mind, she could already picture them laughing
about it – Kate telling her not to be silly, that she was
imagining things; that it was absurd, that Jason was
devoted to her. As she pictured this conversation,
Lana felt a sudden rush of affection for her – her
oldest, dearest friend. Thank God for Kate.

Or is that bullshit?

Did Lana secretly suspect something? Why else race

to the theatre like that? I'll tell you one thing: after decades of being styled and photographed, modelling one piece or another, Lana had developed a photographic memory regarding clothing and items of jewellery. I find it hard to believe that she would think the earring familiar yet be strangely unable to recall where she had seen it – or on whom. Perhaps I'm wrong. But I don't suppose we'll ever know for sure.

By the time Lana arrived at the Old Vic, she had calmed herself down, convinced it was all in her mind; she was just being paranoid.

Lana knocked at the stage-door window, presenting the old man in the booth with her famous smile. His face lit up as he recognized her.

'Afternoon. Looking for Miss Crosby, are you?'

'That's right.'

'She's in rehearsal at the moment. I'll buzz you in.' He lowered his voice, confidentially. 'Even though you're not on the list.'

Lana smiled again. 'Thank you. I'll wait in her dressing room, if that's all right.'

'Very good, miss.' He pressed a button.

There was a loud buzz, as the stage door unlocked.

Lana hesitated for a second. Then she opened the door and went inside.

7

Lana made her way along the stuffy, narrow corridor until she reached the star's dressing room.

She knocked on the door. No reply. So she cautiously opened it. The room was empty. She went inside, shutting the door behind her.

It was not a large room. It had a tatty couch against one wall, a narrow shower-room – essentially a cubicle – and a large, well-lit dressing table. Typical of Kate, it was a mess, with half-unpacked bags and clothes everywhere.

Lana took a breath. Then she began – at last – to be honest with herself. By that I mean she quickly and methodically started looking through Kate's belongings.

Even as she did this, Lana remained mentally disassociated from her actions. She stayed calm and detached, as if her hands were operating beyond her control, her fingers rifling through the bags and boxes of their own accord. Nothing to do with her.

In any case, the search yielded nothing.

What a relief, she thought. *Thank Christ for that.*

Of course she found nothing: *there was nothing to be found*. Everything was okay. This was all in her head.

Then she noticed the large black make-up bag, sitting on the dressing table. She froze. How had she not seen it? It was right there.

145

Lana reached out, with trembling fingers. She unzipped the bag – opening it up . . .

And there, inside the bag . . . was a half-crescent moon earring, glinting at her.

Lana pulled out the other earring from her pocket. She compared both earrings, but there was no need. They were obviously identical.

The dressing-room door suddenly opened behind her.

'Lana?'

Lana dropped one earring back in the make-up bag. Her hand closed around the other.

She quickly turned around.

Kate walked in, smiling. 'Hello, love. Oh, *shit* – we haven't made plans, have we? I can't get away for hours yet. Today's a fucking disaster. I could happily murder Gordon.'

'No, Kate, no plans. I was just passing the theatre. I thought I'd say hi.'

'Are you okay?' Kate peered at her, concerned. 'Lana – you don't look well. Do you want some water? Here, sit down –'

'No, thanks. You know, I don't feel great. Too much walking, I – I should go.'

'Are you sure? Shall I get you a cab?'

'I can manage.'

'Will you be okay?'

'I'm fine. I'll call you later.'

Before Kate could object, Lana hurried out of the dressing room.

She left the theatre. She didn't stop until she was on

146

the street. Her heart was thudding in her chest. She felt like her head might explode. She was finding it hard to breathe. She felt panicked; she had to get home.

Lana saw a passing taxi, and hailed it. As she waved down the cab, she realized she still had the earring in her fist.

She opened her hand and looked at it. The earring had dug so deep into her palm, it had drawn blood.

8

As she returned to Mayfair, Lana was in a state of shock.

The physical ache in her palm, where the earring dug into her hand, was her only sensation. She focused on it, feeling it pulse and throb.

When she got home, she knew, she would have to face her husband. She had no idea what to say or how to say it. So, for the moment, she would say nothing. Jason was bound to see how upset she was, but she'd do her best to hide it.

It was typical of Jason, however, that when he did finally return that evening, he didn't notice anything was wrong. He was preoccupied by his own problems – on a tense business call as he walked into the kitchen; then sending emails on his phone, while Lana prepared two steaks for their dinner.

It was interesting, Lana thought, how heightened her senses were. Everything felt so vivid – the smell of the steaks, the sizzling, the sensation of the knife in her hand as she chopped a salad – as if her brain had slowed itself right down to the present second. *Right now* was all she could deal with. She didn't dare think of the future. If she did, she'd crumple on to the kitchen floor.

Lana managed to keep going and the evening passed,

much like any other. A couple of hours after dinner, they went upstairs. Lana watched Jason undress and get into bed. He soon fell asleep.

But Lana was wide awake. She got out of bed. She stood above Jason, watching him.

She didn't know what to do. She had to confront him. But how? What could she possibly say? That she suspected him of having an affair with her best friend? Based on what? An *earring*? It was ridiculous. Jason would probably laugh – and offer a perfectly innocent explanation.

If this were a movie, she thought – like one of those candyfloss romantic comedies she used to make – it would turn out that Kate met Jason secretly, in order to help him select a birthday present for Lana – or perhaps an anniversary gift? – and somehow, involving a moment of heightened physical comedy, Kate's earring had got attached to the lapel of his jacket.

There you go, perfectly innocuous.

But Lana didn't buy it. As she watched Jason sleep, she began to admit the truth to herself. The truth was she had known for some time that there was something – some kind of feeling – between Kate and Jason. Perhaps it had always been there, right from the start. From the very beginning?

Kate met Jason first, you see. They even went out a few times. And the night Lana met Jason, he was there as Kate's date.

You can imagine what happened – the instant Jason saw Lana, like so many others before him, he fell; and from then, only had eyes for her. Kate graciously stepped aside. And it was all resolved quite amicably. She gave Lana her blessing and assured her she had no hard feelings; that there had been nothing serious between them.

Even so, Lana had felt guilty about it. Perhaps this guilt is what blinded her. Perhaps that was why she kept ignoring her nagging suspicion that, for all her protestations, Kate's eyes always lingered on Jason when he was in the room, and she would pay him odd, unexpected compliments, or flirt with him after a couple of drinks, and try to make him laugh. It was all there, everything Lana needed to know, right there in front of her.

She had shut her eyes to it.

But now, her eyes were open.

Lana quickly got dressed and hurried out of the bedroom. She felt her way along the darkened passage and climbed up the steps to the roof terrace, where she kept a secret pack of cigarettes and a lighter, protected from the weather in a tin box. She rarely resorted to smoking these days. But now, she needed a cigarette.

Lana stood on the roof and opened the box. She took out the packet of cigarettes. Her hands trembled as she lit one. She inhaled deeply, trying to calm herself.

As Lana smoked, she looked over the rooftops at the lights of London, and the stars sparkling above.

And then – peering over the edge – she stared at the pavement down below. She flicked the cigarette butt over the edge. The red ember disappeared into darkness.

Lana felt a sudden desire to follow it.

It would be so easy, she thought – just a couple of steps, and she'd be over the edge – her body falling, slamming against the pavement. Then it would be over.

What a relief that would be. She wouldn't have to face any of the horrors that lay ahead – the pain, the betrayal, the humiliation. She didn't want to feel any of it.

Lana took a small step forward towards the edge. And then another . . .

She stood right at the edge of the roof. *One more step – and it will be over – yes*, she thought, *yes, do it* . . . She lifted her foot –

Then her phone vibrated in her pocket.

A small distraction, but enough to wake her from her trance. Lana pulled back from the edge, catching her breath.

She took out her phone and glanced at it. It was a text message. Guess who from?

Yours truly, naturally.

Fancy a drink?

Lana hesitated. And then – at last – she did the very thing she should have done first.

She came to see me.

9

This is where my story begins.

If I were the hero of this tale, instead of Lana, I would start the narrative right here – with Lana banging on my door at eleven-thirty at night.

This was my *inciting incident*, as it's known in dramatic technique. Every character has one – it can be as unusual or violent as a tornado, whirling you into a different world, or as commonplace as a friend turning up unexpectedly one night.

I often apply theatrical structure to my own life, you know. I find it extremely helpful. You'd be surprised how often the same rules apply.

I learned how to structure a story through a fiery apprenticeship: years of compulsively writing crap play after crap play, spewing them out, one after the other, a production line of unperformable dramas, each worse than the last – stilted construction, endless inane dialogue, sheet after sheet of pointless, passive characters doing nothing – until I slowly and painfully learned my craft.

Considering I lived with a world-famous writer, you might think Barbara West would be the obvious person to mentor me. Do you imagine she gave me any helpful hints or slivers of encouragement? No, never. Her default position, it must be said, was to be unkind.

She only ever made one comment on my writing, incidentally – after reading a short play I'd written. 'Yuk. Your dialogue stinks,' she said, handing it back to me. 'Real people don't talk like that.'

I never showed her anything again.

Ironically, the best teacher I ever had was a book I found on Barbara's shelf. An elderly, obscure-looking volume, published in the early 1940s. *The Techniques of Playwriting*, by Mr Valentine Levy.

I read it one spring morning, sitting at the kitchen table. As I read it, I had a lightbulb moment. Finally, things made sense. Finally, someone explained storytelling in words I could understand.

Both theatre and reality, said Mr Levy, came down to just three words – *motivation, intention* and *goal*.

Every character has a *goal* – wanting to be rich, say. This is fulfilled by an *intention* designed to achieve it – like working hard, marrying the boss's daughter, or robbing a bank. So far, so simple. The final component is the most important and, without it, characters remain two-dimensional.

We need to ask *why*.

Why isn't a question we tend to ask often. It's not easy to answer – it requires self-awareness and honesty. But if we ever want to understand ourselves or other people – real or fictional – we must explore our *motivation* with all the diligence of a Valentine Levy.

Why do we want something? What is our motive?

According to Mr Levy, there is only one answer:

'Our motivation,' he writes, 'is to remove *pain*.'

There you have it. So simple, and yet so profound.

Our motivation is always pain.

It's obvious, really. All of us are trying to escape the pain and be happy. And all the actions we take to achieve this – that's the stuff of story.

That's storytelling. That's how it works.

So if we consider that moment Lana turned up at my flat, you can see how my motivation was pain. Lana was in so much pain that night – it caused me distress just to witness it. And my misguided attempt to allevi-ate her suffering – and my own – was my intention. And my goal? To help Lana, of course. Did I succeed? Well, that's where theatre diverges from reality, sadly.

In real life, things don't work out quite as you planned.

Lana was a mess when she got to my place. She was barely holding it together, and it didn't take much – just a couple of drinks – to unlock the floodgates, and then she completely fell apart.

I'd never seen anything like this before. I'd never once seen Lana lose control. I won't say it wasn't fright-ening; but then, uncontained emotion is always distressing to be around, isn't it? Particularly when it's someone you love.

We went into my living room – a small room, crammed mainly with books, a large bookcase cover-ing the entirety of one wall. We sat on the two armchairs by the window. We started off with martinis, but soon Lana was knocking back straight vodka from a glass.

Her story was confused and incoherent – coming out in pieces, in disjointed bits, occasionally unintelligible through her tears. When she had got it all out, she demanded my opinion – whether I believed it was possible that Kate and Jason were having an affair.

I hesitated, reluctant to reply. My hesitation spoke more eloquently than any words.

'I don't know,' I said, avoiding Lana's eyes.

Lana gave me a look of dismay. 'Jesus, Elliot. You're such a bad actor. You *knew*?' She sank back in the armchair, drained by this confirmation of her worst fears. 'How long have you known? *Why didn't you tell me?*'

'Because I don't know for sure. It's just a feeling . . . And, Lana – it's not my place to say anything.'

'Why not? You're my friend, aren't you? My only friend.' She wiped the tears from her eyes. 'You don't think Kate planted it, do you? The earring? So I'd find it?'

'What? Are you joking? Of course not.'

'Why not? It's just the kind of thing she would do.'

'I don't think she has the brains, quite frankly. I don't think either of them are particularly bright. Or kind.'

Lana shrugged. 'I don't know.'

'I do.' Warming to my theme, I opened another bottle of vodka, refilling our glasses. '*Love is not love*,' I said, '*which alters when it alteration finds. Love isn't affairs and lying and sneaking around.'

Lana didn't reply. I tried again, because it was important.

'Listen to me. Love is mutual respect, and constancy – and *friendship*. Like you and me.' I took her hand and held it. 'These two nitwits are too shallow and selfish to know what love is. Whatever they have, or think they have, *it will not last*. That's not love. It will crack under the slightest pressure. It will fall apart.'

Lana didn't say anything. She stared into space, desolate. I felt like I couldn't reach her. Seeing her like this was unbearable. I suddenly felt angry.

'How about I take a baseball bat and beat the crap out of him for you?'

I was only half-joking. Lana managed the ghost of a smile.

'Yes, please.'

'Tell me what you want – *anything* – and I will do it.'

Lana looked up and stared at me with bloodshot eyes. 'I want my life back.'

'Okay. Then you must confront them. I will help you. But you must do this. For the sake of your sanity. Not to mention your self-respect.'

'Confront them? How do I do that?'

'Invite them to the island.'

'What?' Lana looked surprised. 'To Greece? Why?'

'They won't be able to run away on Aura. They'll be trapped. Where better for a conversation? A confrontation?'

Lana thought about this for a second. She nodded. 'Okay. I'll do it.'

'You'll confront them?'

'Yes.'

'On the island?'

Lana nodded. 'Yes.' Then she gave me a sudden, frightened look. 'But, Elliot – after I confront them – what then?'

'Well,' I said, with a small smile, 'that's up to you, isn't it?'

10

The following day, I was in Lana's kitchen, drinking champagne.

Lana was on the phone to Kate. I was watching closely.

'Will you come?' she said. 'To the island – for Easter?'

I was impressed. Lana was giving a flawless performance, achieved with minimal rehearsal. There was no hint in her manner of the upset of the night before – she looked and sounded fresh, light and carefree.

'It'll be just us,' Lana went on. 'You, me, Jason, Leo . . . And Agathi, of course . . . I'm not sure if I'll ask Elliot – he's been annoying me lately.'

She winked at me as she said this. I stuck out my tongue at her.

Lana laughed, and then returned her attention to Kate. 'Well,' she said, 'what do you say?'

We both held our breath.

Lana breathed out, and smiled. 'Great. Great. Okay. Bye.' She ended the call. 'She's coming.'

'Well done.' I applauded.

Lana took a slight bow. 'Thank you.'

I raised my glass.

'The curtain rises,' I said. 'And so it begins.'

Over the next few days, life continued to hold a theatrical flavour for Lana.

It felt as if she were taking part in an extended improvisation – remaining 'in character' from morning until night, pretending to be someone else. Except, of course, the person she was pretending to be was *herself*.

Deep breath, shoulders down, big smile – that was the mantra Otto taught her to recite to herself before an audition. It served Lana well now.

She was acting as if she was still the same person she had been a few days ago. Acting as if she wasn't heartbroken – as if she wasn't desperate, and full of pain.

I often think life is just a performance. None of this is real. It's a pretence at reality, that's all. And only when someone or something we love dies do we wake up from the play, and see how artificial it all is – this constructed reality we inhabit.

We suddenly realize that life is in no way lasting or permanent; no future exists – and nothing we do matters. And, in desolation, we howl and scream and rail at the heavens, until, at some point, we do the inevitable: we eat, dress and brush our teeth. We continue with the marionette-like motions of life, however unhinged it feels to do so. Then, ever so slowly, the illusion takes over again – until again, we forget that we are just actors in a play. Until the next tragedy strikes, of course – to wake us up.

And having just been woken, Lana felt hyperconscious of how performative all her relationships were – how brittle and false her every smile; and how badly she was acting. Thankfully, no one seemed to notice.

What hurt the most was how easy it was to deceive Jason. She felt sure he'd sense her pain – how something as simple as brushing past him, talking to him, was incredibly difficult for her. Looking into his eyes was terrifying. Surely, all her feelings were right there, in plain sight, for him to see?

But he didn't see. *Has he always been like this?* Lana wondered. *So uncaring? – he must think I'm a fool. He must have no conscience at all . . .*

Yet – and surely Lana had to acknowledge this possibility – perhaps there was nothing on Jason's conscience, because he was *innocent*?

I didn't know this for sure – but I suspected that, as she packed their belongings for the trip to the island, Lana started thinking of those hours at my place as a bad dream. The hysteria, the tears, the vows of vengeance – none of it was real, just vodka-induced psychosis.

This was real, right now, the clothes in her hand, clothes she'd selected and bought for the man she loved. Could Lana feel herself slipping, sliding back – back into ignorance?

'Denial' is the word I'd use.

And Lana must have known this, I thought, which was why she avoided me for the next few days. She ignored my calls, and remained monosyllabic in her texts. I understood. Don't forget, we were so close, Lana and I – I could practically read her mind.

Of course she resented telling me about the affair; telling me made it *real*. And now, having unloaded all of her suspicion and misery on to me, Lana intended to leave it there, in my apartment.

She wanted to forget all about it.

What a good thing, then, I was there to remind her.

I 2

From the moment I landed on Aura, I sensed that Lana was avoiding me.

She was friendly, of course, but there was a certain distance in her manner. A coolness. Invisible to the others, but I felt it.

I went up to my room and unpacked. I was very fond of that room. It had faded green wallpaper, pine furniture, a four-poster bed. It smelled of old wood, stone, and fresh linen. Over the years, I made it my own, intentionally leaving parts of myself behind – favourite books of mine on the shelves, my aftershave, suntan lotion, swimming goggles and bathers, all waiting faithfully for me.

As I unpacked, I wondered what my next move should be. I decided the best way to deal with the situation was to face it – to find Lana and remind her why we were here. I rehearsed a little speech, designed to bring her out of denial and back to reality.

I tried to talk to her all evening but couldn't get her alone. I felt convinced she was trying to avoid me.

I watched her carefully over dinner. I studied her, trying to read her mind.

I marvelled it was the same woman who – just three days ago – had been hysterical on my couch. Now she was expertly wielding a knife, not to thrust into her worthless husband's heart, but to serve him another slice of steak. And with such a convincing smile on her face, so sincere, such a relaxed and happy expression, that even I was almost taken in.

Lana's capacity for denial was simply breathtaking, I thought. In all likelihood, unless I intervened, she would sail through the entire weekend as if nothing had happened.

Kate, on the other hand, seemed to be doing everything she could to be provocative. She was being even less discreet than usual.

The business with the crystal, for instance.

After dinner, we were sitting outside by the fire pit, and Kate leapt up with a sudden request. 'Agathi's crystal,' Kate said. 'Where is it?'

Lana hesitated. 'I'm sure Agathi's asleep by now. Can it wait?'

'No. It's incredibly urgent. I'll sneak in and get it from her room. I won't wake her.'

'Darling, you won't find it. It's probably at the back of a drawer somewhere.'

This was a lie. Lana knew perfectly well that the crystal was never far from Agathi's person; always on the bedside table, next to her as she slept.

'Agathi's still awake,' Leo said, nodding at the house. 'Her light's on.'

Kate bounded into the house, a little unsteady on her feet but clearly quite determined. She returned a few minutes later – holding up the crystal triumphantly.

'Got it.'

Kate sat by the fire pit, the flames lighting up her face. She dangled the crystal over her left palm. It sparkled in the firelight. Her lips moved as she whispered a silent question.

I guessed what Kate was asking. No doubt some variant of — *will he leave her for me?* — or, *should I end it with him?*

Unbelievable, isn't it? Such callousness — flaunting her affair with Jason in Lana's face like that. How stupid of her to feel so secure, so above suspicion.

Or am I being unfair? Was Kate just too drunk to filter her thoughts — unaware what she was saying, how close she was coming to revealing her secret?

Or was this display for Jason's benefit — as a veiled threat? A warning to him that she was at the end of her rope? If so, she was wasting her breath. Jason wasn't affected in the slightest. He seemed more concerned about Leo beating him at backgammon.

Kate watched, as the crystal began to twitch in the air. It swung back and forth, back and forth, back and forth — like a metronome, in a sharp, straight line.

The answer to her question was a firm 'no'.

Kate's face clouded over. She looked pained. Then she grabbed the crystal with her fist and stopped it swinging. She thrust it at Leo. 'Here — you have a go.'

Leo looked up from the backgammon set, shaking his head.

'No. I'm totally over it. I figured out how it works.'

'Did you? How is that?'

'It's *you*. You don't even know you're doing it. Your hand makes it move the way you want.'

'No, love,' Kate said with a sigh. 'You're wrong. Or I would have got a different answer.'

What was the question Kate asked the crystal?

I have often wondered, over the years. I have wondered to what extent it affected the next twenty-four hours. And all the wicked things Kate did.

Was everything that happened at the crystal's command? Did Kate simply surrender to its decision – wherever it led?

Even if she did, you know, I don't believe Kate had any idea where it would end. How could she?

It went so much further than any of us could ever possibly imagine.

13

I didn't get a chance to talk to Lana alone until the following morning.

We had just arrived at the little beach with the picnic hamper. We arranged the towels and blankets on the ground. I waited until Leo was a little way off, then I made my move.

'Lana,' I said in a low voice. 'Can we have a chat?'

'Later,' she said, brushing me off. 'I'm going for a swim.'

I watched her make her way to the water's edge. I frowned. I had no choice but to follow her.

The water was flat like glass. Lana swam all the way to the raft. I swam after her.

When I reached the raft, I climbed up the ladder and on to the platform – and flung myself on my back, gasping for air.

Lana was fitter than me, scarcely out of breath. She sat there, hugging her knees, staring at the horizon in the distance.

'You're avoiding me,' I said, when I finally caught my breath.

'Am I?'

'Yes. Why?'

Lana didn't reply for a second. She shrugged. 'You can't guess?'

'Not unless you tell me. I'm not psychic.'

I had decided the best way to handle Lana now was to play dumb. So I gave her an innocent look and waited.

Finally, she spoke. 'That night at your apartment . . .'

'Yes.'

'We said a lot.'

'I know we did.' I shrugged. 'Now you're avoiding me. What am I supposed to make of that?'

'I need to know something.' Lana studied me for a second. 'Why are you doing this?'

'Doing what? Trying to help you?' I met her gaze directly. 'I'm your friend, Lana. I love you.'

Lana looked at me for a moment, like she didn't believe me.

I felt a flicker of irritation. Isn't that crazy? In all these years, never one cross word or a disagreement with Lana — a mutually adoring friendship, free of all conflict — until I got involved in her marriage problems.

No good deed goes unpunished, I thought. Who said that? They were right.

I was in a tricky position, I knew. I mustn't press her too hard. I risked losing her, but I couldn't stop myself.

'I'm sorry,' I said. 'I cannot stand by and watch you be abused. It's not okay, letting them treat you like this.'

No reply.

'Lana.' I frowned. 'Answer me, for Christ's sake.'

But Lana didn't answer me. She just stood up — and dived off the raft. She disappeared in the water.

*

After the picnic, we walked back to the house. But Lana didn't go inside.

She lingered on the veranda, acting as if the climb up the steps had tired her, and she was catching her breath. I knew better. She was watching Kate, on the lower level.

Kate was wandering away from the summerhouse, in the direction of the olive grove – towards the ruin.

I knew what was in Lana's mind. I pretended to yawn.

'I'm going to have a shower,' I said. 'See you in a bit.'

Lana didn't reply. I wandered inside into the living room – then stopped just inside the door. I hovered there a moment. Then I went back outside.

And Lana had gone. Just as I expected, she was descending the steps to the lower level.

I followed – keeping my distance, so she wouldn't see. I needn't have worried; Lana didn't look back once. Nor did Kate, as she made her way through the trees, blissfully unaware she was being followed not by one, but two people.

At the clearing, Lana hid behind a tree. I stood a little further back, at a safe distance. We both watched the scene unfold at the ruin.

Jason and Kate spoke for a while. Then Jason put down his gun and approached Kate. They started kissing. How strange it must have been for Lana to watch them kissing. I imagined all her defences collapsing at that moment – her denial, delusion, her projection of her anger on to me – crumbling into dust. How can you deny what's right in front of you?

171

Lana's legs suddenly gave way. She sank to the ground. She fell on to her hands and knees, in the dirt. It looked like she was kneeling in prayer, but she was crying. It was a pitiful sight. My heart went out to her. But it would be dishonest not to admit that part of me was relieved. For if Lana needed more proof than an earring, then fate had just supplied it.

Jason sensed Lana's eyes on him. He looked up. But he was blinded by the sunlight and didn't see her there.

Lana turned, and lurched away from the ruin. She went back through the olive grove, towards the house. She was walking fast. I followed.

I had an uneasy feeling about what she might do next.

14

Lana circled around behind the house. She went in the back door.

She hurried along the passage – and entered Jason's gun room. He had taken a couple of guns out with him – but a couple were still there, on the rack.

Lana reached out and she took hold of a handgun.

She left the room and marched along the corridor, into the living room. She went out through the French windows, on to the veranda. She stood by the low wall, overlooking the lower level.

Below her, Jason was walking back towards the house, clutching a couple of dead wood pigeons. Lana slowly raised the gun – and aimed it straight at him.

Did she intend to kill Jason? Or just scare him?

I honestly don't know how conscious Lana was of what she was doing. She was so beaten up mentally at this point, so destabilized. Perhaps an old, primitive instinct for survival had taken hold – a need to feel a weapon in her hands? If there had been an axe nearby, like Clytemnestra, she might have seized that. As it was, she held a gun.

Go on, I thought, *do it. Squeeze the trigger. Fire* –

But just then, Leo appeared on the lower level, walking to the pool. And Lana immediately lowered the gun, hiding it behind her back.

Leo looked up and saw his mother. He waved. Lana forced a smile and waved back.

Woken from her trance, Lana turned and hurried back into the house. She went along the passage. But she didn't return the gun. She kept walking, past the gun room, and took the handgun upstairs.

In her bedroom, Lana sat at her dressing table. She stared at herself in the mirror – with the gun in her hand. She felt rather frightened by what she saw.

Then, hearing the door open, she thrust the gun into the drawer. She glanced in the mirror, and saw Agathi walk in, smiling.

'Hi,' Agathi said. 'Is there anything you need?'

'No.' Lana shook her head.

'Any thoughts about dinner?'

'No. Maybe we'll go out. I can't think now . . . I'm going to have a bath.'

'I'll run it for you.'

'I can manage.'

Agathi nodded. She watched Lana for a moment. It was unlike her to offer an unsolicited opinion. But she was about to make an exception.

'Lana,' Agathi said. 'Are you – okay? You're not, are you?'

Lana didn't reply. Agathi went on:

'We can leave right now – if you want.' She gave Lana an encouraging smile. 'Let me take you home.'

'Home?' Lana looked confused. 'Where's that?'

'London, of course.'

Lana shook her head. 'London isn't home.'

'Then where?'

'I don't know. I don't know where to go. I don't know what to do.'

She got up. She walked into the bathroom. She turned on the taps and ran her bath. When she returned to the bedroom, a few minutes later, Agathi was no longer there. But she had left something behind.

The crystal pendant was there, on the dressing table, glinting in the sunlight.

Lana picked it up. She looked at it. She didn't believe in magic, but she didn't know what to believe in any more. She dangled the pendant over her palm.

She stared at it, her lips moving – as she murmured a silent question.

Almost at once, the crystal began to twitch, jolt, dance in the air.

A tiny circular movement – that grew and grew, above her outstretched palm – wider, and higher . . . a circle, spinning in the air.

Outside the house, on the ground, a solitary leaf moved.

The leaf was lifted up into the air by an unseen force – spinning it in a circle. The circle grew bigger and wider, higher and higher . . . as the winds appeared . . .

And *the fury* began.

15

The fury was an apt name, I thought, given Kate's mood.

She had been spoiling for a fight all through dinner at Yialos. And now we were back at the house, she seemed intent on finding one.

I thought it best to keep out of her way. So I remained outside, by the French windows, smoking the joint. From that safe vantage point, I watched the drama unfold in the living room.

Kate was pouring herself another large whisky. Jason went over to her. He stood there awkwardly and spoke in a low voice.

'You've had enough to drink.'

'This one is for you.' Kate thrust the tumblerful of whisky at him. 'Take it.'

He shook his head. 'No. I don't want it.'

'Why not? Go on, drink it.'

'No.'

'I think,' Lana said firmly, 'we should all go to bed.'

She stared at Kate for a moment; a warning look, if ever I saw one. And for a second, it looked like Kate might back down.

But no. Kate accepted the challenge. She tore off her red shawl, twirling it in the air, like a red flag in a bullfight – and threw it on to the back of the couch.

Then she brought the glass of whisky to her lips, and drank it all in one go.

Lana was poker-faced, but I could tell she was furious.

'Jason,' she said, 'can we go upstairs? I'm feeling tired.'

Kate reached out and grabbed hold of Jason's arm. 'No, Jason. Stay right there.'

'Kate –'

'I mean it,' Kate said. 'Don't go. You'll regret it if you go.'

'I'll take that risk,' he said.

He removed Kate's hand from his arm – a bad move, I thought. I knew it would enrage her. I was right.

'*Fuck you*,' she hissed.

Jason looked startled. He wasn't expecting that level of anger. My heart went out to him – almost.

I understood now. Kate's anger had betrayed her: this whole charade was for *Jason*'s benefit, not mine or Lana's. It was Jason that Kate was really mad at.

Lana understood this too. She had the unnerving instinct of a great actor. And she knew this was her cue. As always, she underplayed her delivery:

'Jason,' she said. 'Make a decision, please.'

'What?'

'You must choose.' Lana nodded at Kate, not taking her eyes off Jason. 'Me or her.'

'What are you talking about?'

'You know damn well what I'm talking about.'

There was a slight pause. Jason's face was a sight to

behold – like witnessing a car crash in slow motion. Caught between these two women, this was about to end badly for him. Unless he managed somehow to prevent it.

What Jason did next would be most revealing. There's an old writing trick Barbara West once told me – where you give currency to a specific person, or object, by including them in a choice between two alternatives. What you are prepared to give up for something tells us everything about how much you value it.

Jason had a very clear choice here – between Kate and Lana. We were about to discover – if we were in any doubt – whom he valued the most.

Barbara would have loved this, I thought. Just the kind of situation she'd steal, and put into a book.

Thinking of Barbara made me smile – which was unfortunate, as I realized Jason was staring at me, a look of fury on his face.

'What the fuck?' Jason said. 'You think this is *funny*, you evil prick?'

'Me?' I laughed. 'I think I'm the least of your problems, mate.'

At this, Jason lost his temper. He leapt towards me, lunging at me, grabbing me by the throat. He pinned me to the wall, raised his first – like he was going to punch me in the face.

'Stop it! Stop it.' Kate was pummelling his back. 'Leave him alone! Jason –'

Eventually, Jason let me go. I caught my breath and adjusted my collar, with all the dignity I could muster.

'Feel better now?'

Jason didn't reply. He glared at me. Then, remembering his priorities, he turned around – to appeal to Lana.

'Lana,' he said. 'Listen –'

But Lana wasn't there. She had gone.

16

Nikos was in his cottage, sitting in the armchair by the fireplace. He was drinking ouzo, and listening to the wind outside.

He liked listening to the wind, in all its different moods. Tonight, it was in a rage. Other nights, it groaned like an old man in pain, or wailed like a small child lost in the storm. Sometimes, Nikos could convince himself it was a girl outside, lost in the gale, crying. He'd step out and look into the night, into the dark – just to be sure. But it was always the wind, playing tricks.

He poured himself another ouzo. He was a little drunk, his mind as cloudy as the ouzo in his glass. He leaned back in his chair and thought about Lana. He imagined what it would be like if she lived here, on Aura, with him. This was a favourite fantasy of his.

He felt sure Lana would be happy here. She always came alive on the island – it was like a light shone from inside her, the moment she got off the boat. And if she were here, Lana could rescue him from his solitude. She would be like rain falling on parched earth; a cool drink of water, to quench his dry salty lips.

Nikos shut his eyes, drifting into an erotic daydream. He imagined waking up at dawn, in bed with Lana – she was facing him, her golden hair spread over the pillow . . . how soft it was, how sweet she smelled, like orange blossom. He'd take her smooth body into his arms, nuzzle her neck, kiss her skin. He'd press his lips against her mouth . . .

Nikos was half-aroused, half-drunk, half-asleep – and thought he was dreaming, when he opened his eyes . . . and there she was.

Lana.

Nikos blinked. He sat up, suddenly wide awake.

Lana was standing there, in the doorway. She was there, in reality, not his imagination. She looked beautiful, dressed all in white. She looked like a goddess. But a sad goddess. A frightened one.

'Nikos,' Lana said in a whisper. 'I need your help.'

17

Jason, Kate and I were left alone in the living room. I waited to see who would speak first. It was Kate, sounding chastened.

'Jason,' she said. 'Can we talk?'

There was an emptiness to her voice. Her anger had gone, burnt out – nothing left but ashes. 'Jason?' she repeated.

Jason glanced at Kate – and looked right through her. A chilling look, I thought. As if she didn't exist. He turned and walked out of the room.

Kate suddenly looked like a little girl, about to burst into tears. I felt sorry for her, despite myself.

'Do you want a drink?' I said.

Kate gave a brief shake of the head. 'No.'

'I'm making you one anyway.'

I went to the drinks cabinet and made us a couple of drinks. I made small talk about the weather, to give Kate a chance to pull herself together. But I could tell she wasn't listening.

I held out the glass in front of her for a good twenty seconds before she saw it.

'Thanks.' Kate took the drink, absently placing it on the table in front of her. She reached for her cigarettes.

I rubbed my neck. It was sore from where Jason

grabbed it. I frowned. 'You know, Kate,' I said, 'you really should have come to me. I could have put you straight. I could have warned you.'

'Warned me? About what?'

'He will not leave Lana for you,' I said. 'Don't delude yourself.'

'I'm not deluding myself.' Kate tapped the unlit cigarette violently against the table. She planted it in her mouth and lit it.

'I think you are.'

'You know fuck all about it.'

Kate smoked for a moment – I noticed her hand was trembling. Then she suddenly stubbed out the cigarette in the ashtray. 'The question is,' she said, turning on me, with a spark of her old anger, 'why *you* care? Why are you so invested in Lana's marriage? Even if they split up, she's hardly going to marry *you*.'

Kate was joking. But then she saw the flicker of hurt in my eyes. She gasped. 'Oh, my God. Is *that* what you think? You really think . . . that *you* and *Lana* –?'

Kate couldn't finish her sentence – she was overcome by laughter. Unkind, mocking laughter.

I waited until she had stopped laughing. Then I said, coolly, 'I'm trying to help. That's all.'

'No, no, you're not.' Kate shook her head. 'Can't fool me, Prince Machiavelli. But you'll get your comeuppance in the end. Just you wait.'

I ignored this. I was determined that she hear me. It was important.

'I mean it, Kate. Don't put Jason in a position where he has to choose between you. You'll regret it.'

'Fuck off.'

But her rebuke was only half-hearted – her mind was clearly on Jason. Her eyes were on the door.

Then she made a sudden decision. She got up and hurried out.

Alone in the living room, I tried to imagine what might happen next.

Kate had obviously gone to find Jason. But Jason wasn't interested in Kate – he made that quite clear just now.

Jason's priority was Lana. He would try and win her back. He'd comfort her; reassure her there was nothing going on between him and Kate. He'd lie, insist upon his innocence, swear he had never been unfaithful.

And Lana? What would she do? That was the key question. Everything hinged on it.

I tried to picture the scene. Where were they? On the beach, perhaps? No, *by the ruin* – a more romantic setting – a midnight meeting by the moonlit columns.

I had a sense of how Lana might play it. Come to think of it, I felt sure I had seen her play a similar role in one of her movies. She would be stoic and self-sacrificing – what better way to appeal to her leading man's better instincts? To his sense of honour and duty?

She'd give Jason a chilly reception at first, then slowly allow her reserve to weaken. She wouldn't admonish him. No, she'd blame herself – fighting tears as she spoke; she was good at that.

Finally, she would gaze at Jason with her special

look, the one she saved for close-ups: widening those huge, hypnotic eyes, vulnerable, full of pain, yet tremendously brave – 'mugging for camera', Barbara West called it – but extremely effective.

Before he knew it, Jason would be bewitched, swept along by Lana's performance, on his knees, begging for forgiveness, promising to be a better man – and meaning it. Kate would fade into the background of his mind. *The end.*

For one desperate moment, I thought about running to find Lana and Jason myself – and trying to intervene. But no. I had to have faith in Lana.

After all, it was entirely possible she might surprise me.

18

'Well?' Lana said. 'Will you do it?'

Nikos stared at her, astounded. He couldn't believe his ears. He couldn't believe the words that had just come out of Lana's mouth – or what she had asked him to do.

He felt unable to reply, so he didn't.

'What do you want?' she said.

Again, no reply.

Lana reached behind her neck and undid the chain of diamonds. She coiled it in her palm. She held out the sparkling pile of stones.

'Take this. Sell it. Buy whatever you want.' And then, reading his mind in that way of hers, she added: 'A boat. That's what you want, isn't it? You can buy a boat with this.'

Nikos still didn't reply.

Lana frowned. 'Are you insulted? Don't be. It's a fair exchange. Tell me what you want, to do what I ask.'

He wasn't listening. All Nikos could think was how beautiful she was. Before he knew it, the words came out of his mouth:

'Kiss me.'

Lana looked at him as if she hadn't heard. 'What?'

Nikos didn't reply. Lana searched his eyes, confused.

'I don't understand – that's it? That's your price?'

He didn't reply. He didn't speak or move. He just stood there.

There was a pause.

Then Lana took a small step forward. Their faces were inches apart.

They looked into each other's eyes. Lana had never noticed his eyes before. There was a kind of beauty to them, she realized; a clear blue light. A crazy thought popped into her head: *I should have married Nikos. Then I could have lived here, and been happy.*

Then she leaned forward and pressed her lips to his mouth.

As they kissed, Nikos, who was dried up inside, caught fire – and was engulfed. He had never known a feeling like this. He would never be the same, he knew that.

'I'll do it,' he whispered, between kisses. 'I'll do what you want.'

Lana left Nikos's cottage, and made her way along the path. She walked through the olive grove and into the clearing, to the ruin.

The ruin was sheltered from the worst of the wind, by thickset olive trees that surrounded it. Lana sat on a broken column for a moment. She closed her eyes and sat there, deep in thought.

Then, in the undergrowth, behind her, a twig snapped underfoot.

Lana opened her eyes and turned her head to see who it was.

Three gunshots rang out.

Moments later, Lana lay on the ground, in a pool of blood.

19

Leo was the first to arrive at the ruin. He was followed by Agathi, before Jason and I appeared.

As we gathered around Lana's body, time seemed to stop for a moment. It held us suspended – while all around us everything moved. The wind swirled and screamed, the trees swayed; while we stood still, frozen, held in a timeless state, unable to think or feel.

It only lasted a few seconds, but it felt like an eternity – until Kate appeared and broke the spell. She looked disoriented and confused. Her expression changed from confusion to disbelief, to horror.

'What *happened*?' she kept saying. '*My God* –'

Somehow Kate's arrival spurred us into action. I knelt by Leo. 'We need to lie her down,' I said. 'Leo? You have to let her go –'

Leo rocked her back and forth, crying. I tried to coax him to let go of her. 'Come on, Leo, please –'

'Put her down, Leo,' Jason said. Losing patience, he made a sudden movement towards him.

Leo reacted as if he'd been bitten by a snake. He screamed at Jason, his bloodstained face a horrible sight. '*Get away from her! Get away!*'

Jason was startled, and backed down. 'Just put her on the ground, for Christ's sake.'

I threw Jason an exasperated look. 'I'll deal with him. Call an ambulance!'

Jason nodded, feeling in his pockets for his phone. He found it and unlocked it – thrusting it into Agathi's hands.

'Call the station in Mykonos,' he said. 'Say we need an ambulance – and the police. They need to be here *now*!'

Agathi nodded, dazed. 'Yes, yes –'

'I'm going to get a gun. Wait here. Don't move.'

With that, Jason started running back to the house. Kate hesitated, then ran after him.

Agathi and I managed to get Leo to relinquish Lana's body. We carefully laid her on the ground.

Leo looked up, with wide eyes. He spoke in a strangled voice.

'The *guns*.'

'What?'

But Leo was already up – and running after the others.

20

Kate hurried into the house. She looked around but couldn't see him anywhere.

'Jason?' she whispered. 'Jason –'

Suddenly, he appeared – emerging from the gun room. He stared at her, with a strange, confused look on his face.

'They've gone.'

Kate didn't know what he meant. 'What?'

'The guns. They're not there.'

'What do you mean? Where are they?'

'I don't fucking know. Someone's taken them.'

They heard footsteps at the end of the corridor. They looked up.

Leo was standing there, staring at them. He was a frightening sight – covered in blood, wild, wretched. He looked out of his mind.

'The guns,' Leo said. 'I –'

Jason tensed up. 'What?'

'I moved them. I hid them. It was meant to be a joke, I –'

But Jason was already on him – grabbing hold of him. 'Where are they? *Tell me!*'

'Jason, let him go!' Kate said.

'Where are the guns?'

'Let him go!'

Jason released him, and Leo sank to the floor, against the wall, weeping, hugging his knees.

'*She's dead,*' Leo screamed. '*Don't you even care?*'

He covered his face with his hands. Kate went over to him and pulled him into her arms. 'Darling, shh, shh. Please – tell us. Where are the guns?'

Leo raised one hand and pointed at the wooden chest. '*In there.*'

Jason charged up to the chest. He threw open the lid.

He scowled. 'Is this a joke?'

'What?' Leo got up and made his way over. He looked inside.

The chest was empty.

Leo was astonished. 'But – I put them there –'

'When?'

'Before dinner. Someone's moved them.'

'Who? Why would anyone do that?'

Kate frowned as something occurred to her. 'Where's Nikos?'

'I am here,' said a voice behind them.

They spun around. Nikos was standing in the doorway. He was holding a gun.

There was a slight pause, and Jason spoke in a guarded tone.

'Lana's been shot.'

Nikos nodded. 'Yes, I know.'

Jason glanced at the gun in Nikos's hand. 'Where did you get that?'

'This is my gun.'

'Are you sure? All mine are missing.'

Nikos shrugged. 'It is mine.'

Jason held out his hand. 'Well, you better give it to me.'

Nikos shook his head – a definite no.

Jason decided not to press him for it. Instead, he said slowly and emphatically: 'We need to search the island. Do you understand? There's an intruder. He is armed and dangerous. We need to find him.'

Then I entered – the bearer of bad tidings. I didn't know how to say it, so I just came out with it.

'Agathi spoke to the police in Mykonos.'

Jason looked up. 'And? When are they getting here?'

'They're not.'

'What?'

'They're not coming. It's the wind. They can't get a boat across.'

Kate stared at me. Her face tightened. 'But they have to – they must –'

'They said it'll calm down by dawn . . . They'll try then.'

'But – that's in *five hours*.'

'I know.' I nodded. 'Until then, we're on our own.'

21

It was decided that Jason, Nikos and I should search the island for an intruder. I told them it was a waste of time.

'That's madness. You seriously think someone landed here – in this weather? That's impossible!'

'What other option is there?' Jason said, glaring at me. 'Someone's here, and we're going to find him. Now move.'

And so, armed with battery-powered torches, we ventured into the night.

We began patrolling the path through the olive grove, shining our torches into the dark. The olive trees were thickset, revealing only spiderwebs and birds' nests.

As we walked, Jason kept glancing at the gun in Nikos's hand. He clearly didn't trust him. I didn't trust either of them with a gun, to be honest – I kept as close an eye on them as they kept on each other.

We made our way to the coast and began to search the beaches. This was an arduous task, with the wind attacking us as we walked. The fury was relentless, slashing our faces, hurling sand at us; screaming in our ears, shoving us off-balance every chance it got. But we persevered, and it took us a little over an hour, following the dirt path that snaked around the perimeter of the island, rising and falling along the shoreline.

Finally, we reached the north side of the island: a sheer cliff-face, dropping down to the water below – where it was impossible for anyone to moor a boat; and there was nowhere to hide amongst the bare rocks.

At last, what I said earlier now became apparent to the others. There was no boat, no intruder. No one else was on this island.

No one, but the six of us.

22

Perhaps this is a good place to pause – and take stock, before we proceed.

I am aware of the conventions of this genre. I know what's meant to happen next. I know what you're expecting. A murder investigation, a denouement, a twist.

That's how it's supposed to play out. But as I warned you at the start, that's not the way this is going to go.

And so, before our story deviates entirely from this familiar sequence of events – before we take a series of dark turns – let us consider how an alternative narrative might unfold.

Let us, for a moment, imagine a detective – a Greek version of Agatha Christie's Belgian, perhaps? He appears on the island, a few hours later, once the wind has died down.

He is an older man, cautiously stepping off the police boat, assisted by a junior officer. He is tall and lean, with grey hair and a small, neatly clipped black pencil moustache. His eyes are dark and piercing.

'I am Inspector Mavropoulos, of the Mykonian police,' he says, with a strong Greek accent.

His name, Agathi informs us, means 'blackbird' – messenger of death.

And, looking rather like a bird of prey, the inspector

perches at the head of the kitchen table. Once he and his officers drink their little cups of Greek coffee, devouring the sweet biscuits conjured up by Agathi, the inspector begins his investigation.

Brushing away some crumbs from his moustache, he requests to see us all – one by one – for an interrogation.

During these interviews, Mavropoulos quickly establishes the facts.

The ruin, where Lana's body was found, was roughly a twelve-minute walk from the main house – along the path, through the olive grove. The murder itself took place at midnight – when the shots were heard. The body was found soon afterwards.

As Leo was the first to appear at the ruin, he is the first to be interviewed by Mavropoulos.

'My boy,' he says gently, 'I am very sorry for your loss. I'm afraid I must ask you to put your grief aside for a moment and answer my questions as clearly as you can. Where were you when you heard the gunshots?'

Leo explains that he was throwing up – in the newly dug vegetable garden that he and Nikos had been working on. The inspector assumes Leo was sick from alcohol – and Leo decides not to disillusion him, suspecting marijuana might still be illegal in Greece.

The inspector, taking pity on Leo's raw emotional state, doesn't press him – and releases him after a few questions.

Next to be interviewed is Jason. His responses strike Mavropoulos as evasive, even strange. He insists that, at midnight, he was on the other side of the island, by the cliffs.

When pressed for a reason, Jason claims he was looking for Lana, as he couldn't find her anywhere in the house. The cliffs seem an odd place to search, but the inspector doesn't comment – for the moment.

He simply notes Jason has no alibi.

Nor does Kate, alone in the summerhouse. Nor does Agathi, asleep in bed. Nor does Nikos, dozing in his cottage.

And where was I, you ask? Boozing in the living room – but you've only my word for it. In fact, none of us can prove where we were.

Which means any of the six of us could have done it. But why would we?

Why would any of us kill Lana? We all loved Lana.

At least, I did. Although I'm not sure Inspector Mavropoulos fully grasps the concept of *soulmates*, but I do my best to explain to him I had no motive to murder Lana.

Which isn't strictly true.

I don't inform him, for instance, that Lana left me a fortune in her will.

How do I know this? She told me, when I was arranging the sale of the house Barbara West left me in Holland Park. Lana asked why I was selling the house, and I said that apart from the fact I loathed that place and all its memories, the bottom line was I needed some cash. I needed something to live on – otherwise I would end up destitute on the street. I was joking, but Lana looked grave. She told me she wouldn't let that happen – that she'd always take care of me, as long as she lived; and she had left me seven million pounds in her will.

I was stunned by her generosity, and deeply moved. Lana, perhaps regretting her indiscretion, asked me to forget what she had said – in particular, she requested I never mention it to Jason. The unspoken implication was that Jason would be furious. Of course he would – Jason was greedy, mean-spirited, ungenerous. The opposite of me and Lana, in fact.

Knowing about this inheritance didn't make the slightest bit of difference to my feelings, by the way. I certainly didn't plot Lana's murder, if that's what you're thinking.

But you can think what you like – that's the fun of a murder mystery, isn't it? You can bet on whichever horse you choose.

If I were you, I'd put my money on Jason.

We all know how desperate he was, how much he needed money – which he doesn't admit to Mavropoulos. But Jason has an air of guilt clinging to him like cigarette smoke. Any inspector worth his salt should pick up on it, and become suspicious.

And Kate? Well, her motive was not financial – in Kate's case, it would be a *crime passionnel*, wouldn't it? But the question remains, whether Kate would actually kill Lana in order to steal her husband? I'm not convinced she would.

Nor am I convinced that Agathi is a realistic suspect. She was also to receive an inheritance, like me – and, like me, was intensely loyal. There's no reason to think she'd harm Lana. She loved Lana, perhaps even a little too much.

Who is left?

I don't seriously consider Leo. Do you? Would a son really kill the mother he adored simply because she wouldn't let him go to drama school? Although, to be fair, I'm sure people have committed murder for less compelling reasons. And if it did turn out to be Leo, it would prove to be a sufficiently shocking surprise; a dramatic end to our tale.

But a more savvy armchair detective might be likely to go for Nikos – shady from the get-go, increasingly obsessed with Lana, isolated and eccentric.

Or is Nikos too obvious a suspect? A Greek-island version of 'the butler did it'?

But then, who is left?

There's only one other possible solution. A trick that Christie herself sometimes used. An outsider: someone whose name was not on the list of six suspects. Someone who landed illegally on the island, despite the bad weather, armed with a gun and the desire to kill. Someone from Lana's past?

Was it possible? Yes. Probable? No.

But let's not dismiss this idea entirely – not until Inspector Mavropoulos has reached his conclusion; when he asks us all to meet for the solution of the murder.

The inspector gathers us in the living room of the main house – or at the ruin, if he's feeling particularly theatrical. Six chairs, arranged in a row, in front of the columns.

We sit and watch Mavropoulos pace back and forth, taking us through his investigation, all the twists and turns his thinking took. Finally, he deduces that, in fact, to everyone's immense surprise, the murderer is . . .

Well – that's as far as I can go, for the moment.

All of the above is what might have happened – if this tale were being written by a firmer hand than my own – by Agatha Christie's implacable, unshakeable pen.

But my hand isn't firm. It's weak and wildly erratic, like me. Disorganized and sentimental. You couldn't imagine worse traits for a mystery writer. Thankfully I'm just an amateur – I'd never make a living at this.

The truth is, none of it played out the way I have just described.

There was no Inspector Mavropoulos, no investigation, nothing so orderly, methodical, or safe. When the police finally did arrive – by then, it was daylight, and the identity of the murderer was well known. By then, there was chaos.

By then, all hell had broken loose.

So what happened? Allow me to refill your glass, and I'll tell you.

The truth, as they say, is often stranger than fiction.

Act Three

It is not unnatural that the best writers are liars. A
major part of their trade is to lie or invent and they
will lie when they are drunk, or to themselves, or
to strangers.

—Ernest Hemingway

I

At this point, I suppose – like that poor bastard harangued by the Ancient Mariner, and forced to endure his weird tale – you must be wondering what the hell you let yourself in for, agreeing to hear my story.

It only gets weirder, I'm afraid.

I wish I knew how you felt about me, right now. Are you slightly charmed, even beguiled, as Lana used to be? Or, like Kate, do you find me irritating, self-dramatizing, self-indulgent?

All of the above is probably closest to the truth. But we like to keep moral questions simple, don't we? Good/bad, innocent/guilty. That's fine in fiction; real life is not so clear-cut. Human beings are complex creatures, with shades of light and dark operating in all of us.

If this sounds like I'm trying to justify myself, I assure you I'm not. I am well aware that as we proceed, and you hear the rest of this tale, you might not approve of my actions. That's fine. I don't seek your approval.

What I seek – no, what I demand – is your *understanding*. Otherwise my story will never touch your heart. It will remain a two-a-penny thriller that you might pick up at an airport to devour on the beach – only to discard, forgotten, by the time you get home. I will not allow my life to be reduced to pulp. No, sir.

If you are to understand what follows – if any of the incredible events I'm about to relate are to make any sense to you – there are some things I must explain about myself. Some things I felt I couldn't reveal to you when we first met. Why not? I wanted you to get to know me a little better, I suppose. I hoped you might then excuse some of my less attractive traits.

But now it has overtaken me – this desire to unburden myself. I couldn't stop, even if I wanted to. Like the Ancient Mariner, I need to get it off my chest.

I must warn you, what follows is, at times, hard to take. It's certainly hard to write about. If you thought Lana's murder was the climax of this sordid tale, you were sadly mistaken.

The real horror is yet to come.

Once again, I must turn back the clock. Not to the Soho street in London, this time – but much, much further.

I will tell you about me and Lana – about our friendship, strange and extraordinary as it was. But that's just the tip of the iceberg, to be frank. My relationship with Lana Farrar began a long time before we ever met.

It began when I was someone else.

2

It's funny, whenever the novelist Christopher Isherwood would write about his younger self, it was always in the third person.

He would write about '*him*' – a kid named 'Christopher'.

Why? Because, I think, it allowed him to access empathy for himself. It's so much easier to feel empathy for other people, isn't it? If you see a scared little boy on the street, bullied, shamed, disrespected by an abusive parent, you instantly feel sympathy for him.

But in the case of our own childhoods, it's hard to see so clearly. Our perception is clouded by the need to comply, justify and forgive. It takes an impartial outsider sometimes, like a skilled therapist, to help us see the truth – that as kids, we were alone and afraid in a frightening place, and no one took any notice of our pain.

We couldn't admit this to ourselves, back then. It was too scary – so we swept it under an enormous carpet, hoping it would go away. But it didn't. It remained there, lingering forever, like nuclear waste.

High time, don't you think, to lift up the rug and take a good look? Although, for safety's sake, I shall borrow Christopher Isherwood's technique.

What follows is the kid's story – not mine.

*

The kid's early years were not happy.

Having a child was no doubt an inconvenience to his parents. A failed experiment, never to be repeated. They provided him with food and shelter, but gave him precious little else – apart from occasional lessons in drunkenness and brutality.

Home was bad. School was worse. The kid wasn't popular. He wasn't sporty, or cool, or clever. He was shy and withdrawn, and lonely. The only classmates who spoke to him with any regularity were the bullies – a gang of four mean boys in his class. He nicknamed them the Neanderthals.

The Neanderthals would wait for the kid every morning by the school gates and empty his pockets, taking his lunch money, shoving him, tripping him up and playing other pranks. They had a fondness for kicking footballs at his head – attempting to knock him over – while hurling insults at him, like *weirdo* and *freak*, or worse.

And when he was face-down in the dirt, there was always, behind his back, a chorus of laughter. High-pitched children's laughter. Jeering, malevolent.

I read somewhere that laughter is evil in origin – as it requires an object of ridicule, a butt, a fool. A bully is never the butt of his own jokes, is he?

The leader of the Neanderthals was a real joker, called Paul. He was popular, in that way mean kids can be. He was a wag, a prankster. He sat at the back of the class, mocking teachers and students alike.

Demonstrating a precocious grasp of psychological warfare, Paul decided that none of his classmates were allowed to speak to the kid. He was deemed a leper – too disgusting, too gross, too smelly and too damn weird to be talked to, acknowledged or touched. He must be avoided at any cost.

From then on, girls would delight in running off, in fits of excited giggles and screams, if the kid neared them in the playground. Boys would pull faces and make retching noises if they passed him on the stairs. Cruel notes, wishing him harm, were left in his desk for him to find. And always, behind his back, that high-pitched, mocking laughter.

There were occasional respites from this misery.

When he was twelve years old, he was in a play for the first time. A school production of that glorious old American warhorse – *Our Town* by Thornton Wilder. Possibly an odd choice of play for a comprehensive school outside London, but his drama teacher, Cassandra, hailed from the US. She was probably homesick when she decided to stage this love letter to small-town America in Basildon, Essex.

The kid liked Cassandra. She had a friendly horse face, and wore a necklace of amber beads with pre-historic flies trapped in them. And she gave him some of the closest moments he had ever known to happiness.

She cast him (presumably without irony) as Simon Stimson, a cynical alcoholic choirmaster who ends up hanging himself. It was a part he relished to the full. Existential angst, sarcasm, despair – he had no idea what his lines meant in any literal sense – but trust me, he got the gist.

That first night of the performance, the kid experienced applause for the first time in his life. He'd never
known anything like it – it felt like a wave of affection,
of love, flooding the stage, drenching him. The kid
shut his eyes, and drank it in.

But then he opened his eyes – and saw Paul, and the
other Neanderthals, sitting in the back row, laughing,
making faces and obscene gestures. Their vengeful
expressions told him there'd be a price to pay for his
brief moment of happiness.

He didn't have to wait long. The following morning,
at breaktime, he was dragged into the boys' toilets. He
was told he was going to be punished, for showing off.
For thinking he was special.

One Neanderthal stood guard by the door, making
sure they weren't disturbed. The other two pushed the
kid down, on to his knees, and held him there, by the
stinking urinal.

Paul reached into his locker. He produced, with a
magician's flourish, a large carton of milk.

I've been saving this for weeks, he said, *brewing it – for a
special occasion.*

He opened the carton slightly, cautiously sniffing
it – and then pulled a disgusted face, like he might
throw up. The other boys tittered in anticipation.

Get ready, said Paul.

He ripped open the carton – and he was about to
turn it upside down, over the kid's head – when he
suddenly had a better idea.

He held the carton out to the kid. 'You do it.'

The kid shook his head, trying not to cry.

'No. Please . . . no, please . . .'

'It's your punishment. Do it.'

'No –'

'*Do it.*'

I wish I could say the kid fought back. But he didn't. He took hold of the carton that was being thrust into his hands.

And, slowly, ceremoniously, under Paul's supervision, the kid poured the contents over his head. Rotten milk, white, sludgy, green, foul-smelling slime slid down his face – covering his eyes, filling his mouth. He gagged on it.

He could hear the boys laughing, shrieking. Their side-splitting laughter was almost as cruel as the punishment itself.

Nothing can be worse than this, he thought. The shame, the humiliation, the anger bubbling inside – nothing could ever be as bad.

He was wrong, of course. He had so much further to fall.

Writing this, I feel such anger. Such outrage on his behalf. And even though it's too late, and even though it's only me, I'm glad someone is at last empathizing with him. No one else did – least of all himself.

Heraclitus was right, you see – *character is fate*. Other children, who had more successful childhoods, brought up to respect and stand up for themselves, might have fought back, or at least alerted the authorities. But in the kid's case, sadly, every time he took a beating, he felt he deserved it.

He started skipping school, after that. He'd hang

around alone in town, at the shops, or sneak into the movies.

And it was there, in the dark, where he first encountered Lana Farrar.

Lana was only a few years older than him, barely more than a child herself. It was one of Lana's first films he saw, *Starstruck*, an early misfire – an unfunny romantic comedy about a movie starlet falling in love with a paparazzi photographer, played by an actor old enough to be her father.

The kid was oblivious to all the sexist jokes and contrived comic situations. All he could see was her. Those eyes, that face – projected up on the screen, thirty feet high – the loveliest face he'd ever seen. As every cinematographer who worked with her discovered, Lana had no bad angles; just perfect planes – the face of a Greek goddess.

She cast a spell on the kid, in that moment. He never recovered.

He kept going back to the cinema. Just to see her, to gaze at her. He saw every film she made – and God knows, she churned them out in those early days. Their variable quality was of little interest to him. He happily watched them all, again and again.

The kid was at his lowest ebb when he encountered Lana. He was close to despair. And she gave him beauty. She gave him joy. It wasn't much, perhaps. But it was enough to sustain him; to keep him alive.

He would sit alone, in the middle of the cinema, in the fifteenth row, and gaze at Lana in the dark.

No one could see it, but there was a smile on his face.

3

Nothing lasts forever. Not even an unhappy childhood.

The years passed, and the kid grew older.

As he grew, a flood of hormones signalled growth spurts in all kinds of peculiar places. The need to shave was something he agonized over for months. He'd stare despondently at his ever-increasing beard in the mirror, dimly aware that learning to shave was some kind of ancient masculine rite of passage – a bonding moment between father and son, initiating the boy into manhood. The thought of sharing that rite with his own father made him feel physically sick.

The kid decided to circumnavigate embarrassment by sneaking off to the corner shop and buying razors and shaving foam – which he kept hidden, like porn, in his bedside drawer.

He permitted himself one question to his father. He felt it was innocuous enough.

'How do you not cut yourself?' he said casually. 'When you're shaving, I mean – do you make sure the razor's not too sharp?'

His father threw him a look of contempt. 'It's a blunt razor that cuts you, idiot, not a sharp one.'

That ended their conversation. So, with no other recourse in that pre-internet age, the kid smuggled the foam and razors into the bathroom. Through trial and bloody error, he taught himself how to be a man.

He left home soon after that. He ran away, a few days after his seventeenth birthday.

He went to London, like Dick Whittington, in search of fame and fortune.

The kid wanted to be an actor. He assumed all he had to do was appear at one of the cattle-call auditions advertised in the back pages of *The Stage*, and he would be discovered and catapulted to stardom. It didn't work out quite like that.

Easy to see why, looking back. Never mind the fact he wasn't a very good actor – too self-conscious and too unnatural – he wasn't handsome enough to stand out in the crowd. He had a ragamuffin look, more unkempt with each passing day.

Not that he could see this at the time. If he had, he might have swallowed his pride, gone home with his tail between his legs – and come to much less grief. As it was, the kid reassured himself success was just around the corner. He just had to tough it out for a while longer, that's all.

Unfortunately, he soon ran out of what little money he had. He was now penniless, and kicked out of the youth hostel in King's Cross where'd been staying.

That's when things got really bad, really fast.

You wouldn't think it, now it's gentrified and cleaned up – all gleaming steel and exposed brick – but back then, my God, King's Cross was *rough*. A shadowy place, full of danger – a Dickensian underworld, populated by drug dealers, prostitutes and homeless kids.

It makes me shudder now, to think of him there alone, so spectacularly ill-equipped to survive. He was destitute and sleeping on benches in parks – until his luck changed, during a rainstorm, when he found refuge in Euston cemetery.

He climbed over the wall into the graveyard, looking for shelter. He discovered, along one side of the church, a subterranean bunker – a dug-out concrete space – big enough for two or three people to lie down comfortably. Well, as comfortable as you can get in an empty crypt – for that's what it was. But it provided a level of protection.

And, for the kid, this was a minor miracle.

He was a little unhinged, by this point. He was hungry, scared, paranoid – and increasingly cut off from the world. He felt dirty, like he stank – he probably did – and he didn't like getting too close to people.

But he was desperate – and so he did some things for money that he –

No, I can't bring myself to write about that.

I'm sorry – I don't mean to be coy. I'm sure you have a few things you'd rather not tell me about. We all have a skeleton or two in our closet – so to speak. Let this be mine.

The first time he did it, he felt entirely disassociated and he blanked it out, like it was happening to someone else.

The second time it was much worse, so he shut his eyes and thought of the madwoman who lived on the church steps, shouting at passers-by to fling themselves into the arms of Jesus. He imagined throwing himself into Jesus's arms and being saved. But somehow salvation felt a long way off.

Afterwards, feeling overwhelmed and afraid, the kid sat up all night until dawn, clutching a cup of coffee in Euston Station. Trying not to think, trying not to feel.

He sat there through the early-morning rush hour – a depressed waif, ignored by the sea of commuters. He counted the minutes until the pubs opened, and he could get a drink.

Finally, the dingy pub across the road opened its doors, offering sanctuary for the lost and disheartened.

The kid went inside and sat at the bar. He paid cash for a vodka – it was the first time he had ever tasted vodka, come to think of it. He knocked it back, wincing as it burned in his throat.

Then he heard a husky voice at the end of the bar:

'What's a pretty thing like you doing in a shithole like this?'

This was – on reflection – the first, and last, compliment she ever paid him.

The kid looked up, and there was Barbara West. A lined older woman, dyed red hair, an excess of mascara. She had the darkest, most piercing eyes he had ever seen; penetrating, brilliant and scary.

Barbara laughed – a distinctive laugh, a throaty cackle. She laughed easily, he discovered, mostly at her own jokes. The kid would grow to hate her laugh. But that day, he merely felt indifferent. He shrugged – and tapped his empty glass in answer to her question.

'What's it look like?'

Barbara took the hint, nodding at the barman. 'Give

him another, Mike. Me too, while you're at it. Doubles.'

Barbara had gone to the pub that morning, direct from signing books in Waterstone's bookshop next door, because she was an alcoholic. Character is fate; and without Barbara's need for a gin and tonic at eleven a.m., she and the kid would never have met. They were from two different worlds, those two. And were destined, in the end, only to cause each other harm.

They had a couple more drinks. Barbara kept her eyes on him the whole time, sizing him up. She liked what she saw. After one more drink for the road, she called a cab. She took the kid home with her.

It was only meant to be for one night. But one night led to another, and another – and he never left.

Yes, Barbara West used him, taking advantage of this desperate child in his hour of need. She was indeed a predator; even if, unlike her alcoholism, this was not immediately apparent. She was one of the darkest human beings I ever encountered. I dread to think what she would have done with her life if she hadn't had a knack for writing novels.

But let's not underestimate the kid, here. He understood perfectly well what he was getting into. He knew what Barbara wanted, and he was happy to supply it. If anything, he got the better deal. In return for his services, not only did he receive a roof over his head, but an education, which he needed just as urgently.

In that house in Holland Park, he had access to a private library. A world full of books. 'Can I read one?' he said, staring at them in awe.

Barbara seemed surprised at his request. Perhaps she doubted he could read. 'Take your pick,' she said with a shrug.

He randomly chose one book from the shelf. *Hard Times* by Charles Dickens.

'Oh yuk, Dickens,' said Barbara, pulling a face. 'So *sentimental*. Still, I suppose you've got to start somewhere.'

But the kid didn't find Dickens sentimental. He found him wonderfully entertaining. And funny, and profound. So he read *David Copperfield* next; and his enjoyment grew, along with his appetite. Not just for Dickens, but for whatever he could find on Barbara's shelves – devouring all the great authors he could lay his hands on.

Every day spent in that house was an education – not just from her books, but from Barbara herself, and from the circle she moved in – the literary salon she ran from her living room.

As time went on, and the kid was exposed to more and more of her life, he kept his eyes and ears open. He tried to absorb as much as he could from her guests' conversations; what all these sophisticated people said, and how they said it. He would memorize phrases and opinions and gestures, practising them when he was alone, in front of a mirror; trying them on, like uncomfortable clothes he was determined to squeeze into.

Don't forget the kid was an aspiring actor. And, frankly, this was his only role, which he tirelessly and meticulously rehearsed over the years – until he honed it to perfection.

And then, one day, staring at himself in the mirror, he could see no trace of the kid.

Someone else was staring back at him.

But who was this new person? The first thing he had to do was find a name for him. He stole one from a play on Barbara's shelf: from *Private Lives* by Noël Coward.

Barbara thought this was hilarious, of course. But despite mocking him, she went along with it. She preferred this new name, she said, as it was less hideous than his real one. But between you and me, I think the idea just appealed to her sense of the perverse.

That evening, over a bottle of champagne, he was christened Elliot Chase.

I was born.

And then, with perfect timing – Lana appeared.

4

I have forgotten many things in my inebriated life. Numberless names and faces, places I've been, whole cities have fallen into a void in my mind. But something I will never forget until I die – forever emblazoned on my mind, engraved upon my heart – is the moment I first met Lana Farrar.

Barbara West and I had gone to see Kate in a play. It was a new translation of *Hedda Gabler* at the National. It was the first night, and though the production was a pretentious stinker, in my humble opinion, it was received with wild acclaim and heralded as a triumph.

There was a first-night party afterwards – which Barbara begrudgingly agreed to attend. Any unwillingness on her part was pure bullshit, believe me. If there was free booze and free food on offer, Barbara was always the first in line. Especially at a party of luvvie theatricals, who would queue up to tell her how much her writing meant to them, and generally kiss her arse. She loved all that, as you can imagine.

Anyway, I was standing next to her, bored to death, concealing a yawn, idly casting my gaze over a motley crew of actors and wannabe actors, producers, journalists and so on.

Then I noticed, across the room, a large group of people, admirers and hangers-on, gathering around someone – a woman, judging by the glimpse I caught through the jostling crowd. I craned my neck to see who it was, but her face kept being obscured by the shifting bodies surrounding her. Finally, someone moved, a gap was created – and I caught a momentary flash of her face.

I couldn't believe my eyes. Was it really her? Surely not?

I craned my neck to get a better look, but I didn't need one. It was her.

Feeling excited, I turned and nudged Barbara. She was mid-lecture to an unhappy-looking playwright, about why he wasn't more commercially successful.

'Barbara?'

Barbara waved away my interruption. 'I'm talking, Elliot.'

'Over there. Look. It's Lana Farrar.'

She grunted. 'So?'

'So, you know her, don't you?'

'We've met once or twice.'

'Introduce me to her.'

'Certainly not.'

'Go on. Please.' I looked at her, hopefully.

Barbara smiled. Nothing gratified her more than refusing a heartfelt request. 'I don't think so, duck.'

'Why not?'

'Yours not to reason why. Go and get me another drink.'

'Get your own fucking drink.'

In a rare act of rebellion, I left her. I knew she'd be furious and make me pay for it later, but I didn't care.

I walked across the room, straight up to Lana.

Time seemed to slow down as I approached her. I felt as if I were departing reality, entering a heightened state. I must have pushed my way through the crowd; I don't remember. I was oblivious of everyone but her.

I found myself there, in the inner circle, standing to one side of her. I stared at her, starstruck, while she listened politely to some man talking. But she couldn't fail to notice me standing there. She glanced at me.

'I love you,' I said.

These were the first words I ever said to Lana Farrar.

The people around her were all startled. They burst out laughing.

Thankfully, Lana also laughed.

'I love you, too,' she said.

And that's how it began. We kept talking all night – meaning I successfully fended off interruptions from would-be competitors. I made her laugh, making fun of the overwrought production we had just been forced to endure. And I let slip that Kate was a mutual friend; a discovery that made Lana visibly relax in my company.

Even so, I had my work cut out for me. I knew I had to convince Lana I wasn't some weirdo, or obsessive fan, or potential stalker. I had to persuade her I was an equal, in intellect, at least – if not in fame or fortune. I badly wanted to impress her. I needed her to like me. Why? I don't think I knew myself, to be honest. Dimly, subconsciously, I wanted to keep hold of her. Even then, it seems, I couldn't bear to let her go.

Lana was cautious, at first, but receptive to my conversation. Now, I'm not quick-witted at the best of times – I can supply you with a witty riposte, but only if you give me three days to write it. However, that night, miraculously, the stars all aligned in my favour. For once, my shyness didn't get the better of me.

On the contrary, I was confident, lucid, lubricated with just the right amount of wine, and found myself talking intelligently, entertainingly, even wittily, on a variety of subjects.

I talked knowledgeably about the theatre, about plays that were currently on, what was coming, and recommended a couple of lesser-known productions to Lana that I said were worth seeing. And I suggested some exhibitions and galleries that she hadn't heard of. In other words, I gave a completely convincing performance of the person I had always wanted to be: a confident, sophisticated, razor-sharp man about town. That's the man I saw reflected in Lana's eyes. In her eyes, that night, I shone.

Barbara West eventually gave in and joined us, all smiles, greeting Lana as an old friend. Lana was perfectly civil to Barbara, but I got the sense that she didn't like her, which was entirely in Lana's favour.

At one point, Barbara went to the Ladies, leaving us alone. Lana took the opportunity to enquire about the nature of our relationship.

'Are you a couple?' she said.

I must confess to being a little evasive. I said I was Barbara's 'partner' and left it at that.

I understood why Lana was asking. She was single

when we met, you see – Jason had yet to come on the scene. I suspected Lana was making sure she was 'safe' with me; determining that I was someone else's property – and therefore less likely to pounce, or make any sudden moves. I imagine she got a lot of that.

By the end of the night, we agreed to meet again on Sunday, for a walk along the river. I asked for Lana's number, when Barbara wasn't looking.

And to my utter joy, she gave it to me.

As Barbara and I left the party that night, I couldn't stop smiling. I felt as if I were walking on air.

Barbara, on the other hand, was in a foul mood. 'What a shitty production,' she said. 'I give it three weeks, before they put it out of its misery.'

'Oh, I don't know.' I glanced at the poster of Kate as Hedda Gabler, holding up a pistol. I smiled. 'I had a pretty good time.'

Barbara shot me a poisonous look. 'Yes, I know you did. I *saw*.'

She didn't comment further – for the moment.

Barbara waited a long time to make me pay for my insolent behaviour that evening. But she made me pay in the end, as you will see.

Oh, yes. She made me pay dearly.

5

It's hard for me to write about my friendship with Lana.

There is too much to say. How can I possibly describe, in a series of well-chosen vignettes, the slow and complicated process of the growing bond of trust and affection between us?

Perhaps I should select a single moment from our years together, as you might pick a random card from a deck in a magic trick, to conjure up the merest feeling of what it was like. Why not?

In which case, I choose our very first walk together – a Sunday afternoon, in late May. It explains everything; about what came later, I mean. And how two people, who were so close in every regard, could, in the end, misunderstand each other so completely.

We met up on the South Bank, for a walk along the Thames. I turned up with a red rose that I had bought from the stall outside the station.

I could tell at once, from Lana's expression when I presented the rose to her, that this was a mistake.

'I hope this doesn't mean we're starting off on the wrong foot,' she said.

'Which foot is that?' I said, stupidly. 'Left or right?'

Lana smiled, and let it go at that. But that wasn't the end of it.

We walked for a while. Then we sat outside a pub, on a bench along the river. We each had a glass of wine.

We sat there in silence for a moment. Lana played with the rose in her fingers. Finally, she spoke.

'Does Barbara know you're here?' she said.

'Barbara?' I shook my head. 'I assure you, she takes very little interest in my comings and goings. Why?'

Lana shrugged. 'I was just curious.'

'Were you afraid she might come too?' I laughed. 'Do you think Barbara's spying on us now from behind those bushes? With a pair of binoculars and a gun? I wouldn't put it past her.'

Lana laughed. Her laugh, so familiar to me from her films, made me grin.

'Don't worry,' I said. 'You have me all to yourself.'

That was clumsy. I cringe now, remembering it.

Lana smiled but didn't reply. She toyed with the rose for a moment. Then she held it up and tilted her head, to look at the rose and me at the same time.

'And this? What does this mean?'

'Nothing. It's just a rose.'

'Does Barbara know you bought me a rose?'

I laughed. 'Of course not. It doesn't mean anything. It's just a flower. I'm sorry it made you uncomfortable.'

'It's not that.' She looked away for a moment. 'It doesn't matter. Shall we go?'

We finished our wine and left the pub.

We continued strolling along the Thames. As we walked, Lana glanced at me, then said, very quietly:

'I can't give you what you want, you know. I can't give you what you're looking for.'

I smiled, even though I was nervous. 'What I'm looking for? You mean friendship? I'm not looking for anything.'

Lana half-smiled. 'Yes, you are, Elliot. You're looking for love. Anyone can see that.'

I could feel my cheeks reddening. I looked away, in embarrassment.

Lana tactfully moved the conversation on. We neared the end of our walk.

And that was that – with the lightest of touches, Lana had firmly and politely let me know that she did not think of me as a potential lover. She had dispatched me to the realm of friendship.

Or so I thought at the time. Looking back now, I'm not so sure. So much of how I interpreted that moment was coloured by my past, and who I thought I was; and the distorted lens through which I viewed the world. At the time, I felt so convinced of my own undesirability – if that's even a word. It's how I felt, ever since I was a kid. Ugly, unattractive. Unwanted.

But what if, for one second, I had put down my self-obsessed emotional baggage that I insisted on carrying about with me?

What if I had actually listened to what Lana was saying? Well – then I might have discovered that her words had very little to do with me, and everything to do with her.

With the benefit of hindsight, I can hear what Lana was saying. She was saying she was sad, she was lost;

and she was lonely – or she would never have been sitting there with me, a relative stranger, on a Sunday afternoon.

And when she accused me of wanting love, what she really meant was that I wanted to be saved. *I can't save you, Elliot*, Lana was saying. *Not when I need saving myself.*

If I had realized this at the time – if I hadn't been so blind, so fearful, if I'd had more courage – well, I might have acted very differently in that moment.

And then, perhaps, this story would have had a happier ending.

6

From then on, I began to accompany Lana on her walks around London.

We'd walk for hours, and spent many happy afternoons crossing bridges, trudging along canals, roaming through parks – discovering old and peculiar pubs tucked in, around, and sometimes even under, the city.

I often think about those walks. About all the things we talked about – and the things we didn't. All the things that were skirted over, ignored, dismissed. The things I failed to notice.

I said to you earlier that Lana always saw the best in you, making you rise to the challenge, and try to be that person: embody the best possible version of yourself. Well, it was true of her, too. Lana was trying to be the person I wanted her to be, I can see that now. Both of us performing for each other. It makes me so sad to write that. Sometimes I look back, and wonder if that's all it ever was – a performance?

But no, that's not fair. It was real enough, deep down. In her own way, Lana was as much a fugitive from her past as I was – or, to put it less poetically, just as fucked up. Isn't that what brought us together in the first place? What connected us? The fact we were both so lost?

I couldn't see any of this back then. My omniscience is entirely retrospective. I sit here now, knowing what I know, and peer into the past, trying to see the end in the beginning, and piece together all the hidden clues and signs I missed then; when I was young, and in love, and starstruck.

The truth is, I didn't want to see the sad, wounded woman walking by my side. The damaged, frightened person. I was far more invested in her performance, and the mask she wore. I'd squint a little, as I gazed at Lana, so I wouldn't see the cracks in it.

Sometimes, as we walked, I'd ask Lana about her old movies. She was so quick to dismiss them, I'll admit it hurt my feelings, rather – all these films I cherished and had seen so many times.

'You made a lot of people happy,' I said. 'Including me. You should be proud of that.'

Lana shrugged. 'I don't know about that.'

'I do. I was a fan.'

That's as far as I went. I didn't want to make her uncomfortable. I didn't want to reveal the extent of my – my what? Let's be kind; let's not call it obsession. Let's call it love – for that's what it was.

And so, we became friends. But were we ever just friends, really?

I'm not so sure. Even a man as – I'm struggling for inoffensive adjectives here – unthreatening, unmanly, as timid as myself, is not immune to beauty. To desire. Wasn't there an unacknowledged tension between us, even then? It was so subtle, a gossamer-thin frisson; a whisper of sexuality. But it was there, hanging like a spider's web in the air around us.

*

The closer Lana and I became, the less time we spent outside. We spent most of our time at her house – that huge, six-storey mansion in Mayfair.

God, I miss that house. Just the smell of it – the fragrance upon entering the doorway. I used to pause in the vast hallway, shut my eyes – and breathe it, drink it in. Smell is so evocative, isn't it? It's similar to *taste*: both senses are time-machines, transporting you – beyond your control, against your will, even – to somewhere in your past.

Nowadays, if I sniff a bit of polished wood or cold stone, I'm right back there, in that house – with its scent of chilly Venetian marble, dark polished oak, lilies, lilac, sandalwood incense – and feel such a burst of contentment; a warm glow in my heart. If I could bottle that smell and sell it, I'd make a bloody fortune.

I became a permanent fixture there. I felt like part of the family. It was an unfamiliar feeling, but wonderful. The sound of Leo practising his acoustic guitar in his bedroom; the enticing smells emanating from the kitchen, where Agathi performed her magic; and – in the living room – Lana and me: talking, or playing cards or backgammon.

How mundane, I hear you say. How trivial. Perhaps – I don't deny it. Domesticity is a peculiarly British trait. Never let it be said that an Englishman's home is not his castle.

All I wanted was to be safe within those walls, with Lana – drawbridge firmly up.

I had longed for love, whatever that means, all my life. I longed for another human being to see me, accept me – care for me. But when I was a young man, I was so invested in this *fake* person I wanted to be, this false self. I simply wasn't capable of engaging in a relationship with another human being – I never let anyone get close enough. I was always acting, and any affection I received felt curiously unsatisfying. It was for a performance, not for me.

These are the mad hoops damaged people jump through: so desperate to receive love – but when it is given to us, it can't be felt. This is because we don't need love for an artificial creation, a *mask*. What we need, what we desperately long for, is love for the only thing we will never show anyone: the ugly, scared kid inside.

But with Lana, it was different. I showed the kid to her.

Or at least, I let her glimpse him.

7

My therapist used to sometimes quote that famous line from *The Wizard of Oz*.

You know the bit. It's where the Scarecrow, confronted by the dark and frightening Haunted Forest, says:

'Of course, I don't know – but I think it'll get darker before it gets lighter.'

Mariana meant this metaphorically, of course, referring to the process of therapy itself. And she was right: things do get darker before they get lighter; before the therapeutic dawn.

Funnily enough – as an aside – I have a pet theory that everyone in life corresponds to one of the characters in *The Wizard of Oz*. There's Dorothy Gale, a lost child, looking for a place to belong; an insecure, neurotic Scarecrow, seeking intellectual validation; a bullying Lion, really a coward, more afraid than everyone else. And the Tin Man, minus a heart.

For years, I thought I was a Tin Man. I believed I was missing something vital inside: a heart, or the ability to love. Love was out there, somewhere, beyond me, in the dark. I spent my life groping for it – until I met Lana. She showed me I already had a heart. I just didn't know how to use it.

But then, if I weren't the Tin Man . . . who was I?

To my dismay, I realized I must be the Wizard of Oz, himself. I was an *illusion* – a conjuring trick, operated by a frightened man, cowering behind a curtain.

Who are you, I wonder? Ask yourself this honestly; and you might be surprised at the answer. But will you be honest, though?

That's the real question, I think.

A frightened child is hiding inside your mind, still unsafe; still unheard and unloved.

The night I heard Mariana utter those words, my life changed forever.

For years, I had pretended my childhood didn't happen. I had erased it from my memory – or thought I had – and I lost sight of the kid. Until that foggy January evening in London, when Mariana found him for me again.

After that therapy session, I went for a long walk. It was bitterly cold. The sky was white, and the clouds heavy. It looked like it might snow. I walked all the way from Primrose Hill to Lana's house in Mayfair. I needed to burn off nervous energy. I needed to think – about me; and the kid, trapped in my head.

I pictured him, small and afraid, shivering; languishing undeveloped, undernourished – chained up in the dungeon of my mind. And as I walked, all kinds of memories started coming back to me. All these injustices; the cruelties I had deliberately forgotten – all the things he endured.

I made a promise to the kid, there and then. A pledge, a commitment – call it what you will. From now on, I would listen to him, I would look after him. He wasn't ugly, or stupid, or worthless. Or unloved. He was *loved*, for Christ's sake – I loved him.

From now on, I would be the parent he needed – too late, I know, but better late than never. And this time, I'd bring him up properly.

As I walked, I glanced down – and there he was, the little boy, walking by my side. He was struggling to keep up, so I slowed down my pace.

I reached out and held his hand.

It's okay, I whispered. *Everything's okay now. I'm here. You're safe, I promise.*

I arrived at Lana's house, shivering with cold, just as it started to snow. No one was home but Lana. We sat by the fire, drinking whisky, watching the snow fall outside. I told her about my – I don't know what the right word is – *epiphany*, shall we call it?

It took me a while to explain it all to her. As I spoke, I struggled with the fear I wouldn't be able to make myself understood. But I needn't have worried. As Lana listened, and the snow fell outside, it was the first time I ever saw her cry.

We both cried, that night. I told her all my secrets – almost all – and Lana told me hers. All the dark secrets we were both so ashamed of, all the horrors we believed had to be kept hidden – they all came tumbling out that night, with no shame, no judgement, no self-consciousness – just openness, just truth.

It felt like the first *real* conversation I'd ever had with another human being. I don't know how to describe it – for the first time, I felt alive. Not performing at life, you understand, not pretending, not faking it, not *almost* living . . . but just *living*.

This was also the first time I glimpsed the other Lana – the secret person she kept hidden from the world, and whom I had not wanted to find. Now I discovered her, in all her naked vulnerability, as I heard the truth about her childhood: about that sad, lonely girl, and the terrible things that happened to her. I heard the truth about Otto and the frightening years of their marriage. It seemed he was just one in a long line of men to treat her badly.

I swore to myself that I would be different. I'd be the exception. I would protect Lana, cherish her, love her. I'd never betray her. I'd never let her down.

I reached out, across the couch, and squeezed her hand.

'I love you,' I said.

'I love you too.'

Our words hung in the air like smoke.

I leaned forward, still holding on to her hand – as, ever so slowly, staring into her eyes, I inched closer, and closer . . . until our faces met.

My lips were against hers.

And I kissed her, gently.

It was the sweetest kiss I'd ever known. So innocent, so tender – so full of love.

Over the next few days, I spent a lot of time thinking about that kiss, and what it meant. It seemed like a final acknowledgement of the long-standing tension between us – the fulfilment of an ancient unspoken promise.

It was, as Mr Valentine Levy might have put it, the conclusion of a deeply cherished goal on my part. And what was that goal?

To be loved, of course. I finally felt loved.

Lana and I were meant to be together. This was clear to me now. This was deeper than anything I ever imagined.

This was my destiny.

8

I'm going to tell you something I've never told anyone.

I was going to ask Lana to marry me.

I understood now, you see – that's where we had been heading all this time; drifting, slowly but surely, into romantic territory. Maybe not great flames of passion, which, by the way, blow cold as fast as they blow hot. I mean a slow, steady burning ember of true, deep affection and mutual respect. That's what lasts. That's love.

Lana and I were now spending almost every second of the day together. The next step, it seemed to me – the logical progression – was for me to move out of Barbara West's house, and to move in with Lana. For us to get married, and live happily ever after.

What's wrong with that? If you had a child, you'd want that for them, wouldn't you? To live in a world of beauty, prosperity, safety. To be happy, secure – and loved. Why is it wrong for me to want that for myself? I would have made a good husband.

Talking of husbands, I've seen plenty of photos of Otto – and he was no oil painting either, believe me.

Yes – I stand by my claim. Despite the discrepancy in our appearances and our bank balances, Lana and I made a great couple. Not sexy or glamorous, perhaps, like her and Jason. But less self-conscious, and more content.

Like two kids, happy as clams.

I decided to proceed formally – as you might in an old-fashioned movie. I felt some kind of romantic declaration would be appropriate: a confession of my feelings; the story of a friendship turned to love, that kind of thing. I practised a little speech, concluding in a marriage proposal.

I even bought a ring – a cheap thing, admittedly; a plain silver band. It was the best I could afford. My intention was to replace it with something more valuable, one day, when my ship came in. But even though it was just a prop, as a symbol of my affection, that ring was as meaningful or significant as any island Otto might buy her.

One Friday evening, with the engagement ring in my pocket, I went to meet Lana at a gallery opening at the South Bank.

My plan was to sneak her on to the roof, under the stars, and propose above the Thames. What could be a more appropriate backdrop, given all our walks along the river?

But when I arrived at the gallery, Lana wasn't there. Kate was, though, holding court at the bar.

'Hello,' she said, giving me a funny look. 'I didn't know you were coming. Where's Lana?'

'I was about to ask you the same question.'

'She's late, as usual.' Kate gestured at the tall man standing next to her. 'Meet my new fella. Isn't he devilishly handsome? Jason, this is Elliot.'

Just then, Lana arrived. She came over, and was introduced to Jason. And then – well, you know the rest.

Lana acted completely out of character that night. She was all over Jason, flirting shamelessly with him. She threw herself at him. And she was being so weird with me, so cold and dismissive. She rebuffed all my attempts to talk to her – as if I didn't exist.

I left the gallery, feeling confused and dejected. The cold, hard ring was in my pocket, and I turned it over and over in my fingers. I found myself giving in to a familiar feeling of despair, a feeling of inevitability.

I could hear the kid sobbing in my head: *of course*, he cried, *of course she didn't want you. She's embarrassed by you. You're not good enough for her, can't you see that? She regretted kissing you. And tonight was her way of putting you in your place.*

Fair enough, I thought. Perhaps it was true. Perhaps I never really stood a chance with Lana. Unlike Jason, I was no practised seducer. Except of old women, apparently.

My jailer was waiting for me when I got back to the house. She had been writing all evening, and was now relaxing with a large scotch in the living room.

'Well, how was it?' Barbara said, as she poured herself another drink. 'Fill me in on all the gossip. I want a full report.'

'No gossip. Very dull.'

'Oh, come on. Something must have happened. I've been working hard all day, earning our daily bread. At least you can entertain me a little before bed.'

I was in no mood to indulge her, and remained monosyllabic. Barbara could sense my unhappiness. And like a true predator, couldn't resist going in for the kill.

'What's the matter, dear?' she said, peering at me.

'Nothing.'

'You're being very quiet. Is something wrong?'

'Nothing.'

'Are you sure? Tell me about it. What is it?'

'You wouldn't understand.'

'Oh, I bet I can guess.' Suddenly, Barbara laughed, full of glee – like an impish child delighting in a mean prank.

I felt unaccountably nervous.

'What's so funny?'

'It's a private joke. You wouldn't understand.'

I knew better than to react. She was trying to provoke me, but there was no point in getting into a fight with Barbara. I have learned from bitter experience that you never win an argument with a narcissist. It doesn't work like that. Your only victory is to leave.

'I'm going to bed.'

'Wait.' She downed her drink. 'Help me upstairs.'

Barbara walked with a stick by then, which made climbing stairs difficult. I supported her with one arm. She held on to the banister with her other hand. We slowly made our way upstairs.

'By the way,' Barbara said. 'I saw your chum today. Lana. We had tea – and a nice cosy chat.'

'Did you?' That didn't make sense. They weren't friends. 'Where was that?'

'Lana's house, naturally. My, my, isn't it grand? I had no idea you were so ambitious, duck. Mustn't set your sights too high. Remember what happened to Icarus.'

'Icarus?' I laughed. 'What are you on about? How many whiskies have you had?'

Barbara grinned, showing her teeth. 'Oh, you're right to be scared. I would be too, if I were you. I had to put a stop to it, you see.'

We reached the top of the stairs. Barbara let go of my arm, as I handed her stick back to her. I tried to sound amused.

'A stop to what?'

'To you, duck,' Barbara said. 'I had to put the poor girl straight. She doesn't deserve you. Few do.'

I stared at her, feeling frightened. 'Barbara. What have you done?'

She laughed, delighting in my distress. As she spoke, she hammered her stick on the floorboards, under-scoring the rhythm of her speech. She was clearly relishing every word.

'I told her all about you,' Barbara said. 'I told her your real name. I told her what you were, when I found you. I told her I've had you followed – that I know what you get up to in the afternoons, and the rest. I told her you're dangerous, a liar, a sociopath – and you're after her money, like you're after mine. I told her I caught you messing about with my medication not once, but twice, recently. "If anything should happen to me in the near future, Lana," I said, "you mustn't be surprised."'

Barbara drummed her stick on the floor, as she laughed, and went on:

'The poor girl was *horrified*. Do you know what she said? "If all this is true," she cried, "how can you *bear* to live with him in the same house?"'

I spoke in a low voice, flat, expressionless. I felt strangely tired.

'And what did you say?'

Barbara drew herself up, and spoke with dignity.

'I simply reminded Lana that I am a writer. "I keep him around," I said, "not out of pity or affection, but to *study* – as an object of repulsive fascination. Very much as one might keep a reptile in a cage."'

She laughed and pounded her stick on the floor repeatedly, as if applauding her witticism. I didn't say anything.

But let me tell you, I hated Barbara in that moment. I hated her so much.

I could have killed her.

It would be so easy, I thought, to kick that stick of hers, and knock her off-balance.

Then just the lightest of touches would send her falling backwards down the stairs – her body thumping down the steps, one by one, all the way to the bottom . . . until her neck broke, with a crack, on the marble floor.

9

You'd be forgiven for thinking, after everything Barbara West told her about me, that Lana would never speak to me again. Friendships have floundered on less.

Thankfully, Lana was made of strong stuff. I imagine how she reacted to Barbara's character assassination – that cruel attempt to discredit me in her eyes, and destroy our friendship.

'Barbara,' Lana said, 'the majority of what you said about Elliot is untrue. The rest, I knew already. He is my friend. And I love him. Now get out of my house.'

That's how I like to picture it, anyway. The truth was, there was a definite coolness between Lana and me after that.

It was made worse by the fact we never spoke about it. Not once. I only had Barbara's word for it that the conversation had even taken place. Can you believe it? Lana never mentioned it. I often thought about bringing it up, forcing her to confront it. I never did. But I hated the fact there were secrets between us now, subjects to be avoided – we, who had shared so much.

Mercifully, Barbara West died soon afterwards. No doubt, the universe sighed with relief at her passing. I certainly did. Almost immediately, Lana started calling me again, and our friendship resumed. It seemed as if Lana had decided to bury Barbara's poisonous words along with the old witch herself.

But it was too late for me and Lana, by then.

Too late for 'us'.

By then, you see, Jason and Lana had embarked on their 'whirlwind romance' – as the *Daily Mail* breathlessly called it. They were married a few months later.

Sitting in the church, watching the wedding ceremony, I was keenly aware I wasn't the only guest with a broken heart.

Kate was sitting right next to me, tearful and more than a little inebriated. I was impressed she had brazened it out, to be honest – in true Kate style – and attended the wedding, head held high, despite having ignominiously lost her lover to her best friend.

Perhaps she shouldn't have gone. Perhaps what Kate should have done, for the sake of her mental health – and this goes for me too – was pull away at that point, and distance herself from Lana and Jason. But she couldn't do that.

Kate loved them too much to give either of them up. That's the truth.

And after Lana married Jason, Kate tried to bury her feelings for Jason and put the past behind her.

Whether she succeeded or not is open to question.

I may as well come clean. I had known about Kate and Jason's affair for quite some time.

I discovered it entirely by chance. It was a Thursday afternoon. I happened to be in Soho, for – well, let's call it an appointment – and I was a little early. So, I thought I'd pop into a pub for a quick drink.

As I turned on to Greek Street, guess who I saw, emerging from the Coach and Horses?

Kate was exiting the pub, looking rather furtive, glancing from left to right.

I was about to call out her name when Jason emerged, just behind her, with that same sheepish look.

I watched them from across the street. They could have seen me, either of them – if they had looked up. But they didn't. They kept their heads low, parting without a word to each other. They hurried off in opposite directions.

Hello, I thought. *What's going on here?*

What odd behaviour. Not to mention informative. It told me something I hadn't known before: that Jason and Kate were meeting independently of Lana.

Did Lana know about this? I made a mental note to ponder this further – and think how I might best use it to my advantage.

I hadn't given up hope, you see. I still loved Lana. I still believed that one day, we would be married. There was no question about that in my mind. Obviously she was now married to Jason – which made things trickier – but my *goal*, as Mr Levy would say, remained the same.

When Lana and Jason got married, I assumed – like everyone else – it wouldn't last. I thought after a few months of being married to a bore like Jason, Lana would come to her senses. She would wake up to what a terrible mistake she had made – and she would see me there, waiting for her. Compared to Jason, I'd appear as suave and sophisticated as Cary Grant in an old movie – reclining against a piano, cigarette in one hand, martini in the other, witty, self-effacing, warm, lovable – and, just like Cary, I'd get the girl in the end.

But to my astonishment, their marriage endured. Month after month, year upon year. It was torture for me. No doubt it was Lana's sheer loveliness that kept it going. Jason would have tried a saint's patience, and Lana was clearly something more than a saint. A martyr, perhaps?

And therefore, as far as I was concerned, this surprise encounter with Kate and Jason in Soho was nothing short of a divine intervention.

I had to make the most of it.

I decided it would be a good idea if I started following Kate.

Which, of course, makes it sound more cloak and dagger than it was. You didn't need to be George Smiley to spy on Kate Crosby. She wasn't inconspicuous; you didn't lose her in a crowd – whereas I always melt into the background.

At that time, Kate was appearing in a successful revival of Rattigan's *The Deep Blue Sea*, which had transferred to the Prince Edward Theatre in Soho. So it was just a matter of lurking across the street from the stage door, watching from the shadows; waiting for the play to finish, and Kate to emerge and sign autographs for the crowd of fans.

Then, when Kate left, and made her way along the street, I followed.

I didn't have to follow far – just from stage door to pub door. Kate walked around the corner and slipped in through the side door of – yes, you guessed it – the Coach and Horses. And, peering through one of the pub's narrow windows, I saw Jason waiting for her at a corner table, with a couple of drinks. Kate greeted him with a long kiss.

I was shocked, to be honest. Not so much by the revelation that they were lovers – which, to be frank, had a kind of sordid inevitability to it – but by their total, unbelievable lack of discretion. They were all over each other that night – drunker and messier as the evening wore on. They were so oblivious to their surroundings, I felt secure enough to leave the window and venture inside the pub.

I sat at the other end of the bar, ordered a vodka tonic, and watched the proceedings from there. Appropriately enough, some old dear was sitting at the upright piano, belting out 'If Love Were All' by Noël Coward: 'I believe the more you love a man, / The more you give your trust / The more you're bound to lose.'

When they finally left the pub, I followed. I watched them kissing in an alley for a moment.

Then, having seen enough, I hopped in a cab and went home.

10

From then on, I kept a detailed record in my notebook of everything I saw — all the dates, times, locations of their clandestine meetings. I wrote it all down. I had a feeling it might come in useful later on.

Often, during my surveillance, I would ponder the precise nature of Kate and Jason's affair — what they got out of it (apart from the obvious) — and why they were so intent on pursuing a course that, to me, seemed destined for disaster.

Sometimes, I would apply Valentine Levy's system to their affair, breaking it down, in terms of intention, motivation and goal. As usual, motivation was key.

Presumably Jason's motive for embarking on the affair had to do with boredom, sexual attraction or selfishness? Maybe that's unkind.

If I were being generous, I might say Jason found Kate easier to talk to — Lana was wonderful, of course, but her habit of always seeing the best in you made you determined to rise to that challenge. Kate, on the other hand, was far more cynical in her view of human nature, and therefore much easier to confide in — not that Jason was entirely honest with her, either.

But truthfully, I believe the real reason for Jason's infidelity lay in the darkest of places. He liked to think he was a powerful man. He was competitive and aggressive – he couldn't even lose a game of backgammon without flying off the handle, for God's sake.

So what happens when a man like that marries a woman like Lana? A woman who is infinitely more powerful in every regard. Might he not wish to punish that woman; to crush her, break her – and call it love? His affair with Kate was an act of *revenge* on Jason's part. An act of hatred, not love.

Kate's motive for pursuing the affair was quite different. It reminds me of what Barbara West used to say, that emotional betrayal was much worse than sexual infidelity. 'Screw another woman, fine,' she would say. 'But take her out for dinner, hold her hand, tell her your hopes and dreams – then you've screwed *me*.'

And that's precisely what Kate wanted from Jason – dinner conversations and held hands and passionate romance – a love affair, in other words. Kate wanted Jason to leave Lana and be with her. She kept pressing him on this. Jason kept putting her off.

Who could blame him? He had far too much to lose.

Late one night, I followed Kate to a bar in Chinatown. She met a friend there – a redhead called Polly. They sat by the window and talked.

I stood across the street, lurking in the shadows. I needn't have worried about them seeing me – Polly and Kate were engrossed in an animated and heated conversation. At one point, Kate was in tears.

I didn't need to be able to lip-read, to work out what was being said. I knew Polly quite well. She was Gordon's stage manager – and they had been involved in a lengthy affair. Everyone knew about it – except Gordon's wife.

Polly was a troubled person, in many ways. But I liked her. She was outspoken and direct, so I could imagine how her conversation with Kate played out.

Kate confided in her, no doubt hoping for a sympathetic ear. From where I was standing, it didn't look like she was getting one.

'End it,' Polly was saying. 'End it *now*.'

'What?'

'Kate. Listen to me. If he doesn't leave his wife *now*, then he never will. It will just drag on and on. Give him an ultimatum. Thirty days to leave her – one month – or you end it. *Promise me.*'

I suspect these words grew to haunt Kate. Because thirty days came and went and she didn't follow Polly's advice. And as time passed, the reality of what she was doing started sinking in. Kate's conscience began to plague her.

This shouldn't come as a surprise. Unless I have spectacularly bungled my job, it should be abundantly clear that, despite her many faults, Kate was fundamentally a good person – with a conscience and a heart. And this prolonged betrayal of her oldest friend – the heinous cruelty of it – began to torment Kate.

Her guilt grew, obsessing her – until she became fixated on the idea of 'clearing the air', as she put it. She wanted to have it out with Lana and Jason. A frank and open conversation between the three of them. Which, needless to say, Jason was determined to prevent.

Personally, I think Kate's intention was naive, at best. God only knows what she imagined would happen. A confession, followed by tears, then forgiveness and reconciliation? Did she really think Lana would give them her blessing? That it would all end happily?

Kate should have known better. Life doesn't work like that.

In the end, it seems that Kate, too, was a romantic. And that is precisely what she and Lana, so different in every other regard, had in common. They both believed in love.

Which, as you shall see, proved their downfall.

11

Considering how indiscreet Kate and Jason were being, I knew I couldn't be the only one who knew about their affair. The theatre world in London is not a large one. Gossip about them must be rife.

Surely it would only be a matter of time before it filtered back to Lana?

Not necessarily – for all her fame, and her immersive walks around London, Lana lived a quiet life. Her social circle was small. There was only one person in that circle who I suspected knew the truth, or at least had guessed it: Agathi. And she would never breathe a word.

No, it fell to me to break the bad news to Lana. Not an enviable task.

But how to do it? One thing was clear: Lana must not hear the news from me directly. She might question my motives. She might decide to be suspicious – and refuse to believe me. That would be catastrophic.

No, I must be entirely independent of this unsavoury business. Only then could I appear, as her saviour – her *deus ex machina* in shining armour – to rescue her, and carry her off in my arms.

Somehow, I had to engineer Lana's discovery of the affair invisibly, undetectably; making her believe she had discovered it all by herself. Easier said than done. But I've always enjoyed a challenge.

I began with the simplest and most direct approach. I tried to contrive a coincidental, 'accidental' meeting – where Lana and I would bump into the guilty pair unexpectedly, *in flagrante delicto*, as it were.

There followed a period of high comedy – or low farce, depending on your taste – as I attempted to manoeuvre Lana into Soho on various pretexts. But this was a hopeless effort and, in the best tradition of farces, went nowhere fast.

The obvious reason was, of course, that it was impossible to manoeuvre Lana Farrar anywhere inconspicuously. The one time I managed to coax her into the Coach and Horses, just as Kate's play was finishing, Lana's arrival caused a mini-riot of jovial drunks, surrounding her, begging her to autograph their beer mats. If Kate and Jason had even neared the pub, they would have seen this whole circus, long before we ever saw them.

I was forced to grow bolder in my methods. I began dropping comments into our conversations: carefully rehearsed phrases that I hoped would register and linger with Lana – *isn't it funny how Jason and Kate have exactly the same sense of humour, they're always laughing together.*

Or else – *I wonder why Kate isn't dating anyone, it has been a while, hasn't it?*

And, one afternoon, I told Lana off for not inviting me for lunch at Claridge's – then, when it was obvious that Lana had no idea what I meant, I looked flustered, brushing it off, saying Gordon saw Kate and Jason eating there – and I assumed Lana was with them – but Gordon must have been wrong.

Lana just gazed at me with those clear blue eyes, unfazed, free of all suspicion, and smiled. 'It couldn't possibly be Jason,' she said. 'He hates Claridge's.'

In a play, all my little hints would have stayed with Lana, creating a general subliminal patina of suspicion, impossible for her to ignore. But what works on stage doesn't, apparently, work in real life.

Even so, I persevered. I am nothing if not persistent – if occasionally absurd. For instance, I bought a bottle of Kate's perfume – a distinctive floral scent, with hints of jasmine and rose. If that didn't make Lana think of Kate, nothing would. I kept the bottle in my pocket, and whenever I was in the house, I would pretend I was going to the bathroom – and sprint along the corridor to their laundry room, to liberally spray Jason's shirts with the perfume.

How much direct contact Lana ever had with Jason's laundry was open to question. But even if Agathi smelled it and made the connection, I thought, that might help.

I stole a few long hairs from Kate's coat, when we were both at Lana's for dinner; then attached them carefully to Jason's jacket. And I toyed with leaving condoms in Jason's washbag, but decided against it, as it felt too obvious.

It was hard to get the balance right – too subtle a hint and it went undetected; too much and I'd give the game away.

The earring proved just right.

And so simple to engineer. I had no idea it would work so well, or provoke the reaction it did. All I did was suggest Lana and I pay a surprise visit to Kate's house; and I stole an earring from Kate's bedroom – which I then pinned to Jason's suit lapel, back at Lana's house. Lana did the rest herself, with a little help from Agathi – and Sid, the dry cleaner.

The fact that Lana reacted so violently to the earring suggests she already secretly suspected the affair. Don't you think?

She just didn't want to admit it to herself.

Well, now she had no choice.

12

This brings us neatly back to that night in my flat. The night Lana came over, distraught, having found the earring.

She sat across from me in an armchair, red-eyed, tear-stained, vodka-soaked. She told me about her suspicions that Jason and Kate were sleeping together. I confirmed her fears, saying I suspected it too.

I was feeling triumphant. My plan had worked. It was hard to conceal my excitement. It took an effort not to smile. But my elation was short-lived.

When I tactfully suggested that Lana would now be leaving Jason, she looked mystified.

'Leaving him?' Lana said. 'Who said anything about leaving him?'

Now it was my turn to look mystified. 'I don't see what other option you have.'

'It's not so simple, Elliot.'

'Why not?'

Lana looked at me, eyes full of baffled tears, as if the answer were obvious.

'*I love him*,' she said.

I couldn't believe it. Staring at her, I realized to my increasing horror, that all my efforts had been in vain. Lana wasn't going to leave him.

I love him.

I had a sick feeling in my stomach, like I was going to throw up. I had been wasting my time. Lana's words crushed all my hopes.

She wasn't going to leave him.

I love him.

I clenched my hand into a fist. I'd never felt so angry before. I wanted to hit her. I wanted to punch her. I felt like screaming.

But I didn't. I sat there, looking sympathetic, and we continued talking. The only outward sign of my distress was the clenched fist by my side. The whole time we talked, my mind was racing.

I understood my mistake now. Unlike her husband, Lana clearly meant her vows. *Until death do us part.* Lana might well cut Kate out of her life, but she wasn't about to relinquish Jason. She would forgive him. It would take more than the revelation of an affair to end their marriage.

If I wanted to get rid of Jason, I had to go much further. I had to destroy him.

Finally, Lana drank herself into oblivion and passed out on my couch. I went to the kitchen, to make a cup of tea – and to think.

While I waited for the kettle to boil, I daydreamed about sneaking up behind Jason, armed with one of his own guns, pointing it at him – and blowing his brains out. I felt a sudden rush of excitement as I imagined this; a weird, perverse feeling of pride; the way you feel standing up to a bully – which is exactly what Jason was.

Unfortunately, it was just a fantasy. I'd never go

through with it. I knew I'd never get away with it. I had to think of something cleverer than that. But what?

Our motivation is to remove pain, Mr Valentine Levy said.

And he was right. I had to take action – otherwise I'd never be free of this pain. I was in such pain: believe me, I felt so close to despair at that moment, standing there in the kitchen at three a.m. I felt thwarted. Vanquished.

But no – not entirely vanquished.

For thinking about Mr Levy had sparked an association in my mind. The beginnings of an idea.

If this were a play, I suddenly thought, *what would I do?*

Yes – what if I were to approach my dilemma in those terms, as if I were staging a theatrical work, a drama?

If this were a play I was writing, and these were my characters, I'd use my knowledge of them to predict their actions – and provoke their reactions. To shape their destiny, without them knowing it.

Could I not, similarly, in real life, contrive a series of events, that would – without me lifting a finger – end in Jason's death?

Why not? Yes, it was risky, and might well fail – but that element of danger is what live theatre is all about, isn't it?

The only hesitation in this was Lana. I didn't want to lie to her. But I decided – and judge me harshly for this if you like – that, in the end, it was for her own good.

After all, what was I doing? Nothing but freeing the woman I loved from a faithless, dishonest criminal – and replacing him with a decent, honest man. She would be so much better off without him. She would be with *me*.

I sat down at my desk. I switched on the green lamp. I pulled out my notebook from the top drawer. I opened it and turned to a fresh page. I reached for a pencil, sharpened it – and I began to plot it out.

As I wrote, I could sense Heraclitus standing above me, watching over my shoulder, nodding with approval. For even though my plan went so wrong, even though it ended in such disaster, there – in the designing of the plot, in its conception – it was beautiful.

That's my story, in a nutshell. A tale of beautiful, well-intentioned failure – ending in death. Which is a pretty good metaphor for life, isn't it?

Well – my life, anyway.

There we have it. I'm aware this has been a lengthy aside. It is, however, integral to my narrative.

But that's not up to me, is it? It what *you* think that counts.

And you don't say anything, do you? You just sit there, listening, silently judging. I'm so conscious of your judgement. I don't want to bore you, or lose your interest. Not when you've given me so much of your time already.

Which reminds me of something Tennessee Williams used to say. His writing advice to aspiring dramatists:

Don't be boring, baby, he'd say. *Do whatever it takes to keep the thing going. Blow up a bomb onstage, if you have to. But don't be boring.*

Okay, baby – so here comes that bomb.

13

Let us return to the island – and the night of the murder.

Just after midnight, there were three gunshots in the ruin.

A few minutes afterwards, we all arrived at the clearing. A chaotic scene followed, as I tried to take Lana's pulse, and to disentangle her from Leo's arms. Jason gave Agathi his phone – to call an ambulance, and the police.

Jason went back to the house to get a gun. He was followed by Kate, then Leo. Agathi and I were alone.

This much you know.

What you don't know is what happened next.

Agathi was in a state of shock. She had gone completely pale, like she might faint. Remembering the phone in her hand, she lifted it up, to call the police.

'No.' I stopped her. 'Not yet.'

'What?' Agathi looked at me blankly.

'Wait.'

Agathi looked confused – then she looked at Lana's body.

And for a split second, did Agathi think of her grandmother – and wish she were here now? And that the old witch would shut her eyes and sway and mutter an incantation; an ancient magical spell to resurrect Lana, to make her live again – and return from death?

Lana, please, Agathi prayed silently, *please be alive – please live – live –*

Then, as in a dream or a nightmare – or on hallucinatory drugs – reality began to distort itself at Agathi's command . . .

And Lana's body began to move.

14

One of Lana's limbs twitched, ever so slightly, of its own accord.

The blue eyes opened.

And her body began to sit up.

Agathi went to scream. I grabbed hold of her.

'Shh,' I whispered. 'Shh. It's okay. It's okay.'

Agathi squirmed, and threw me off. She seemed about to lose her balance. But she managed to stay upright, unsteadily, breathing hard.

'Agathi,' I said. 'Listen. It's okay. It's a game. That's all. A *play*. We're acting. See?'

Agathi, slowly, fearfully, moved her eyes past me. She looked over my shoulder, at Lana's body. The dead woman was now on her feet, holding out her arms for an embrace.

'Agathi,' said the voice she thought she'd never hear again. 'Darling, come here.'

Lana wasn't dead. In fact, judging by the sparkle in her eyes, she'd never felt more alive. Agathi was overcome with emotion. She wanted to fall into Lana's arms, sob with joy and relief, hold Lana tight. But she didn't.

Instead, she found herself staring at Lana with increasing anger.

'A *game* –?'

'Agathi, listen –'

'What kind of *game*?'

'I can explain,' said Lana.

'Not now,' I said. 'There isn't time. We'll explain later. Right now, we need you to play along.'

Agathi's eyes welled up with tears. She shook her head, unable to bear it any longer. She turned and marched off, disappearing in the trees.

'Wait,' Lana called after her. 'Agathi –'

'Shh, keep quiet,' I said. 'I'll deal with it. I'll talk to her.'

Lana looked doubtful. I could tell her resolve was wavering. I tried again, more forcefully: 'Lana, please don't. You'll ruin everything. Lana –'

Lana ignored me. She ran after Agathi into the olive grove.

I watched her go, aghast.

I don't know if I'm saying this with the benefit of hindsight – or if I had some inkling of it at the time – but it was at this precise moment that my perfect plan began to unravel.

And everything went to hell.

Act Four

Truth or illusion, George; you don't know the difference.

—Edward Albee, *Who's Afraid of Virginia Woolf?*

I

A good rule of thumb, you know, when telling a story, is to delay all exposition until absolutely necessary.

Nothing is more suspect, to my mind, than unsolicited explanation. It's best to keep quiet, to refrain from any elucidation until you have to.

Now, it seems, we have reached that crucial point in the narrative. I owe you an explanation – I can see that.

Remember that night in my flat, what I said about Jason and Kate?

Whatever they have – or think they have – it will crack under the slightest bit of pressure. It will fall apart.

What better way to test them, I said to Lana, than a little *murder*?

'Like one of the plays you used to stage at the ruin,' I said, 'in the old days – remember? A little more gory, that's all.'

Lana looked confused. 'What are you talking about?'

'I'm talking about a play. For an audience of two – for Kate and Jason. A murder, in five acts.'

Lana listened, as I began to explain my idea. I said that, by faking Lana's murder, and casting suspicion on Jason, we'd watch his relationship with Kate disintegrate.

'They'll turn on each other in an instant,' I said. 'Don't think they won't. If you want to end their affair, just put that kind of pressure on it for a few hours.'

The two lovers would tear each other apart, each suspecting the other. And the moment they each accused the other of murder, Lana could reveal herself. She would emerge from the shadows, having returned from death. She'd stand before them, gloriously alive – giving them the fright of their life. And leaving them in no doubt how they truly felt about each other – how shallow and tawdry, how easily polluted their feelings really were.

'It will be the end of them, forever,' I said.

This is no doubt what appealed to Lana about my idea – the prospect of ending Jason and Kate's affair. Perhaps she was hoping to win Jason back. But Lana also had another reason for agreeing – a secret reason – which, as you will see, brought her little joy.

The idea had a lovely poetic symmetry to it, I said. It provided the perfect revenge for Lana; and the superlative artistic challenge for me. Of course, Lana didn't know quite how far I intended to take the performance. I didn't lie to her. All I did – you might say – was not burden her with a lot of unnecessary exposition. Instead, I concentrated on the practicalities of staging our drama.

As we talked, we discovered the story together.

Drowning? I said.

No, shooting, said Lana, with a smile – *that would be much better; we could use the guns in the house – then easily incriminate Jason in Kate's eyes.*

Yes, I said, *that's it. Good idea.*

What about the others? Should we involve them or not?

I knew we had to, to a certain extent. Lana and I couldn't pull this off on our own. For the illusion to work, Jason and Kate must never be allowed to get too close to Lana's body. I couldn't manage that by myself. I needed help.

And Leo – hysterical, screaming – demanding they keep away from Lana . . . would do the trick nicely.

I worried about how little acting experience Leo had – what if he wasn't up to the challenge? *What if he corpsed* – no pun intended – *and gave the game away?*

Lana promised she'd rehearse him diligently until he was perfect. It seemed a matter of parental pride for her that he be given the part. Ironic, considering how much she disapproved of him becoming an actor.

I agreed to her demands, even though I had my doubts about Leo. As I did about keeping Agathi in the dark. But Lana overruled me on both counts.

What about Nikos? she said. *Should we tell him or not?*

Let's keep him out of it, I said. *Too many cooks, and all that.*

Lana nodded. *Okay. You're probably right.*

And so it was agreed.

Three days later, on the island, a few minutes before midnight, I went to meet Lana at the ruin. I was armed with a shotgun.

Lana was waiting for me, sitting on one of the broken columns. I smiled as I approached. She didn't smile back.

'I wasn't sure you'd be here,' I said.

'Neither was I.'

'Well?'

Lana nodded. 'I'm ready.'

'Okay.' I raised the gun and pointed it at the sky.

I fired three times.

I watched as Lana applied the fake blood and the stage make-up to herself. The bullet wounds were latex, very gory and effective – at night, anyway. I wasn't sure how well they'd play in daylight.

The special effects were the model's own, procured for her by a make-up artist she had worked with on several movies. She'd said she needed them for a private performance – an apt description of our little production, I thought.

Lana lay on the ground, in the pool of fake blood. Then I pulled Kate's red shawl out of my back pocket and wrapped it around her shoulders.

'What's that for?' Lana asked.

'Just a final touch. Now try not to move. Lie completely still. Let your limbs go limp.'

'I know how to play dead, Elliot. I've done it before.'

Then, hearing the others approach, I went and hid behind the column. I stuffed the shotgun into a rosemary bush.

Then I emerged, a couple of minutes later – acting as if I had just arrived, breathless and confused.

From then on, I followed my dramatic instinct. Though, to be honest, seeing Lana lying there, in a pool of blood, with Leo hysterical at her side, it wasn't difficult to get caught up in the drama. It felt surprisingly real, in fact.

I see now, that's exactly where I took a wrong turn in my thinking. I didn't anticipate how real it would feel. I got so caught up with the twists and turns of the plot, I didn't think of how it would affect everyone emotionally. And that, therefore, people might react in highly unpredictable ways.

You might say I forgot my most fundamental rule: *character is plot*. And I paid the price for it.

2

Lana hurried through the olive grove, in search of Agathi.

She needed to find her. She had to calm her down, before she ruined everything.

It had been a mistake not to tell Agathi, to keep the plan a secret from her. But Lana felt she had no choice. Agathi would have certainly refused to take part, and she would have done her best to talk Lana out of it. Now Lana rather wished she had.

There was a small figure in the distance, through the trees, at the end of the path . . . it was Agathi, hurrying into the house.

Lana quickly followed. At the back door, she took off her shoes, leaving them outside. She crept in, barefoot, silently, stealthily. She looked around.

There was no sign of Agathi in the passage. Had she gone to her room? Or the kitchen?

Lana deliberated which direction to go in – when heavy footsteps heading down the corridor made up her mind for her.

Lana turned and quickly climbed the stairs.

A few seconds later, Jason appeared at the foot of the staircase. He nearly collided with Kate, who walked in through the back door.

They had no idea Lana was there, at the top of the stairs, watching them.

'They're gone,' Jason said.

Kate stared at him. 'What?'

'The guns. They're not there.'

Outside the back door – from the wings – I nudged Leo onstage. 'Go on,' I whispered. 'Now's your cue.'

Leo ran inside, and told Kate and Jason he had hidden the guns.

The fact the guns weren't in the chest where Leo had hidden them was a surprise to him. I had decided not to tell Leo that I had moved them; I thought it would aid his performance if he was ignorant of that fact.

As it was, I could see that Leo required no acting aid. *The kid's a natural*, I thought. *A chip off the old block.* His performance was frighteningly real, in its hysteria and its grief. A tour de force.

'*She's dead,*' Leo screamed. '*Don't you even care?*'

And Lana, watching from the gallery, craned her neck, trying to see Jason's reaction.

This was what she had been waiting for. This was Lana's real reason for agreeing to my plan. She wanted to observe Jason's reaction to her death – to test his love. She wanted to see if Jason's heart would break; or at least glimpse some proof that he possessed one. She wanted to see him cry; see him weep for his beloved Lana.

Well, she saw. Jason didn't shed a single tear. As Lana watched him from the top of the stairs, she saw he was angry and afraid, trying to not lose control. But he wasn't heartbroken, or grief-stricken. He was entirely unmoved.

He doesn't care, she thought. *He doesn't give a damn.*

And in that moment, Lana felt herself die a second time.

Tears filled her eyes; but not her tears – no, they belonged to a little girl from long ago, who had once felt so unloved. A girl who used to crouch in this exact same position, at the top of the stairs, clutching the banister, watching her mother entertain her 'men friends' down below – feeling unwanted and ignored. That is, until her mother's friends began noticing her precocious beauty, and her troubles really began.

Lana had gone through so much since then – since those bleak, frightening days – to ensure that she became safe, respected, unassailable – and loved. But now, watching Jason from the top of the stairs, all that Cinderella magic vanished. Lana found herself right back where she had started: a suffering little girl, alone in the dark.

Lana realized she was going to be sick. She pulled herself up. She ran to her bedroom, into the bathroom.

She fell to her knees in front of the toilet, and threw up.

3

When Lana came out of the bathroom, she found Agathi was in her bedroom, waiting for her.

There was silence for a moment. The two women stared at each other.

Lana realized she needn't have worried about Agathi losing control. There was no danger of an emotional outburst. Agathi looked entirely calm. Only her red eyes showed she had recently been crying.

'Agathi,' Lana said. 'Please let me explain.'

Agathi spoke in a low, flat voice. 'What is this? A joke? A game?'

'No.' Lana hesitated. 'It's more complicated than that.'

'Then what?'

'I can tell you, if you'll let me –'

'How could you do this, Lana?' Agathi searched her eyes, incredulous. 'How could you be so cruel? You let me think you *died*.'

'I'm sorry –'

'No. I do not accept your apology. Let me tell you something, Lana. You are a most selfish, self-deluding person. I see all this – and I love you. Because I thought you loved me.'

'I do love you.'

'No.' Agathi rolled her eyes in angry contempt.

Tears streamed down her cheeks. 'You are not capable. You don't know how to love.'

Lana stared at her, deeply pained. 'Selfish, and self-deluding? Is that what you think? Perhaps . . . you're right. But I am capable of love. I love you.'

They stared at each other for an instant. Then Lana went on, quietly. 'I need your help, Agathi. Let me try and explain. Please.'

Agathi didn't reply. She just stared at her.

4

Meanwhile, I reluctantly agreed to accompany Jason and Nikos on their search of the island – looking for a non-existent intruder.

I felt increasingly resentful as we made our way along the coast, battered by the wind. I was exhausted, and my newish shoes had been ruined from wading through undergrowth, mud and sand. I was also anxious to get back to Lana – and Agathi.

But Jason was proving annoyingly methodical in his search, intent on examining every square foot of the island. Even when we reached the cliffs – and it was finally obvious no boat was moored on the island – Jason refused to accept defeat. I think in some perverse way, he was enjoying himself, acting like a hero in a bad movie.

'Let's keep going,' he shouted, to be heard over the wind.

'Where?' I shouted. 'There's no one here. Let's go back.'

Jason shook his head. 'We have to search the buildings first.' He shone his torch into Nikos's face. 'Starting with his place.'

Nikos glared at him, blinking in the light. He didn't respond.

Jason smiled. 'That a problem?'

Nikos shook his head, frowning. He didn't take his eyes off Jason.

'Good,' Jason said. 'Come on.'

'Not me,' I said. 'I'll see you back at the house.'

'Where are you going?'

'To check on the others.'

Before he could object, I marched off.

As I hurried along the path, back to the house, I wondered whether Lana had managed to placate Agathi. Hopefully she had smoothed things over and persuaded her to play ball.

But, knowing Agathi, I felt far from confident Lana would succeed.

As I entered the house through the French windows, I looked around. There was no sign of anyone. I took the opportunity of crouching down by the long sofa and, reaching underneath, I felt for the guns I'd hidden there earlier.

I pulled out a revolver.

I looked at it for a moment, feeling its weight in my hand. I checked the barrel. It was empty. I took out the bullets from my pockets – I'd stolen a handful from the box in the gun room. I carefully loaded it.

I didn't know much about guns. Just the basics – taught to me by Lana, when Jason first acquired them. She learned to shoot on the set of a western she did, and we had a practice session, she and I, one afternoon, on the island. I wasn't a bad shot, as it happens.

Even so, I was afraid of this weapon I was holding. My fingers were slightly trembling as I placed the gun in my pocket. I kept one hand on it, cautiously, through my trousers.

I checked my reflection in the mirror.

And there, reflected in the mirror, right behind me, was Lana's bloodstained corpse – staring at me with bloodshot eyes.

I jumped and spun around.

Lana looked a fright – covered in bullet wounds, dried blood and dirt. An incongruous sight in this elegant living room. I laughed.

'Christ, you scared me. What are you doing here? Get back to the ruin before Jason sees you.'

Lana didn't reply. She walked in and poured herself a drink.

'You went a bit off-piste back there, love,' I said. 'Running after Agathi like that. Take it from me – nothing is more catastrophic than when an actress starts writing her own script. Always ends in tears.'

I was joking – trying to make her laugh. But it didn't work. Lana didn't even crack a smile.

'Where is everyone?' I said. 'Where's Kate?'

'In the summerhouse,' Lana said. 'With Leo.'

'Good. He gave a marvellous performance, by the way. He's inherited your talent. He'll go far.'

Lana didn't reply. She took one of Kate's cigarettes from the table, and lit it. I watched her smoke, feeling uneasy.

'You spoke to Agathi?'

Lana nodded, and blew out a long line of smoke.

I frowned. 'And? Did you square it with her? Has she given you her blessing?'

'No, she has not. She's very upset.'

I laughed. 'You should have told her it was my idea.'

'I did.'

'And? What did she say?'

'That you're evil.'

'That's a little dramatic. Anything else?'

'That God will punish you.'

'I think he already has.'

'It's over, Elliot.' Lana stubbed out the cigarette. 'She said this must stop. Now.'

Ah, I thought. So that was it. I tried not to sound too annoyed.

'It's not finished yet. We still have the final act. Agathi has to wait until the curtain.'

'It's curtain now. It's over.'

'What about Jason?'

Lana shrugged. She whispered, more to herself than to me, 'Jason doesn't care. He thinks I'm dead – and he doesn't care.'

She looked wretched as she said this.

At last, I thought. At last, Lana was awake. At last, she had seen the light. I had been waiting for this moment. Now we could begin again, she and I – on an equal footing, this time. We could begin again – with honesty, and truth.

'Very well,' I said. 'It's over. What now?'

Lana shrugged. 'I have no idea.'

'I have an idea – if you care to hear it.'

Despite herself, Lana glanced at me with faint curiosity. 'Well?'

It seemed like the moment for truth. So I went for it.

'Remember that night you first met Jason? On the South Bank? We've never spoken about that night.'

'What about it?'

'I had a ring on me . . . I was going to ask you to marry me.'

Lana looked up at me. I could see the surprise in her eyes.

I smiled. 'But Jason got there first, unfortunately. I've often wondered what would have happened if you hadn't met him that night.'

Lana looked away. 'Nothing would have happened.'

Now it was my turn to look surprised. 'Nothing?'

She shrugged. 'You and I were friends, that all.'

'Were?' I smiled. 'I was under the impression we still are. And a damn sight more than that – and you know it.' I felt suddenly quite angry. 'Why can't you be hon-est with yourself, just for once? I love you, Lana. Leave him. Marry me.'

Lana stared at me, silent, as if she hadn't heard me.

'I mean it. Marry me – and be happy.'

It took all of my courage to say this. I held my breath.

There was a pause. Lana's response, when it came, was brutal. She laughed. A cold, hard laugh, like a slap in the face.

'And then what?' she said. 'Fall down the stairs, like Barbara West?'

I felt like I'd been punched. I stared at her, stunned.

I felt – well, you know me as well as anyone, by now – you can imagine how I felt. I didn't trust myself to speak. I was afraid I might say something unforgivable, something that would cross an uncrossable line.

So, I didn't say anything. I turned and walked out.

5

I exited the same way I had entered. I went out through the French windows, on to the veranda.

I made my way down the steps, buffeted by the wind – and by my thoughts. I couldn't believe what Lana had said to me. That mean joke about Barbara West – it was so unlike her. I didn't understand.

Even now, as I write this, I struggle to comprehend her cruelty in that moment. It was so out of character; I couldn't believe it of my friend, of Lana. But perhaps I could believe it of that other, hidden person; that frightened girl lurking beneath the skin, so full of pain and wanting to lash out.

I would forgive her, of course. I had to. I loved her. Even if, sometimes, she could be cruel.

I was lost in a cloud of thought, I didn't see Jason coming. I collided with him at the bottom of the steps.

Jason shoved me back. 'What the fuck –?'

'Sorry. I was looking for you. Did you search Nikos's place?'

He nodded. 'Nothing there.'

'Where is Nikos now?' I asked.

'In his cottage. I told him to wait there until the police get here.'

'Okay, good.'

Jason tried to pass me and climb the steps. I stopped him.

'Wait a minute,' I said. 'I have good news. Agathi just spoke to the police.'

'And?'

'The wind has dropped. They're on their way over right now.'

'They are?' A look of relief appeared on Jason's face. 'Oh, thank Christ for that.'

'Shall we go and wait for them on the jetty?'

Jason nodded. 'Good idea.'

'I'll meet you there.'

'Wait a second.' He gave me a suspicious look. 'Where are you going?'

'To tell Kate.' Unable to resist, I added, 'Unless you prefer to?'

'No.' Jason shook his head. 'You do it.'

Jason turned on his heel, heading towards the beach – and the jetty.

I watched him go, smiling to myself.

Then, keeping a firm grip on the revolver in my pocket, I went to find Kate – to finish this.

As I made my way to the summerhouse, I felt grimly determined to continue with my plan – whatever the cost.

I won't lie and say my anger towards Lana at that moment didn't spur me on. But there was no way I could stop this now, despite Lana's objections. No more than you can stop a boulder you've sent rolling down a hill. It was bigger than all of us now; it had taken on its own momentum. We had no choice but to let this drama play out. As an actor, Lana should have understood that.

I neared the summerhouse and saw the door open. Leo came out. I quickly hid behind a tree. I waited until he passed by. Then I crept over to the summerhouse window and peered inside.

Kate was alone, inside. She looked a mess. Scared, paranoid, upset. It had been a rough night for her.

Unfortunately, it was about to get worse.

I walked to the door. I reached out to open it – then, unaccountably, I froze.

I stood motionless – paralyzed by a sudden and unexpected attack of stage fright. It had been many years since I'd done any acting – and never before had I played such an important role. Everything depended on my performance in this scene with Kate. This was the final magic trick I had to pull off. I needed to be one hundred per cent convincing – everything I said and did must seem entirely innocent and believable.

In other words, I had to give the performance of my life.

I steeled myself, then knocked loudly on the door.

'Kate? It's me. We need to talk.'

6

Seeing it was me, Kate unlocked the door. I pushed it open, and went inside the summerhouse.

'Lock it,' she said, gesturing at the door.

I did as she asked, sliding the bolt across. 'I just saw Leo outside,' I said. 'I told him to meet us at the jetty.'

'The jetty?'

'The police are on their way. We're going there, to wait. All of us.'

Kate didn't reply for a moment. I watched her closely. There was a slight sway to her movements, a slur to her words, but hopefully she was sober enough to take in what I had to say.

'Kate, did you hear me? The police are coming.'

'I heard. Where's Jason? Did you find anything? What happened?'

I shook my head. 'We searched the island, top to bottom.'

'And?'

'Nothing.'

'No boat?'

'No boat. No intruder. No one's here but us.'

This clearly didn't come as much of a surprise to her. She nodded to herself. 'It's *him*. He killed her.'

'Who are you talking about?'

'Nikos, of course.'

'No.' I shook my head. 'It's not Nikos.'

'Yes, it is. He's *crazy*. You just have to look at him. He's –'

'He's dead.'

Kate stared at me, open-mouthed. 'What?'

'Nikos is dead,' I repeated quietly.

'What happened?'

'I don't know – I wasn't there.' I avoided eye contact as I said this. I felt Kate staring at me, feverishly trying to work me out.

'They were searching the north side of the island,' I said, 'where the cliffs are – and Nikos fell . . . That's what Jason said. That's what he told me. But I wasn't there.'

'What are you trying to –?' Kate looked frightened. 'Where's Jason?'

'He's at the jetty, with the others.'

Kate stubbed out her cigarette. 'I'm going to find him.'

'Wait. There's something I have to tell you.'

'It can wait.'

'No, it can't.'

Kate ignored me and walked to the door. It was now or never.

'He killed her,' I said.

Kate stopped. She looked at me. 'What?'

'Jason killed Lana.'

Kate half-laughed but it turned into a choke. 'You're mad.'

'Kate, listen, I know we don't always see eye to eye. But you're an old friend – and I don't want you to come to any harm. I need to warn you.'

'Warn me? About what?'

'This isn't going to be easy.' I gestured at a chair. 'Do you want to sit down?'

'Fuck off.'

I sighed, then spoke patiently. 'Okay – how much has Jason told you about his finances?'

Kate was bemused by the question. 'His *what*?'

'So you don't know. He's in serious trouble. Lana found out he set up something like seventeen different company accounts, all in her name, in private banks all around the world. He's been moving his clients' money around, using her like a washing machine – like a fucking laundry.'

I bristled with indignation as I said this. I could see Kate taking it all in, weighing it up, weighing me up, working out whether to believe a word I said or not. I must say, my performance was pretty good – presumably because most of what I said was true. Jason *was* a crook. And I didn't think for one second that Kate didn't know this.

'That's bullshit,' she said, feebly.

But she didn't object further, so I went on, emboldened.

'Jason is about to be caught – if he hasn't been already. He'll be going away for a long time, I imagine. Unless someone bails him out. He needs money very badly –'

Kate laughed. 'You think he killed Lana for *money*? You're *wrong* – Jason wouldn't do that. He wouldn't kill her.'

'I know he wouldn't.'

Kate stared at me, annoyed. 'Then what are you saying?'

I spoke slowly, patiently, as if to a child. 'She was wearing *your* shawl, Kate.'

A slight pause. She stared at me. 'What?'

'That's why Jason followed her to the ruin. Because he thought she was *you*.'

Kate stared at me, silent. She had suddenly gone pale.

'It's true,' I said. 'Jason didn't mean to shoot Lana. He meant to shoot *you*.'

Kate shook her head violently. 'You're sick . . . you're fucking sick.'

'Don't you understand? He's going to frame Nikos – now he's made sure Nikos can't defend himself. I warned you not to make Jason choose between you. Lana was too valuable for him to give up. Whereas you . . . are *expendable*.'

As I said this, I could see the change in Kate's eyes. A kind of pained recognition – that word, *expendable*, it chimed with something deep within her, an old feeling, from long ago – a feeling that she wasn't important, not special in any way, not loved.

She grabbed the back of the chair – like she was going to throw it at me. But she needed it to steady herself. She held on to it, looking like she might faint.

'I need to find Jason,' she whispered.

'What? Haven't you heard a single word I said?'

'I need to find him.'

Suddenly determined, she went to the door.

I blocked her path. 'Kate, stop –'

'Get out of my way. I need to find him.'

'*Wait.*' I reached into my pocket. 'Here –'

I pulled out the revolver. I held it out to her.

'Take it.'

Kate's eyes widened. 'Where did you get that?'

'I found it, in Jason's study – where he hid all the guns.' I pressed the gun into her hands. 'Take it.'

'No.'

'*Take it.* Act like an idiot if you must – but take this with you. Please.'

Kate stared at me for a second. Then she made a decision. She took the revolver.

I smiled. I stood aside, and let her pass.

7

Gripping the gun, Kate walked out of the summer-house. She went along the path in the direction of the coast – towards the beach, and the jetty – in search of Jason.

I waited for a moment. Then I followed.

I felt nervous as I walked along the path. I had but-terflies in my stomach, the way you do on a first night. It felt thrilling to have done all this; written this drama, not with pen and paper, for fictional characters on a stage – but for *real* people, in a *real* place. All of them, performing in a play they had no idea they were in.

In a way, it was Art. I really believed that.

As I approached the beach, I could see the wind was calming down. Soon the fury would have blown itself out, leaving destruction in its wake. I looked around for Kate. And sure enough, she was up ahead, making her way across the sand towards the jetty – where Jason was waiting.

What would happen now? I knew the answer to that. I could predict the future as surely as if I had written it in my notebook. Which, in fact, I had.

Kate would climb up the stone steps to the jetty. Jason would see the gun in her hand. And, being Jason, he would demand Kate hand it over to him.

The question was, given what I had just told Kate – all

the doubts about him that I had planted in her mind – would she give Jason the gun?

And, more importantly, now that I had put a loaded gun in Kate's hand . . . would she use it?

Soon, we would know the answer to the question I posed that night Lana came over, and I stayed up writing until dawn. Would I be able to contrive Jason's death, without pulling the trigger myself?

I felt confident that my plan had every chance of working. Particularly as Kate had played so completely into my hands. She was volatile at the best of times; and right now, she was also terrified, highly emotional and inebriated. There was every possibility that Kate might allow her feelings to overcome her. If I were a betting man, I'd say the odds were damn good.

I took up my position by the tall pines at the end of the beach. Near enough to have a good view, but not close enough to be seen; safely hidden in the shadows. My own private theatre.

Suddenly, I had a last-minute attack of nerves. Every playwright experiences this at some point, you know; an eleventh-hour panic. A fear that the story won't come together. *Have I done enough? Will the structure hold?*

It's imperative to refrain from tinkering at this late stage. Many a great work of art has been ruined by the artist's inability to stop tampering with it. Many a criminal venture too, no doubt.

I had to trust in the work I had already done. What happened next was beyond my control. It was in the actors' hands now; I was merely a spectator.

So I settled in to watch the show.

8

Kate walked across the beach, and over to the jetty. She slowly climbed up the stone steps.

Jason was standing alone on the platform. They stood face to face.

There was silence for a second. Jason spoke first, giving her a cautious look.

'Are you alone? Where are the others?'

Kate didn't reply. She just stared at him, tears welling up in her eyes.

Jason watched her. He seemed uneasy, no doubt sensing something was wrong. 'Kate. Are you okay?'

Kate shook her head. She didn't speak for a second. She gestured at the speedboat, moored below them.

'Can we just go? Get the fuck out of here –'

'No. The police will be here soon. It's okay.'

'No, it's not. Please, let's just go now –'

'What's that?' Jason was staring at the gun in her hand. He spoke in a sharper tone. 'Where the hell did you get that?'

'I found it.'

'Where? Give it to me.'

Jason stepped towards her, holding out his hand. And Kate took a slight step back – an involuntary movement, but it opened up a chasm between them.

Jason frowned. 'Give me the gun. I know how to use it, you don't.' And then: 'Katie, come on. It's me.'

For a second, Kate believed in his authority – but then she saw his hand was trembling. She realized Jason was as scared as she was.

Jason had every reason to be scared. Kate was out of control, clearly; he had to handle her somehow. He had to calm her down, and bring her to a more rational state. He needed to reassure her; persuade her to give him the gun.

So he took a calculated risk.

'I love you,' he said.

It was obvious, from the look on her face, that this gamble failed. Kate's expression hardened.

'Liar,' she said.

And that instant I had been praying for arrived. A suspension of disbelief; a kind of theatrical alchemy – call it what you will. Illusion became truth in Kate's mind. In her imagination, the idea that Jason was not to be trusted took hold. For the first time since knowing him, she felt afraid of him.

This was made worse when Jason tried again, with more force.

'Give me the gun, Kate.'

'No.'

'Kate –'

'Did you kill her?'

'What?' Jason stared at her, incredulous. '*What?*'

'Did you kill Lana?' Kate went on quickly. 'Elliot said you killed her – by mistake. He said – you meant to kill me.'

'What?' Jason groaned. 'He's *insane*. That's a *lie*.'

'Is it?'

'Of course it is!' He made a movement towards her. 'Give me the gun.'

'No.' Kate raised the gun and pointed it at him. She was shaking so much, it took both her hands to keep it steady.

Jason took another step towards her. 'Listen to me. Elliot is a *liar*. Do you know how much she has left him? *Millions*. Think about it – who do you trust, Kate? Me or him?'

Jason sounded so upset, so impassioned, so genuine, Kate found herself wanting to trust him. But it was too late. She didn't trust him.

'Keep away from me, Jason. I mean it. Keep back.'

'Give me the gun. Now.'

'Stop. Don't come any closer.'

But he kept moving towards her, step by step.

'Jason, *stop*.'

He kept coming closer.

'Stop.'

He kept walking. He held out his hand. 'Give it to me. It's *me*, for Christ's sake.'

But it wasn't him. It wasn't Jason, not any more – it wasn't the person she had known and loved. As if in a nightmare, he had transformed from a lover into a monster.

Then he made a sudden lunge towards her –

And Kate's finger squeezed the trigger. She fired.

But she missed. And Jason kept coming . . . Kate fired again –

And again . . .

And again.

Finally, she hit her mark. Jason collapsed, and he tumbled down the jetty steps. He lay there, motionless . . . bleeding to death on the sand.

I wish I could end the story there.

Smashing ending, isn't it? It has everything you need: a man, a woman, a gun, a beach, moonlight. Hollywood would love it.

But I can't end the story like that.

Why not? Because it isn't true, unfortunately.

That's not what happened. It's just a figment of my imagination. It's what I hoped would happen – it's the scene I sketched out in my notebook.

But it's only fiction, I'm afraid.

Real life turned out somewhat differently.

9

As I stood there, in the shadows, watching Kate climb the jetty steps, I had the first unpleasant inkling that reality was diverging from my plans for it.

I felt a small, sharp jab in my back. I quickly turned around.

Nikos was there, standing behind me. He was holding a gun on me, which he prodded me with again. Harder this time.

When I saw it was him, I felt annoyed rather than concerned.

'Back off,' I said. 'Don't point that fucking thing at me. I thought Jason told you to stay in your cottage.'

Nikos ignored my words. He stared at me, suspiciously. 'We find the others,' he said. He gestured at me to walk. 'Go.'

He nodded at the beach – in the direction of the jetty, and Jason and Kate. I immediately felt alarmed.

'No,' I said quickly. 'Not that way. Not a good idea.'

'Go.' Nikos jabbed me again with the gun. 'Now.'

'No, listen. The police are coming. We need to find Leo and Agathi.' I went on, slowly and emphatically, so he'd understand: 'You and me, we go back to the house. And we find them. Okay?'

I went to point him in the right direction. But as

soon as my hand moved, his gun was dug deep into my chest. He pressed it hard between my ribs. I could feel my heart thudding against it.

Nikos wasn't fucking around.

He nodded again at the jetty. 'Go. Now –'

'Okay,' I said, 'okay. Calm down.'

Seeing I had no choice, I accepted my fate with a sigh. Like a sulky child, I walked down on to the beach.

As we crossed the sand, Nikos kept close behind me, digging the gun into my back. He was suspicious of me, and rightly so. How stupid of me to let him catch me, lurking in the bushes, spying on Kate and Jason. It didn't look good, and now I'd have to talk my way out of it – and it wouldn't be easy. I'd have to improvise, which was never my strong suit.

Damn him, I thought. *He's ruining everything.*

We reached the jetty steps. I stopped, unwilling to go on. I felt the gun pressing in to my back, forcing me up, step by step . . . until I stood there, on the stone platform.

I came face to face with Kate and Jason.

Kate was still holding the gun, I noticed – and Jason didn't seem to object, so perhaps I had been wrong about that. Kate looked from me to Nikos, with a look of disbelief, mingled with revulsion. She turned to Jason.

'He said Nikos was *dead*,' she said. 'He said you killed him.'

'What?' Jason looked stunned. '*What?*'

'Elliot said you killed him – like you killed Lana.'

308

Jason gasped. 'What the *fuck*?'

'What a snake you are,' Kate said, turning on me. 'What a fucking snake. I keep expecting you to hiss. Why don't you *hiss*? *Sssssssssssss* –'

'Kate, please stop. I can explain –'

I was about to begin to talk myself out of it – when, over Jason's shoulder, I saw someone on the beach. My heart sank. It was Agathi. She was hurrying over to us.

Now, it was all over. My entire house of cards was about to collapse around me in a heap. Nothing I could do now but resign myself to it.

While I waited for Agathi to reach us, I turned my attention to Kate and Jason – who were talking about me as if I wasn't there. Which was disconcerting, to say the least.

I have often heard other writers describe their characters as 'getting away from them', behaving independently, with 'a life of their own'. I used to scorn this idea, roll my eyes at the pretension of it. But now, to my amazement, I was experiencing it myself. I kept wanting to interrupt them – to say, *no, no, you're not meant to be saying that* and *this shouldn't be happening* . . . But it *was* happening. This was reality, not a play. And it was not going as I planned.

'He's trying to frame you,' Kate said. 'Lana left him millions of pounds. Did you know that?'

'No.' Jason looked furious. 'I did not.'

Agathi appeared at the top of the steps. She gave us all a frightened look.

'What's going on?'

'We know who shot Lana,' Kate said.

'Who?' said Agathi, looking confused.

Kate pointed at me with the gun.

'Elliot.'

IO

We stood there on the jetty, staring at each other. The only sounds were the wind wailing, and the waves crashing around us.

Behind Agathi's eyes, I could see her thinking hard, working out her next move. She spoke cautiously.

'Why would Elliot do that?'

'Money,' said Kate. 'He's broke, Lana told me. She said she left him a fortune.'

This was the one possibility I had never considered: that *I* might end up as prime suspect.

The irony was not lost on me. It took an effort to keep a straight face. I pulled myself together, and presented them with a grave expression.

'I'm sorry to disappoint you,' I said. 'I am guilty of many things – but murdering Lana is not one of them.'

I gave Agathi a defiant look.

Go on, I thought. *Spill the beans, I bet you're dying to tell them it's all a charade.*

But Agathi remained silent. And a hopeful thought suddenly occurred to me. Was it possible that Lana had succeeded in winning her over? Might Agathi play along, after all? Might she help me turn this around?

Meanwhile Kate was talking, in a low, excited voice:

'Elliot killed her. He can't get away with this. He can't, he can't –'

'He won't,' said Jason. 'The police –'

'Fuck the police. He'll talk his way out of it. He *can't* get away with it, Jason. We *cannot* let him.'

'What are you talking about?'

'I'm talking about justice. *He killed Lana.*'

'You want to shoot him? Go ahead. Be my fucking guest.'

'I mean it.'

'So do I.'

There was a slight pause. This had gone far enough, I decided. I didn't like where it was heading, particularly as Kate was waving a loaded gun around. Things might easily get out of hand.

And so, very reluctantly, I felt compelled to end it.

'Ladies and gentlemen.' I held up my hands. 'I hate to spoil the surprise. But I'm afraid this isn't real. This whole evening is a hoax. Lana isn't dead. It's just a joke.'

Jason looked at me with disgust. 'You're fucked in the head, mate.'

So he didn't believe me – which was, in a way, a tremendous compliment.

I smiled. 'Fine. Ask Agathi, if you don't believe me. She'll tell you.'

I glanced at her. 'Go on. Tell them.'

Agathi met my gaze, unblinking. 'Tell them what?'

I frowned. 'Tell them the truth. Tell them Lana's alive –'

Agathi spat in my face. '*Murderer.*'

I gasped, stunned. 'Agathi –'

'*You killed her.*' Agathi crossed herself. 'May God forgive you,' she said.

312

I was incredulous – and furious. I wiped my face. 'What the fuck are you playing at? Stop it, now. Tell them the truth!'

But Agathi just stared at me, with an insolent look. So I controlled my anger, and turned to Jason.

'Come on,' I said. 'Let's go back to the house. You'll find Lana alive and well – knocking back vodka, smoking Kate's fags, and –'

Jason punched me in the face. His fist connected with my jaw. The blow sent me staggering backwards.

I took a moment to steady myself. My hand went to my throbbing, aching jaw. The pain was intense. It hurt to speak.

'I think you broke my jaw . . . *Fuck.*'

'I'm just getting started, mate,' he said, grimly.

'For Christ's sake.' I glared at Agathi. 'Happy now? *Satisfied?* Now will you tell this fucking moron it's just a joke –?'

Jason punched me again. This time, the blow caught the side of my head, knocking me off balance. I stumbled, falling on to my hands and knees. Blood spurted from my nose on to the sandy stone floor. I gasped, trying to catch my breath. I had been thrown off balance psychologically as well as physically. I needed to adjust to the fact that this situation was rapidly getting out of control. I could hear them talking above my head – and what I heard was unsettling, to say the least.

They sounded weirdly excited, almost high.

'Well,' said Jason. 'Are we doing this? Yes or no?'

'We have no choice,' said Kate. 'He killed her. It's *justice.*'

'And what do we tell the police?'

'The truth – Elliot shot Lana ... Then he shot himself.'

They had temporarily lost their minds – and I didn't believe for one second that they would actually go through with it. But despite reassuring myself, I was starting to feel scared. I had to get out of this.

I pulled myself to my feet. I forced a smile, despite my aching jaw.

'Bravo,' I said. 'Quite a performance, guys. You almost got me ... But this charade has gone on too long. Let me give you a tip. You mustn't let the final act drag on forever – you lose your audience.'

With that, I turned to go –

And I heard a dull thud. Then felt a crippling, spreading pain in my lower back. Nikos had hit me from behind with the handle of the gun. I sank to my knees with a groan.

'Hold him,' said Jason. 'Don't let him go.'

Nikos grabbed my shoulders, holding me down, on my knees. I struggled to free myself.

'Get the fuck off me! This is insane! *I've done nothing wrong* –'

They surrounded me. I could hear them above my head, talking in whispers.

'Justice?' said Jason.

'Justice,' repeated Kate.

Starting to panic, I squirmed, fighting to turn my head to Agathi. I appealed to her.

'Why are you doing this? You proved your point, okay? I'm *sorry* – now stop!'

But Agathi wouldn't look at me. '*Justice,*' she said. She translated the word into Greek for Nikos: '*Dikaiosýni.*'

'*Dikaiosýni,*' Nikos said, nodding. 'Justice.'

Jason nodded at the gun in Kate's hands. 'He needs to be holding the gun. Give it to me.'

'Here.' Kate handed it to him. 'Take it.'

'*Let me go!* Lana is alive —'

I fought to get away, but Nikos held me there like a vice. I felt panic rising up inside me.

Jason pressed the gun into my hand, keeping his hand over mine. He raised the gun to the side of my head. I could feel it digging deep into my temple.

'Pull the trigger, Elliot,' he said. 'This is your punishment. Pull the trigger.'

I was fighting tears. '*No, no — I didn't do anything wrong. Please —*'

'Shh.' Jason was being weirdly gentle now, even tender. 'Stop pretending now,' he whispered in my ear. 'Do it. Pull the trigger.'

'*No — no — please.*'

'Pull the trigger, Elliot.'

'No.' I was sobbing now. '*Please . . . stop —*'

'Then I'll do it.'

'No,' said Kate. '*I* will.'

Suddenly, I found myself staring into Kate's eyes. They were huge, wild, terrifying.

'This is for Lana,' she hissed.

'No, no —'

And then, in absolute terror, I started to scream.

I was screaming for Lana, of course. I had no idea

if she was out of earshot, but she had to hear me. She had to save me.

'LANA! LANA!'

I felt Kate's fingers on the gun, slipping over mine – forcing my finger on to the trigger. And I realized, with absolute certainty, that the sensation of Kate's fingers on mine, the gun against my head, the wind against my face . . . were the last things I'd ever feel.

'LAAANA –'

Kate pushed my finger down on the trigger.

'LAN—'

My scream was cut short. I heard a click – and an enormous bang. Everything went dark.

And my world disappeared.

Act Five

I know this is wrong. But stronger than my
conscience is my fury.

—Euripides, *Medea*

I

Lana woke up in the dark.

She wasn't sure where she was – or what the time was. She felt groggy and confused.

Her eyes slowly adjusted to the gloom, and she made out the shape of a large window, with its curtains drawn. Tinges of light were appearing around the edges, creeping in from outside.

It's morning, she thought. *And I'm on Elliot's couch*.

As she took in the debris surrounding her, from the carnage last night – the coffee table, strewn with empty bottles of wine, bottles of vodka, various glasses, loose marijuana buds, ashtrays overflowing with joints and cigarette ends – her memory returned to her. She had come over here late last night. The reason for her visit also came back to her – the discovery of Kate and Jason's affair – and she was flooded with pain.

Lana lay still for a moment. She felt so sad, so weary, utterly broken. It took an effort to summon the strength to stand up. She managed to lean on the arm of the couch, and pulled herself up. She got to her feet. Slightly unsteadily, she started gathering her things.

Then, across the room, she saw the figure of a man – fast asleep, face-down at the desk.

It's Elliot, she thought.

She cautiously made her way through the wreckage.

She stood above the desk. She watched me sleep for a moment.

Memories of last night came back to her – and she remembered, when she needed a friend the most, when she was desperate, out of her depth . . . Elliot Chase was there – supporting her, holding her up, keeping her head above water.

He is my rock, she thought. *Without him, I'd drown.*

Despite herself, Lana smiled suddenly – remembering that crazy plan of revenge we had concocted together, at the height of her lunacy.

We got carried away, she thought. *But we were carried away together – partners in crime. Partners.*

And as she stood there, looking at me, she felt such love in that moment. It felt as though, in Lana's mind, I was emerging from a mist, stepping out of a fog. She felt she was seeing me clearly for the first time.

He looks just like a little kid, she thought.

She studied my face affectionately. It was a face she knew so well, but had never looked at closely before.

It was a pale face, weary-looking. A sad face. *Unloved.*

No, Lana thought. *That's not true. He is loved. I love him.*

And then, peering at me in the dim light, Lana experienced a life-changing moment of clarity. She understood that not only did she love me, but she had always loved me. Not with the mad passion that Jason inspired in her, perhaps; but with something quieter, more lasting – and deeper. A great love, a true love, born of mutual respect and repeated acts of kindness.

Here, at last, was a man on whom she could depend. A man she could trust. A man who would never leave her, or cheat on her, or lie to her. He would only give her what she needed most. He would give her companionship, kindness – and love.

Lana felt a sudden urge to wake me up – to tell me how much she loved me.

I'll leave Jason, she was about to say. *And you and I can be together, my love – and we can be happy. Forever and ever and –*

Lana reached out to touch my shoulder – but something made her stop.

My notebook was on the desk, under my right hand.

It was open, and its pages were covered with scribbled writing. It looked like a draft of a script, perhaps – or a scene from a play.

One word jumped out at her: 'Lana.'

She peered at it more closely. Other words popped out at her – 'Kate' . . . 'Jason' . . . and 'gun'.

It must be that mad idea from last night – *silly man,* Lana thought, *he must have begun writing it down, before he passed out. I'll make him destroy it when he wakes up.* She assumed that, like her, I would wake up soberer, and wiser.

She hesitated a moment – then curiosity got the better of her. Carefully, so as not to wake me up, she slid out the notebook from under my hand. She went and stood by the window. She held it up to the cracks of light, and began to read.

As she read the notebook, Lana frowned, confused. She didn't understand what she was reading. It didn't make sense. So she turned back a few pages. Then a few more . . . then she went all the way back to the first page – and read from the beginning.

As Lana stood there, she began to make sense of what she was looking at, and her fingers trembled. Her teeth chattered. She felt out of control – she felt like screaming.

Get out, howled the voice inside her, *get out, get out, get out, get out* . . .

She made a decision. She was about to stuff the notebook into her bag – but thought better of it. She replaced the open notebook on the desk, edging it under my fingers.

Just as I was beginning to stir, Lana crept out of my flat.

She left without making a sound.

2

It was early morning when Lana stumbled out of my building.

The daylight felt overwhelming to her, blinding her, and she shielded her eyes from it, keeping her head low as she walked. Her heart was pounding in her chest, her breathing coming thick and fast. She felt like her legs might give way. But she managed to keep going.

She didn't know where she was headed. All she knew was that she had to get as far away as possible from the words she had read, and the man who had written them.

As she walked, she tried to make sense of what she had seen in the notebook. It felt horrendous – and too much to take in. Looking at those pages was like peering into the fractured mind of a madman, a glimpse into Hell.

At first, she'd had the disconcerting impression she had been reading her own diary, there was so much of her in it – it was full of her words, her ideas, her sayings, her observations about the world, even her dreams. All faithfully recorded – and written down in the first person, as if she herself were writing it. It felt like an acting exercise, almost – as if she were being studied, as if she were a character in a play, not a real person.

Even worse, and more painful to read, was the long catalogue of meetings between Jason and Kate, that went on for several pages. Each entry was neatly dated, its location noted, with a summary of what had taken place.

There was a list titled Lana – with a column of possible clues to be planted in her house, to make her suspicious of Jason's infidelity.

Another list, Jason, sketched out a variety of alternative methods by which he might be disposed of. But that list had been crossed out. Evidently none of the proposed methods had proved satisfactory.

Finally, in the notebook's last pages, written, then rewritten, was a bizarre plot to murder Jason on the island. Even more disturbingly, it was written in the form of a play – including dialogue and stage directions.

Lana shuddered, thinking about it. She felt like she, too, had gone mad. The last time she felt this kind of unreality was when she had discovered the earring.

The *earring* – which, according to the notebook, had been planted there for her to find. Was this possible? She struggled to reconcile the words she had read with the man who wrote them. A man she thought she knew – and loved.

That's what made it so painful – the love she had. This betrayal felt so profound, so visceral, it was like a physical wound, a gaping hole. It couldn't be true.

Had her best friend really lied to her; manipulated her; isolated her; schemed to end her marriage? And now, planned an actual murder?

Lana knew she had to go to the police with this – right

now, this second. She had no choice. And, emboldened by this decision, she started walking faster. She would go straight to the police station, and she would tell them –

Tell them what? About the scribbled rantings of a madman? Would she not also look crazy – turning up with garbled accusations of gaslighting, affairs, murder plots?

Her pace slowed as she played it out in her mind. The story would get out almost immediately – she'd be on the front page of every tabloid in the world tomorrow. There was enough material there to keep the papers busy for weeks, months. No, she couldn't allow that – for Leo's sake, as well as her own. Going to the police was not a possibility.

Then what? What else could she do? She had no more options.

Her footsteps faltered and came to a halt. She stood still, in the middle of the pavement. She didn't know what to do, or where to go.

The street wasn't busy; it was too early. A handful of people walked past, mostly ignoring her; apart from an impatient man who sighed heavily. 'Come on, love,' he said, pushing past her. 'Get out of the bloody way.'

This prompted Lana to move – to put one foot in front of the other, and keep going. She didn't know where to go, so she just kept walking.

Eventually, she found herself at Euston. She wandered into the train station, and, feeling tired, she sank down on to a bench. She was exhausted.

This was the second brutal psychological assault she had endured in as many days. The first was the discovery of the affair between Jason and Kate – which had prompted an outpouring of emotion, tears and hysteria. But Lana had used up all her tears – for she had none left for this second betrayal. She felt unable to cry, or feel. She only felt weary and confused. She was finding it hard even to think.

Lana sat there, on the bench, for about an hour. Her head remained bowed, as the station came to life around her. No one noticed her – she was invisible, another lost soul, ignored by the steady stream of commuters.

Eventually, someone saw her. An old man who, like Lana, had nowhere to go. He shuffled close to her. He stank of booze.

'Cheer up, sweetheart,' he said. 'Things can't be that bad.' And then, peering more closely, 'Say, you look familiar . . . Don't I know you?'

Lana didn't look up, didn't reply, just kept shaking her head. Eventually, the old man gave up. He ambled off.

Lana forced herself up. She walked out of the station, just as the pub across the road was opening its doors. She hesitated, and considered going inside. But she decided against it. She didn't need to get drunk. She needed her mind to be absolutely clear.

As she walked past the pub, she found herself thinking about Barbara West.

Suddenly Lana was flooded with the memories that she had worked so hard to forget. She recalled all the things Barbara had said to her about Elliot. That he was dangerous, that he was crazy. Lana had refused to believe her. She had insisted that Elliot was a good man, loving and kind.

But she had been wrong. Barbara was telling the truth.

And now, as Lana walked, she felt herself coming into focus. She found herself thinking more easily, with more fluidity. She knew her purpose now. She knew what must be done. She dreaded doing it, but she had no choice – she had to know the truth.

So she walked all the way from Euston to Maida Vale. She went up to the front door of a Victorian terraced house in Little Venice and stood on the doorstep, keeping her finger pressed on the buzzer, until there were angry footsteps in the hallway, and the door was thrown open by the owner, in a rage.

'What the hell –?'

Kate looked a fright. She had only recently got to sleep after a heavy night. Her hair was messy and her make-up smeared. Her anger evaporated when she saw it was Lana. 'What are you doing here? What's wrong?'

Lana stared at her. She said the first thing that came into her head:

'Are you fucking my husband?'

Kate breathed in sharply, practically a gasp. And then, in the same breath, she let out a long, slow audible sigh.

'Oh, *Jesus*. Lana . . . it's over. I ended it. I'm sorry . . . I'm so sorry.'

This wasn't much – but somehow this truthful exchange provided a tiny base, a stepping stone, from which to proceed. The truth liberated them – or at least opened the door a crack. Finally, they could talk honestly.

Lana went inside, and sat at Kate's kitchen table. They sat there for hours, and talked and cried. They were more honest with each other than they had been for years. All the misunderstandings, crossed wires, hurt feelings, lies, suspicions, they all came tumbling out. Kate confessed her feelings for Jason, there since the first day she met him. She buried her head in her hands and wept.

'I loved him,' Kate said quietly. 'And you took him from me, Lana. It hurt so much. I tried to let go, I tried to forget – but I couldn't.'

'So you tried to take him back? Is that it?'

'I tried.' Kate shrugged. 'He doesn't want me. It's you he wants.'

'My money, you mean.'

'I don't know. I know that you and me – that's real. That's love. Can you ever forgive me?'

'I can try,' Lana said faintly.

Perhaps this moving reconciliation isn't that surprising – Lana and Kate were closer than ever now. After all, they were united by a common enemy now.

Me.

Kate furiously chain-smoked cigarettes as she listened, incredulous, to Lana's story.

'Fucking hell,' she said, her eyes wide in amazement. 'Elliot is *evil*.'

'I know.'

'What are we going to do?'

Lana shrugged. 'I don't know. I can't think. I can't believe it's happening.'

'I can,' Kate said, with a grim laugh. 'Trust me.'

Despite her initial astonishment, Kate found the news of my deception easier to accept than Lana. She'd had an instinctive mistrust of me for years, after all. And now, at last, she felt vindicated – even triumphant – and justified in seeking retribution.

'We cannot let that bastard get away with this,' Kate said, as she stubbed out her cigarette. 'We have to do something.'

'We can't go to the police, not with a story like this.'

'No, I know. Honestly, I don't know how seriously they'd take us. To understand how fucking sick this is, you need to *know* him. You need to *know* what a psychopath he is.'

'Kate. Do you think he's crazy? I do.'

'Of course he is. Mad as a hatter.' Kate poured them a couple of whiskies. 'I warned you years ago, remember? I told you not to trust him. I knew there was something weird about him. You should never have let him get close to you. That was your mistake.'

Lana didn't say anything for a moment. She spoke very quietly. 'I think I'm a little afraid of him.'

Kate frowned. 'That's exactly why we can't let him win. Do you understand? We have to act. Have you told Jason?'

'No. I've only told you.'

'You must tell him.'

'Not yet.'

'What about Elliot?' Kate gave her a curious look. 'Are you going to confront him?'

'No.' Lana shook her head. 'He mustn't find out we know. Don't underestimate him, Kate. He's dangerous.'

'I know he is. Then what do we do?'

'There's only one thing we can do.'

'And what's that?'

Lana fixed her eyes on Kate. She didn't speak for a second. When she did, her voice was without emotion, simply stating a matter of fact.

'We must destroy him,' Lana said. 'Or he'll kill Jason.'

They stared at each other. Kate slowly nodded.

'But how?'

They sat in silence for a moment, mulling it over, as they sipped their whisky. Suddenly, Kate looked up, her eyes sparkling.

'I've got it,' she said. 'We beat him at his own game.'

'Meaning?'

'We play along. We follow his script. Then, as soon as he thinks it's all going according to plan . . . we turn the tables on him. We write him a different ending. One he wasn't expecting. One that will be the end of him.'

Lana thought about this. Then she nodded. 'Okay.'

Kate raised her glass, to make a toast. 'To revenge.'

'No.' Lana raised her glass. 'To *justice*.'

'Yes. Justice.'

The two women solemnly drank to the success of their production.

The curtain went up immediately. That afternoon, in fact, when, tired and hung-over, I made my way to Lana's house.

'Love,' I said. 'I came over to check on you. I was worried when I woke up and you were gone. And you've not been answering your phone. Are you okay?'

'I'm fine,' said Lana. 'I was going to wake you, but you looked so peaceful.'

'I feel rough as hell now. We drank far too much last night . . . Talking of which – how about hair of the dog?'

Lana nodded. 'Why not?'

We went into the kitchen, and I opened a bottle of champagne. Then I gently began to remind Lana what we had spoken about last night. I encouraged her to go ahead with our plan, to lure Kate and Jason to the island.

'That's if you still want to proceed,' I said casually.

I waited. I noticed Lana was finding it hard to look at me. But I put it down to her hangover.

She forced a smile in my direction.

'Nothing could stop me.'

'Good.'

Then, at my suggestion, Lana reached for her phone. She rang up Kate, who was at the Old Vic.

Kate answered the phone quickly. 'Hey. You okay?'

'I will be,' Lana said. 'I've worked out what we all need is some sunshine. Will you come?'

'What?' Kate sounded mystified.

'To the island – for Easter?'

Lana went on, in a cheery tone, before Kate could respond: 'Don't say no. It'll be just us. You, me, Jason and Leo. And Agathi, of course. I'm not sure if I'll ask Elliot – he's been annoying me lately.'

This alerted Kate to the fact Lana wasn't alone; that I was in the room with her.

Kate understood. She smiled and played along. She nodded.

'I'm booking my flight right now.'

4

They didn't tell the others about their plan until they were on the island.

Lana kept putting off telling Agathi – she felt sure Agathi would refuse to participate. In the end, she was wrong about that – Agathi proved an all-too-willing participant in the evening's festivities.

Lana told Leo about it on the second day, at the picnic on the beach. She suggested they have a walk together.

'Darling,' said Lana in a low voice, as they strolled along the water's edge, arm in arm. 'There's something you should know. There's going to be a murder tonight.'

Leo listened, amazed, as his mother explained the practicalities of the plot. To his credit, he felt a flicker of uncertainty – an uneasy feeling that what Lana was suggesting was morally wrong, and that there would be some terrible price to pay. But he quickly banished the thought. As a budding actor, he knew he couldn't turn her down. He'd never get offered a part like this again.

And the fact that he detested me helped him overcome his scruples. He figured I had it coming. Perhaps he was right.

Telling Jason, however, was a rather trickier proposition.

Lana attempted to talk to him that afternoon – after the beach. She snuck off to find Jason at the ruin, where he was hunting.

But Jason wasn't alone. Kate was with him.

As Lana watched them kissing, she flew into a rage. It took a while to calm herself down. Then she confronted Kate – on the speedboat, on the way to Yialos.

'You said it was over,' said Lana in a low voice. 'You and him.'

'What?' said Kate. 'It is over.'

'Why did you kiss him?'

'At the ruin? Elliot was watching us – I could see him there, hiding. I had to play along. I had no choice.'

'Well, you were very convincing. Congratulations.'

Kate accepted the rebuke with a shrug. 'Fine, I deserve that.' She gave Lana a wary look. 'When are you going to tell Jason? You need to warn him.'

Lana shook her head. 'I'm not going to tell him.'

'What?' Kate stared at her, astonished. 'If he doesn't know, it won't work. I'll never be able to talk him into it.'

'Oh, you can be very persuasive when you want. Think of it as an acting challenge.'

'You can't do this to Jason. You can't put him through that.'

'That's his punishment.'

'That's so fucked up.' Kate pulled a face. 'And *I* have to watch it?'

'Yes.' Lana nodded. 'That's yours.'

*

334

A few hours later, Lana stood outside the summer-house window. She watched Kate perform inside – all for an audience of one.

'Jason didn't mean to shoot Lana,' I said. 'He meant to shoot *you*.'

Kate shook her head. 'You're sick . . . you're fucking sick.'

Kate ran through the gamut of emotions in this scene – paranoia, fear, anger. It was a bravura performance – if a little over the top, in Lana's opinion.

Kate's overdoing it, she thought. *But he seems convinced – how smug he is. How vain. If he had any self-awareness at all, he'd see through her. But he thinks he's so clever, he thinks he's some kind of god. But he'll learn. He'll be humbled.*

Inside the summerhouse, I took out the gun, pressing it into Kate's hands. Then I sent her out to meet Jason at the jetty.

Lana lurked in the darkness, waiting. She stepped on to the path in front of Kate. Their eyes met, and they exchanged guns.

'Break a leg,' Lana said.

Kate didn't say anything. She stared at Lana for a second. Then she turned and walked away.

Lana followed me down to the beach. She positioned herself in the dark – a little way behind where I was standing. She sent Nikos over to accost me – to march me, at gunpoint, to the jetty; where I was humiliated, brutalized and beaten.

Lana watched all this, her blue eyes glowing in the

dark, like a vengeful goddess, cruel, pitiless. As I, her victim, was forced on to my knees; begging for mercy, screaming her name . . . until a gunshot silenced me.

And Lana's revenge was complete.

5

I promised you a murder, didn't I? Bet you never thought it would be mine.

Well, sorry to disappoint you – I wasn't dead. I just thought I was. I really believed my last moment on earth had come. That gunshot made me pass out. Scared to death, you might say.

I was nudged awake by a prodding foot.

'Wake him up,' Kate said.

Nikos's foot nudged me again, harder this time. I opened my eyes, and the world came into focus. I was lying on the ground, on my side.

I pulled myself up to a sitting position and gingerly touched the side of my head – feeling for any sign of a bullet wound.

'Relax,' said Kate. 'They're blanks.' She threw the gun to the ground. 'It's a prop gun.'

Ah, I thought. *Of course.*

Kate was an actress, not a murderer. I should have known.

Judging by the look on his face, Jason was even more surprised than I was that I was still breathing.

'*What the fuck* –?' Jason stared at Kate, incredulous. 'What is going on?'

'I'm sorry,' Kate said. 'I wanted to tell you. She wouldn't let me.'

'Who? What are you talking about?'

Kate was about to reply, when she fell silent – as she glimpsed Lana on the beach.

Jason followed her gaze, and he stared, open-mouthed, aghast, as Lana walked across the sand, to the jetty. She was holding Leo's hand. Behind them, the sun was rising, and the sky was streaked with red.

Lana and Leo climbed up the jetty steps. They joined the others.

'Lana?' Jason said. 'What the fuck –? *What is this –?*'

Lana ignored Jason, as if he hadn't spoken. She took hold of Kate's hand and clasped it. They stared at each other for a second.

Then they turned and faced me. They were standing in a line – all of them – like actors in a curtain-call. Lana, Kate, Agathi, Nikos, Leo. Only Jason stood to one side, out of place, confused. Even I had a better understanding of what had happened than he did. In fact, I understood all too well.

I got to my feet, with some difficulty. I clapped, sarcastically, three times.

I tried to speak – but my mouth filled with blood. I spat the blood on the ground. I tried again – it wasn't easy with a broken jaw. All I could manage was one word:

'*Why?*'

In response, Lana produced my notebook. 'You shouldn't leave this lying around.' She threw it at me, hard, hitting me in the chest.

'I thought you were different,' she said. 'I thought you were my friend. You're no one's friend. You're *nothing.*'

I didn't recognize Lana. She sounded like a different person. Hard, ruthless. She looked at me with hatred – there's no other word to describe that look.

'Lana, please –'

'Stay away from me. Stay away from my family. If I see you again, ever, you're going to jail.'

She turned to Agathi: 'Get him the fuck off the island.'

Then Lana turned to go. And Jason reached out, to touch her. She batted away his hand, like it revolted her.

Without looking back, she went down the steps. She walked alone across the sand.

There was a momentary pause. Then the mood abruptly changed. Leo broke the silence with a sudden peal of laughter – high-pitched childish laughter.

He was pointing at me and laughing. 'Look,' he said. 'He *pissed* himself. What a *freak*.'

Kate laughed and took Leo's arm. She gave it a squeeze. 'Come on, love. Let's go.'

They walked over to the steps. 'Your acting was amazing,' Leo said. 'You were so real. I want to be an actor too.'

'I know,' Kate said. 'Your mother told me. I think it's a wonderful idea.'

'Will you teach me?'

'I can certainly give you a few tips.' Kate smiled. 'Of course, the most important thing is to have a good audience.'

She threw me one last look of triumph. Then she turned and walked down the steps. Leo followed. And so did the others.

They made their way, in a procession, across the sand. Kate and Leo were first, and a little behind them, Nikos supported Agathi with his arm. Jason trailed behind them, his head bent forward, his fists clenched in anger.

I could hear Kate and Leo talking, as they walked away.

'I don't know about you,' Kate was saying, 'but I think this calls for a celebratory drink. How about a very expensive bottle of bubbly?'

'Good idea,' said Leo. 'Maybe I'll even have a glass.'

'Oh, Leo.' Kate kissed his cheek. 'There is hope for you, after all.'

As they walked further off, their voices faded – but I could still hear Leo's childish laughter.

It echoed in my head.

If I had any sense, I'd stop now. I'd pay for your drinks and hastily stagger out of this bar – leaving you with a cautionary tale, and no forwarding address. I'd get out of town quick – before I said something I shouldn't.

But I must go on – I have no choice. This has been looming over me from the start, casting its shadow on me, ever since I first sat down to tell you this story.

You see, my portrait is not complete. Not yet. It needs a few details filling in. A few final brushstrokes here and there, to finish it.

Strange, I used that word – *portrait*.

I suppose it is a portrait. But of whom?

Initially, I thought it was a portrait of Lana. But now, I'm beginning to suspect it's of me. Which is a frightening thought. It's not something I wish to look at, this hideous rendering of myself.

But we must confront it together one last time, you and I – in order to finish this tale.

I warn you, it's not a pretty sight.

6

It was dawn. I was alone on the jetty.

I was in a lot of pain. I didn't know what hurt the most – my aching lower back, where Nikos hit me with the gun, my cracked ribs, or throbbing jaw. I winced as I lurched down the steps, on to the beach.

I didn't know where I was going – I had nowhere to go. So I just hobbled along the sand, beside the surf.

As I walked, I tried to make sense of what had just taken place.

Suffice to say, my plan didn't work out as I had hoped. In my version of events, Lana and I would be together now, at the house, waiting for the police to arrive. I would be comforting her – explaining that Jason's death was an unfortunate, even tragic accident.

I had no idea things would get so out of hand, I would say to Lana, fighting tears. *That Kate would actually take a gun and use it.*

I'd tell her I would never get over the terrible sight I had witnessed: that of Kate repeatedly shooting Jason on the beach, in a wild, drunken rage.

That would be my story, and I'd stick to it.

Kate might tell a different tale to mine – but it would be my word against hers. That's all that was left now – words, recollections, accusations, suggestions, all blowing in the wind. Nothing real. Nothing tangible.

The police and, more importantly, Lana, would believe me over Kate – who, after all, had just murdered Lana's husband in cold blood.

'I feel so guilty,' I would say. 'It's all my fault –'

'No,' Lana would reply. 'It's mine. I never should have agreed to this crazy idea.'

'I talked you into it – I'll never forgive myself, never –'

And so on – we would comfort each other, each taking the blame. We would both be distraught, but we would recover. We would be united, she and I – united in our guilt. We'd live happily ever after.

That's how it was supposed to end.

Except Lana saw my notebook. Which was unfortunate – it read badly, I can see that. Words written in anger, ideas taken out of context, private fantasies not meant to be seen – certainly not by Lana.

If only she had woken me up, right then, when she found it. If she had confronted me, I could have explained it all. I could have made her understand. But she didn't give me that chance.

Why not? Surely she had discovered equally terrible things about Kate over the past few days? And yet Lana found it within herself to forgive her. Why not me?

I imagine it was Kate who came up with the idea. Like me, she was always having bright ideas. How they must have enjoyed scripting it, then rehearsing their performance. How they must have laughed at me the whole time – watching me make a fool of myself on the island. Allowing me to presume I was the author of this play – when I was just its audience.

344

How could Lana do this to me? I didn't understand how she could be so cruel. This punishment far exceeded my crime. I had been humiliated, terrified, stripped of all dignity, all humanity – reduced to nothing but snot and tears: to a kid snivelling in the dirt.

So much for friendship. So much for love.

As I walked, I felt increasingly angry. I felt like I was back at school. Bullied. Abused. Except this time, there was no hope of escape. No future happiness with Lana to look forward to. I was trapped here, for eternity.

Without realizing it, I found myself back at the ruin. I was standing in the circle of broken columns.

The ruin was eerie and desolate in the dawn light. Along with the dawn had come the wasps.

Wasps were everywhere, suddenly, swarming in the air around me, like a black mist. Wasps, crawling all over the marble columns, crawling on the ground. They were crawling over my hand, as I thrust it into the rosemary bush. Wasps crawled over the gun, as I pulled it out.

I was about to walk away, when I saw something that made me freeze.

They say the wind drives you mad. And that must be what happened to me – I must have been driven momentarily insane. For I was witnessing something that couldn't possibly be real. There, in front of me, gusts of wind were rushing together from all directions – swirling together, forming a giant spiral of wind.

A whirlwind – twisting and turning in the air.

Around it, the air was perfectly still. No hint of a

breeze. Not a leaf moving. All the violence and rage of the gale was concentrated here, in this whirling mass.

I stared at it, awestruck. For I understood what this was.

I knew, with utter certainty, this was Aura herself. This was the goddess, terrifying, vengeful and full of rage. She was the wind.

And she had come for me.

As soon as I thought this, the wind rushed towards me. It entered my open mouth, ran down my throat and filled up my body. It made me expand, grow and swell. My lungs nearly burst with it. It coursed through my veins; it swirled around my heart.

The wind consumed me; and I became it.

I became the fury.

7

Lana walked into the kitchen. She was followed by the others. But she barely registered their presence.

She looked out of the window at the brightening sky.

She was deep in thought – but with no confusion or distress. She felt strangely calm, as though she'd had a restful night, and had just awoken from a deep sleep. She felt clear, in a way she hadn't for a long time.

You might suppose her mind would be on me, but you'd be wrong. I had faded almost entirely from her thoughts, as if I had never existed.

And, with my departure, a new clarity appeared. Everything Lana had felt so scared of – all the loneliness, loss, remorse – meant nothing to her now. All the human relationships she had deemed so necessary for her happiness, meant nothing. She saw the truth at last, that she was alone, and always had been.

Why had that been so frightening? She didn't need Kate, or Jason. She would set them all free, all of them. She would release her hostages. She would buy Agathi some land in Greece, a house, and a life, instead of demanding she sacrifice herself to Lana's fear. Lana was no longer afraid. She would let Leo live his own life, pursue his own dreams. Who was she to hold on to him, to cling on to him?

And Jason? She would throw him on to the street. Let him go to jail, let him go to hell; he meant nothing to her now.

She couldn't wait to leave. She wanted to get as far away from this island as possible. She never wanted to come back. And she would leave London, too. She knew that.

But where would she go? Would she wander the world aimlessly, forever lost? No. She was no longer lost. The fog had lifted, the road was revealed. The journey ahead was clear.

She would go home.

Home. As she thought this, she felt a warm glow in her heart.

She would go back to California, back to Los Angeles. All these years, she had been running away – fleeing who she was, fleeing the only thing that gave her meaning. Now, finally, she would confront her destiny, embrace it. She'd go back to Hollywood, where she belonged. And go back to work.

Lana felt so powerful now, rising like a phoenix from the ashes. Strong and fearless. Alone, but not afraid. There was nothing to be afraid of. She felt . . . what – what was this feeling? Joyful? Yes, joy. She felt full of joy.

Lana didn't hear me enter the kitchen. I had come into the house through the back door. Silently making my way along the passage, I heard them, in the kitchen, congratulating themselves on their successful production. There was laughter, and the sound of champagne corks popping.

As I walked in, Agathi was pouring champagne into a row of glasses. She didn't see me at first, but then she noticed a couple of wasps crawling on the counter. She looked up.

She saw me standing by the door. She gave me a strange look. It must have been the wasps on me that made her look at me like that.

'A water-taxi will be here in twenty minutes,' Agathi said. 'Go get your stuff.'

I didn't reply. I stood there, staring at Lana.

Lana was standing apart from the others, by the window, looking out. I thought how beautiful she looked, in this early morning light. The sun outside made the window glow behind her, creating a halo around her head. She looked like an angel.

'Lana?' I said, in a low voice.

I sounded calm. I looked calm on the surface. But in the padlocked cell in my mind, where I kept him prisoner, I could hear the kid, rising up like a golem, wailing, screaming – battering the cell door with his fists, howling with rage.

Once again, abused; once again, humiliated. And worse, much worse – all his darkest fears, all the terrible things that I promised him weren't true, had just been confirmed, by the only person he ever loved. Lana had exposed the kid, finally, for what he was: unwanted, unloved, a fraud. *A freak.*

I could hear him breaking free, bursting out of his cell – howling like a demon. He wouldn't stop screaming – it was a horrifying, terrifying scream.

I wished he would stop screaming.

And then I realized it wasn't the kid screaming.

It was me.

Lana had turned around and was staring at me, alarmed. Her eyes widened as I took the shotgun out from behind my back.

I aimed it at her.

Before anyone could stop me, I pulled the trigger.

I fired three times.

And that, my friend, concludes the sad story of how I came to murder Lana Farrar.

Epilogue

I had a visitor the other day.

I don't get many visitors, you know. So it was nice to see a familiar face.

It was my old therapist. Mariana.

It turned out she had come to visit a colleague here – but thought she'd kill two birds with one stone; and she popped in to see me too. Which lessened the compliment somewhat – but there you go. These days, I must take what I can get.

Mariana looked well, considering. Her husband died a few years ago, and she was heartbroken. Apparently, she completely fell apart. I know how that feels.

'How are you?' I said.

'I'm okay,' Mariana said with a cautious smile. 'Surviving. And you? How are you finding it here?'

I shrugged and answered with the usual banalities about making the best of things, that nothing lasts forever.

'Plenty of time to think,' I said. 'Too much, perhaps.'

Mariana nodded. 'And how are you doing with it all?'

I smiled but didn't reply. What could I possibly say? How could I begin to tell her the truth?

As if reading my thoughts, Mariana said, 'Have you considered writing it down? Everything that happened on the island?'

'No. I can't do that.'

'Why not? It might help. To tell the story.'

'I'll think about it.'

'You don't sound very enthusiastic.'

'Mariana,' I said, with a smile. 'I am a professional writer, you know.'

'Meaning?'

'Meaning I only write for an audience. There's no point, otherwise.'

Mariana looked amused. 'Do you really believe that, Elliot? There's no point without an audience?' She smiled, as something occurred to her. 'That reminds me of something Winnicott said – about the "true self". He said it is only accessed through *play*.'

I misunderstood what Mariana meant, and my ears pricked up.

'A *play*? Really?'

'Not *a* play.' Mariana shook her head. '*To* play. The verb.'

'Oh, I see,' I said, losing interest.

'He meant our true self only appears when there is no one to perform to – no audience, no applause. No expectation to be met. Playing serves no practical purpose, I suppose, and requires no reward. It is its own reward.'

'I see.'

'Don't write your story for an audience, Elliot. Write it for yourself.' Mariana gave me an encouraging look. 'Write it for the kid.'

I smiled politely. 'I'll think about it.'

Before she left, Mariana suggested I might find it

helpful to talk to her colleague, whom she had come here to visit.

'You should say hello to him, at least,' she said. 'You'll like him, I'm sure. He's very easy to talk to. It might help.'

'Perhaps I will.' I smiled. 'I could certainly use someone to talk to.'

'Good.' She looked pleased. 'His name's Theo.'

'Theo. Is he a therapist here?'

'No.' Mariana hesitated. For a split second, she looked embarrassed. 'He's an inmate, like you.'

As a writer, I am habitually prone to fleeing reality. To making things up and telling stories.

Mariana once asked me about this, in a therapy session. She asked why I spent my life making things up. Why write? Why be creative?

To be honest, I felt surprised she needed to ask. To me, the answer was painfully obvious. I was creative because, when I was a child, I was dissatisfied with the reality I was forced to endure. So, in my imagination, I created a new one.

That's where all creativity is born, I believe – in the desire to escape.

Bearing that in mind, I took Mariana's advice. If I wrote my story down, it might set me free. As she advised, I didn't write it for publication – or performance. I wrote it for myself.

Well, perhaps that's not quite true.

You see, when I first sat down, at the narrow desk in my cell, to write, I felt a strange, dissociated anxiety.

Once, I would have ignored it – lit a cigarette or had another coffee or a drink to distract myself.

But now, I knew it was the kid who was anxious, not me. His mind was racing; he was terrified of this document. Who might read it, and discover the truth about him, and what would the consequences be? I told him not to worry – I wouldn't abandon him. We were in it together, he and I, to the bitter end.

I took the kid, and placed him gently on the single bed beside me. I told him to settle down – and I told him a bedtime story.

This is a story for anyone who has ever loved, I said.

It was a rather unusual bedtime story, perhaps – but full of incident and adventure, with goodies and baddies; heroines and wicked witches.

I must say, I'm rather proud of it. It's one of the best things I've written. It's certainly the most honest. And in the spirit of that honesty, allow me, before we part, to tell you one final story. About me, and Barbara West, and the night she died.

I think you'll find it illuminating.

After Barbara fell down the stairs, I hurried down after her.

I examined the body on the floor, at the foot of the staircase. Once I had made sure she was dead, I went into her study. Before I called the ambulance, I wanted to make sure she hadn't left anything incriminating behind. Perhaps she had written or photographic evidence of all those things she had accused me of? I

354

wouldn't put it past Barbara to keep a secret diary, detailing my misdemeanours.

I methodically went through her desk drawers – until finally, at the back of the bottom drawer, I found something unexpected. Seven thin notebooks, bound together with elastic.

A diary, I thought, as I opened them up. But I quickly realized what I held in my hands wasn't a diary.

It was a handwritten play – by Barbara West.

It was about me and her, and our life together. It was the meanest, most devastating, most brilliant thing I'd ever read in my life.

So what did I do?

I tore off the title page, and made it my own.

I'm not really a writer, you see. I have no real talent for anything, except lying. I'm certainly no good at writing stories.

Let's face it, I couldn't even plot a murder.

I've only ever had one story to tell. And now that I've told it, I can't bring myself to destroy it. Instead, I'll lock it away until I am dead. Then, if everything goes according to plan, this can be published posthumously. The intrigue surrounding it should make it a bestseller – which will give me a great deal of satisfaction, even from beyond the grave.

Joking aside – if you're reading this, then these are the words of a dead man. That's the final twist. I didn't get out alive, either. No one does, in the end.

But let's not dwell on that.

Let us end, instead, as we began – with Lana.

She's still here, you know. I haven't entirely lost her. She lives on in my mind.

When I'm lonely, or afraid, or I miss her – which is all the time – all I have to do is close my eyes.

Then, I'm right back there – a little boy in the cinema, in the fifteenth row.

And I gaze at her, smiling, in the dark.

Acknowledgements

It's impossible for anyone to write a book like this without standing on the shoulders of giants, who did it first and did it much better – so I feel I must begin by acknowledging the debt of gratitude I owe writers like Agatha Christie, Anthony Shaffer, Patricia Highsmith and Ford Madox Ford, for inspiring me and *The Fury*.

They say it takes a village – which was never more true than for this book. So many people helped me along the way. I had a lot of fun writing this story and exploring this world, but I got seriously lost in the woods a few times. My brilliant editors, Ryan Doherty at Celadon, and Joel Richardson at Michael Joseph, and agent extraordinaire, Sam Copeland, always helped me find the path again. Thank you, my friends – you really went above and beyond the call of duty.

I'd like to thank my US and UK publishers for doing such an amazing job. Your tireless dedication and sheer talent bowls me over. At Celadon, I owe a huge thanks to Deb Futter, Jamie Raab, Rachel Chou, Christine Mykityshyn, Anne Twomey. I'd also like to thank Jennifer Jackson, Jaime Noven, Sandra Moore, Rebecca Ritchey, Cecily van Buren-Freedman, Liza Buell, Randi Kramer, Julia Sikora. Thank you, Will Staehle and Erin Cahill for the fab cover. And in Production, thank you, Jeremy Pink, Vincent Stanley,

Emily Walter and Steve Boldt. And a big thank you to the Macmillan sales team.

At Michael Joseph, I'd like to give massive thanks to Louise Moore, Maxine Hitchcock, Grace Long and Sarah Bance. Also, Ellie Hughes, Sriya Varadharajan, Vicky Photiou, Hattie Evans and Lee Motley.

At Rogers, Coleridge & White, I owe a big thank you to Peter Straus, Honor Spreckley, David Dunn, Nelka Bell and Chris Bentley-Smith. And extra-special thanks to the foreign rights agents, who simply are the best in the business – Tristan Kendrick, Aanya Dave, Katharina Volckmer, Stephen Edwards and Sam Coates.

I would also like to thank Nedie Antoniades, for kicking the story around with me in its embryonic form, and for suggesting the character of Nikos. And for your incredibly helpful notes, which elevated the final drafts considerably, thank you to Sophie Hannah, Hannah Beckerman, Hal Jensen, David Fraser, Emily Holt and Uma Thurman.

Thank you, Ivan Fernandez Soto, for your help and sound advice. Thanks, Katie Haines, for being such a star and always making everything so much fun. Thank you, Olga Mavropoulou for lending me your wonderful name.

And finally, thank you to my parents, George and Christine Michaelides and my sisters, Emily Holt and Vicky Holt, for all your support.